T0032208

SAVOR IT

ALSO BY TARAH DeWITT

Rootbound
The Co-op
Funny Feelings

SAVOR IT

A Novel

Tarah DeWitt

ST. MARTIN'S GRIFFIN
NEW YORK

This is a work of fiction. All of the characters, organizations, and events portrayed in this novel are either products of the author's imagination or are used fictitiously.

First published in the United States by St. Martin's Griffin, an imprint of St. Martin's Publishing Group

SAVOR IT. Copyright © 2024 by Tarah DeWitt. All rights reserved. Printed in the United States of America. For information, address St. Martin's Publishing Group, 120 Broadway, New York, NY 10271.

www.stmartins.com

Designed by Gabriel Guma

Library of Congress Cataloging-in-Publication Data

Names: DeWitt, Tarah, author.
Title: Savor it : a novel / Tarah DeWitt.
Description: First edition. | New York : St. Martin's Griffin, 2024.
Identifiers: LCCN 2023058078 | ISBN 9781250329424 (trade paperback) |
    ISBN 9781250329431 (ebook)
Subjects: LCGFT: Romance fiction. | Novels.
Classification: LCC PS3604.E9236 S28 2024 | DDC 813/.6—dc23/eng/20240117
LC record available at https://lccn.loc.gov/2023058078

Our books may be purchased in bulk for promotional, educational, or business use. Please contact your local bookseller or the Macmillan Corporate and Premium Sales Department at 1-800-221-7945, extension 5442, or by email at MacmillanSpecialMarkets@macmillan.com.

First Edition: 2024

10 9 8 7 6 5 4 3 2 1

This one's for the me, who sat in the dark, staring at a glowing screen, dreaming of exactly this. Keep choosing bravery over perfection.

And, okay, this is also a little bit for James Acaster on that episode of The Great British Bake Off *when he said the most relatable thing every creative spirit has experienced:*

"Started making it, had a breakdown. Bon appétit!"

Dear Reader,

While this story is full of warmth, love, and humor, it is also balanced with some heavier and more sensitive topics. A theme I find important to represent in my books is that sometimes Life interrupts our plans with little regard for them. Additionally, even when our best-laid plans do come to fruition, sometimes those successes lead to burnout because we only feel added pressure with each achievement and forget to take the time to savor the good. Some potentially triggering material in this book includes:

-Grief
-Death of a loved one (occurs off-page)
-Career burnout
-Bodily injury (occurs off-page)

As always, I hope I've handled these with accuracy, respect, and care. I hope Fisher and Sage's journey makes you feel seen somewhere along the way, too.

PLAYLIST

"Word to the Trees" by whatever mike
"Backwards Directions" by Abby Sage
"I Wanna Get Better" by Bleachers
"Call It Dreaming" by Iron & Wine
"Wide Open Spaces" by The Chicks
"Cool About It" by boygenius
"Butterflies" by Kacey Musgraves
"Love You for a Long Time" by Maggie Rogers
"Northern Sky" by Nick Drake
"Judy You Hung the Moon" by HARBOUR
"Eat Your Young" by Hozier
"Girl Like You" by bestfriend
"Wildest Dreams" by Taylor Swift
"Dog Days Are Over" by Florence + The Machine
"Walk" by Griff
"My My My!" (Acoustic) by Troye Sivan
"peace" by Taylor Swift
"Wildflowers" by Tom Petty
"Heart of Gold" (with Bon Iver) by Ilsey Juber

"State of Grace" (Acoustic Version, Taylor's Version) by
    Taylor Swift
"Missing You" by Stephen Sanchez, Ashe
"Stupid Cupid" (Acoustic Version) by Jenna Raine
"Boom Clap" by Lennon & Maisy
"I Believe in a Thing Called Love" by Branches
"Lover" (First Dance Remix) by Taylor Swift
"Vienna" by Billy Joel
"The Book of Love" by the Magnetic Fields

CHAPTER 1

SAGE

"Well, it's certainly . . . unexpected," I say.

It is also decidedly phallic, and it is at least fifty feet tall. The dome-shaped tip juts up above the roofline at its back, proudly silhouetted against the early-summer sky.

Wren, my very best friend (and favorite person in the world aside from her equally mature son), barely contains a snicker beside me.

"How'd they get it up so fast?" she asks, a full-out guffaw chasing the words. "Oh god, the jokes are already writing themselves."

"Didn't you have Sam at sixteen? Fairly certain you know how they work," I tease. Her eyes round for a millisecond before we collapse in laughter, curling into each other with our shoulders bumping.

"I see you ladies have taken notice of our new *elevation*," Athena Cirillo says, lips rolled together to hide her own amusement. "Scaffolding for this new bit finally came down yesterday." She strolls down the park path to join us in our gaping, her snow-white waves floating on the breeze.

"Morning, Sprout," I say to the Brussels griffon tucked under her arm. Beady eyes spare me a watery blink.

"Do you know *what* it is?" Wren asks Athena with a nod toward the building. The bookstore owner can always be counted on for the inside scoop, like our very own goddess of small-town knowledge.

Athena turns back to the old warehouse and shakes her head. "All I know is that it's zoned for dining or retail space," she says.

Wren and I hum acknowledgments and go back to curiously studying the sight before us. The old brick building at the front of our coastline park hasn't been operational for years. Not in my lifetime, at least. It'd been absorbed into Spunes, Oregon, and only ever used as a pseudo community center of sorts. The covered patio area up front provided shade for the biweekly farmers market, and the interior was used as town storage for things like banners and holiday decorations.

That is, until it wasn't. Some months back, the place was completely cleared out, everything strewn across the expansive green lawn in tidy piles. Construction began a few weeks after.

"My guess is dining," Athena adds. "Retail would likely be better with other shops surrounding it. Since this is somewhat solitary, I think a restaurant is more probable. Either way, Martha's up in arms. This certainly won't help matters." She waves an arm up and down at the structure, letting out a weary sigh. "Aaanyway. I'm off to open the store. Have a great day, ladies. Stay outta trouble."

We say our farewells before we pivot back, still silently contemplating.

"Huh," I muse. A small twinge of excitement flares at the idea of a new restaurant. I think of my collections of food magazines at home, elaborate dishes I'd love to re-create, but probably never will. Still, my fingers itch to try *something* new. Incidentally, the only specific thing that comes to mind right now is eggplant parm.

Our heads tilt to the side at the same time. "Huh, indeed," Wren supplies.

I break first, a snort tearing its way up my throat until we're both in hysterics again.

"No, but honestly," Wren says, swiping at a rogue tear when we wind back down. "How the *hell* did the phallus palace"—she gestures to the erected structure—"get approved? O'Doyle would never."

"I would never what?"

We suck in twin gasps and immediately stand up straighter. Mrs. Martha O'Doyle of O'Doyle's Feed and Supply—Spunes's one-stop-shop for a myriad of everything from chicken feed to sporting goods—steps slowly into our line of sight. I claw at the wrist Wren's got trapped between us even as she lifts her chin.

"*Meridian*," the self-appointed town ~~dictator~~ preservation-ist intones, gaze narrowed on Wren. It's more of a curse than a greeting. They've had it out for each other since O'Doyle peti-tioned against the bakery's outdoor Christmas display two years ago, all because the elf-inspired vignette clashed with her more classical tastes.

"*O'Doyle*," Wren parrots back.

Cue the spaghetti western ocarina. I chime in before either woman calls for a showdown at high noon. "We just meant that you'd never let any of Spunes's buildings stay so"—I have to bite the inside of my cheek—"monstrous." It'd be best not to push her right now, when we all know this building has been a sore subject for her since it was purchased. It's no secret she's been fighting it, filing petty complaints with the county merely because it's an enigma she hasn't had a say in.

The deep grooves that stitch across her lips purse tighter. "What on earth are you talking about?" But then she slowly rotates toward the new erection, and I shove Wren to make our escape, not glancing back until we scurry a safe distance away. When I do, O'Doyle's head bobs at the capped cylindrical addition, mouth opening and closing in horror.

"Oh my *god*, she's apoplectic," I say, mirth barely contained.

Wren tugs me to an abrupt stop. "All right. Yesterday, you asked Sam if he 'had a case of the morbs' and now *that*. I'm gonna need you to stop channeling Victorian spirit energy and start channeling the energy of a modern-day-woman-not-yet-thirty-and-still-in-her-prime. There are so few of us left in this town."

"You're thirty-one, chuckaboo." Thirty-two, in fact, but she pretends to forget and I'm supportive like this. I scrunch my nose in mock apology, and her chin dips into a baleful glare. "Fine. I'll admit I went a bit rogue with the festival-trivia research. But since you won't do it with me, I'm committed to using my newfound vernacular somehow." I shrug.

She laughs quietly and shakes her head. "I very much doubt that the trivia portion will include anything about the *slang* of the time."

"Tommy-rot! You can't know that for sure! It's always centered around the founding era, and they try to mix up the questions every year."

She blows out a tolerant sigh. "You're sure none of your brothers will do it with you? You've asked all three?"

"No, they won't, and I don't *want* any of my brothers to, anyway. I find that idea even more mortifying." I give her a droll look. "You're *positive* you don't want to?"

She grimaces. "I'm allergic to competition. And Mom needs me at the bakery. Speaking of Mom . . ." Her face turns to something sad and searching, her teeth worrying at her lower lip. Panic starts to thrum beneath my ribs.

"What is it? Is she okay?" I ask.

"Yes, oh god, Sage, I'm sorry. *Yes*, Mom's absolutely fine. It's nothing—nothing like that." She clutches my elbow in reassurance, and I blow out a slow breath, shaking off the surge of dread.

When you experience losing your parents young like my brothers and I did, I think there's always some part of you that stays . . . expectant. Like maybe it's best to forever stay prepared for more loss.

"It's just that Ian came in yesterday with Cassidy," Wren explains.

I school my expression into an indifferent grin and keep it trained on her. "What'd you expect? There's one bakery in town, Wren. I knew they'd come to you." I shrug lightly, albeit stiffly. "Even if there were twelve, Savvy's would still be the best."

"Mom already refused their business," she replies.

I groan. "Wren, *no*. She didn't, did she?!"

"Well, not in those exact terms. But she did have to excuse herself so she could privately call Cassidy a mousy, backstabbing bitch in the walk-in. Then, when she came out, she asked Ian if he was balding and started naming off all the things he should look into, which sent him into a visible spiral. And *then* she told them she had no availability."

A brittle laugh rattles through me. "I don't believe you for a

second. Savannah Meridian is a saint." I've never heard her utter
so much as a *damn* before.

"Precisely! Which is why she won't change her mind, either!"
she happily declares.

"Wren, it's been over a year since we broke up. How would it
make you feel if I told you I wasn't going to talk to Ellis anymore?"

She cocks her head with a pout, caramel-colored curls bouncing. "I think that'd be different, since Ellis is *your brother*." Her
expression sobers. "And he didn't leave me after over five years
with barely an explanation and immediately start dating one of
my friends. Nor did he propose to her in under a year." She looks
away before she adds, "Ellis and I were equally at fault for our
marriage failing."

I snort. I'm tempted to say, *Then maybe you could equally repair
it, too*, but I refrain, recentering on the subject of my own failed
love life instead. "And *you* are my dearest friend," I say, pulling
a face. "Kinda my only friend, actually, which would eventually
make *me* the other woman in that scenario, so maybe that analogy was doomed from the start." I pick up a discarded ice cream
wrapper and toss it in the nearby bin. "I'm truly fine, Wren. The
last thing I want for you and Sav is to lose business over me when
I'm okay." I make sure I look her directly in the eyes when I continue. "You should know more than anyone that there are two
sides to everything. It's too small a town for everyone to take
mine . . . especially because Ian's not going anywhere when his
dad is the goddamn mayor."

We plop down onto our favorite bench at the tip of the park,
the same one we used to meet at when Sam was a baby. I was only
twelve when he was born, but I'd help watch him sometimes. Take
him for walks in his stroller on weekends or after school when

Wren had shifts at Savvy's. At free thirty an hour, I was the only form of childcare Ellis and Wren could afford back then. And despite our four-year age difference and the vastly different walks of life we were in, that time was what led to Wren and me becoming best friends. The kind of friendship that not even their divorce could dissolve.

And really, everyone that could step up to help them, did. Which is how I learned that if something takes a village, the people of Spunes almost always find a way to function as one.

We sit in companionable silence for a time, watching the waves in the distance, gulls screeching through the wind. I scoop fistfuls of hair up the back of my neck and twist them into a bun, happy for the sun warming my skin even though I can practically hear new freckles surfacing. A few sandy-colored pieces escape my hands and gust across my face before I tuck them away, closing my eyes with a happy sound.

Early summer in the Pacific Northwest is always my favorite, especially here in this old town, atop the cliffs where the air is briny and cool. The sun burns off the clouds before most afternoons, but there's typically enough chill wafting off the water to keep us from getting too sticky. When I open my eyes, they follow the thick driftwood fences weaving around the park, along the trails that continue as far as I can see before they curve into the thatch of redwoods that divides Main Street from the homes on the adjacent cliffs.

And then I do a double take when I notice Wren gazing at me sadly again.

"What?!" I laugh.

She searches my face. "It just doesn't seem fair," she says.

Ah, so we're still on the subject of my ex.

I sigh through a smile, tilting my chin. "I like to think it is. I was settling for him, anyway," I say. I spot her proud smirk in my peripheral. "Just make his damned wedding cake, Wren. The whole affair is bound to get a lot of good publicity if the Carvers have any say."

"We'll see," she replies obstinately. "We're not worried about business being slow with the festival, anyway." She gives me a tight smile and darts a glance at her phone. "Gotta go open up the shop. You wanna join? I've got a slice of white chocolate–coconut cake primed and ready."

"Can't. I need to go grab more feed from O'Doyle's and then get the Andersens' place set up. The renters are due today."

Wren rolls her eyes. "The Andersens should have to pay a property management company like all the other vacation home owners do."

"They're only gone for half the year, and the management companies all want yearlong contracts," I explain. "Besides, it's a football field away from me." Quite literally. I measured the meadow that sits between our houses the summer after seventh grade. It'd been an especially unexciting year.

"Which is another thing I don't like," Wren says, stabbing a finger at me. "What if it's some weirdo renting the place all summer? It's just you two on the outskirts of town. And why are they renting it for the *entire* summer? The festival isn't until August. It makes no sense. August is when the tourists show up."

Other towns in nearby counties have multiseason attractions. The beaches are warmer in Yoos Bay, and farther inland you'll find much bigger, more charming properties brimming with Christmas tree farms and wineries. The town over in Gandon is miles more quaint and pleasant to walk around.

Most of Spunes, however, rests on a steep slope, one that only levels out to cliffs that are set high above the water, which means that even a quick stroll feels more like a hike. Our main harbor is too small for major fishing charter vessels, but big enough to pack with smaller boats. The Fourth of July celebration is too big to compete with in the next county over, and June still has too much of the typical cloudy Oregon gloom. Which is why we get August. One month where this place that was built on failures and against all odds stays the driest, when many of our businesses make most of their yearly profits.

"As we've discussed ad nauseam, my friend, I have no clue," I say to Wren. "I don't mind cleaning the place a few times a month or keeping an eye on it when I'm off for the summer." And then I unfold myself from the bench and wrap her in a quick squeeze to cut the tirade short. "Don't be late."

"Yeah, yeah. See you tomorrow." She waves me off.

I blow her a kiss before I head in the opposite direction, ambling past the shops I know too well, waving at the people I know even better. Across Main Street hangs a banner emblazoned with *The Festival of Spunes; celebrating 150 years.*

Every free surface beams with flyers and posters featuring pictures of summer seasons past: photos of Founder's Point packed with canoes, the park filled with vendors and attendees rubbing shoulders. O'Doyle's has an entire wall dedicated to the labyrinth tracings on the beach that small groups of people come to make every year, shapes raked into the sand that outline mazes for folks to take meditative walks through. The majority of the photos are centered on the festivals themselves with the canoe races, carnivals, cooking competitions. . . . And, as I am once again reminded when I walk in, a section of that wall is designated for the contest winners each year. Those pictures are the largest, framed, and impossible to avoid.

Ian and Cassidy smile triumphantly back at me from last year's victory photo when I heave a bag of crumble onto the register counter. Beside them are photos of Ian with my middle brother, Silas, for two years in a row, back when they were still inseparable. Then there's Ian and his father—Mayor Ian Carver Sr.—for six years prior to that. Ian's been winning at this festival since he was eighteen. This year will make ten in a row.

I kiss my fingertips and touch them to the decades-old photo of my mom and dad from the year they won, like I always do.

After I stuff my change into my pocket and say my goodbyes, I dump the feed and myself into the truck, ready to get home, my mind churning the same way it has for months.

As much as it took me by surprise at the time, I have no jealousy over Cassidy being with Ian. She's welcome to him. Better her than me.

The thing that still back-combs against my nerves is that, while I maintain that it's *better her than me*, I also think that she's just *better* than me. She's a doctor, from a family of doctors and lawyers and generations of people that either leave Spunes to do great and important things, or leave Spunes to collect their titles and only return as some sort of concession or out of obligation. Something like, "Well, I needed to be close to Mom, anyway, and the school district in so-and-so county (always one of the next ones over) is rated so excellently!" Like it's a favor for anyone to just . . . stay.

Not the case for my family. Especially not for me.

So truly, it's not so much Ian or Cassidy that bothers me. It's not *that* sort of jealousy that sends something twisting through my gut anymore. It's that this is just as much my town as it is Ian's. I joined the committee that started preparations for this year's festival *two years ago*. I've submitted articles over the years prior to the bigger nearby papers in an effort to generate publicity for the events. I've done marketing and created social media pages for it. I taught other people how to utilize those pages for their own businesses—people who were otherwise spectacularly averse to new technology before my help. *I'm* the one who actually had a hand in building it into a bigger tourist attraction over the last decade.

Dammit, I even gave extra credit to my freshman students before the end of the school year for signing up to volunteer! I gambled on their honor and gave them the credit in advance, but who knows if any of them will actually follow through.

I'd simply like a small victory of my own, I think. Even if I can't *beat* Ian, I'd just like a moment of consideration. I want to be *worth* considering.

I also think I'm just getting sick of being handled with kid gloves all the time. I was already tired of it when I was still with Ian. Fed up with feeling like I was the fortunate one and everyone knew it. Like it was amazing that Ian Carver deigned to be with *me*—the tragic, awkward orphan. The plain, homely girl who grew up to be a woman comfortable and happy in her own skin. Lucky me.

Frankly, it all makes me feel like a fucking loser, and I am *tired*. Tired of being looked upon with pity, when I'm not overlooked entirely. I just want . . . I just want to know what it feels like to win, and I don't think I want too much.

I've never had huge aspirations in life. I've had dreams, but they've all boiled down to very simple things. So as far as I'm concerned, I'm living them. I want to be *happy*. And in the broader picture, I am. I enjoy teaching and working with kids. I'm blessed to have small class sizes, and it helps that I've known every kid their entire life along with most of their families. I don't have a mortgage because our parents' life insurance paid off the house, and I bought out my brothers' shares when I turned eighteen. While the $10,000 prize money would be a welcome cushion, my bills aren't beyond my means, and I get to take my summers off. I love my animals and my garden. I love my home, my town, my people.

And yes. I would love to find a person of my own, but I refuse to let not having a partner preclude me from enjoying my life. It'd just be nice to share it with someone who appreciates and loves me as is.

I meander the truck up my gravel driveway when I get home, smiling at the sight of the place. Two stories, though it's still fairly small—with a little front porch and my beloved sunroom hugging the back. Last year, my farmers market earnings were enough to paint the entire thing white, which makes it pop against the backdrop of the trees in the distance.

That smile plummets when I watch my wolfhound bound across the meadow from the direction of the Andersens', effortlessly leaping over the fence that divides my place from theirs.

"SABLE!" I chide, trying to infuse as much admonishment as I can into two syllables.

She skids to a stop and turns my way, ears flopping. And then she ducks her head and continues hightailing it through the meadow, inconspicuously trying to sneak her way back onto my porch.

"Sable, I can *SEE* you!" I shout to no avail. Nina Andersen is already terrified of her as it is. If she finds out Sable can hop the fence, she's going to want it rebuilt.

By the time I get parked and unload the feed, the pony-sized mutt has her body sprawled out on my front porch, her head dangling from the top step. The picture of innocence.

I quirk a brow and let out a beleaguered sigh. She huffs one right back at me.

"Oh, sure. You're fed up with *my* shit." But I laugh despite myself.

The rest of the day fritters by in a haze. I put the key in the Andersens' lockbox after I make sure things are tidied like they asked. And despite Wren's trepidation, I happen to think it'll be nice to have the same people next door for the summer rather than letting it sit empty from June through July. I won't have to explain myself or my animals multiple times to new people, either. Won't have any weird run-ins over at the barn that sits on the edge of our properties.

I throw on my bikini top with my cutoffs so I can take advantage of the sunshine, but slip a kimono robe over my shoulders so I don't feel like I'm being too negligent with my skin. Eggs are collected from the hens, nose rubs and grain are given to my Clydesdale, Bud. Sable unwittingly terrorizes the geese, and I turn my earbuds up to the max while I tend to my garden and tackle other chores. I busy my body and my mind until there's no room for anything but the small joys in all the *present*. In my colossal dog bumping around at my side, and my cranky three-legged cat when he slinks in from the meadow. Legoless pops Sable once across her snout for good measure before he commandeers a spot on the porch in the rays.

It's everything I need to slip back into my happy place.

It's a beautiful life, and though I am alone, between the people I love and the pets I continue to collect, I am rarely lonely.

I paint my nails in the sunroom after dinner to unwind, pleasantly exhausted by the time dark finally blankets our little hill, content when my head hits the pillow.

The only reason I know that the renters eventually show up is because Sable whines at me sometime in the dead of night, just before I hear the blaring sirens and see the flashing lights of a police cruiser and a fire truck that go streaking past, dust billowing in their wake.

CHAPTER 2

FISHER

Has something ever been so good that you wanted to push it away? Maybe you've seen a film, read a book, or even had a vacation that was so incredible, you didn't want it to end. You wanted to hit Pause and stave off the inevitable.

Some chump once told an interviewer that *that* was what he aimed to capture with his food. He wanted every dish to be so utterly mind-blowing that people would *stop* eating. He wanted to dole out culinary ecstasy. To make people sick with longing for more even before the meal ended.

And yet.

And yet that chump was also once me, which seems ironic given that I cannot get to the *end* of this road trip soon enough.

"Maybe downgrading will be good for you," my niece Indy says bitingly from the back seat. "Maybe greasy spoon fare will expand your horizons."

Even if the comment wasn't laden with teenage disdain, I'd

sense it for the trap that it is. She knows I ran a Michelin-three-starred restaurant up until three months ago, and she knows I'm not on this assignment to *expand* my skill set. She's well aware that I've been humbled plenty. But it's also likely she's getting more agitated the closer we get to our temporary home for the summer.

"Does the new restaurant have a theme yet?" she asks. "Casseroles with a side of ignorance?"

Jesus. We've been on the road for nearly seven exhausting days. I'd thought driving rather than flying would be good for us both, not only because it would allow me to cart all my own culinary tools with me, but because it would give us time to reconnect. The therapist we've been seeing for the last month told me to take my cues from her for a while, to follow her lead, let her open up to me. . . . The problem with that is that she hasn't been budging, so I've had exactly nothing *to* follow. She put in her earbuds back in New York and, aside from the occasional break to recharge, to throw a barb my way, or to let me know at suspiciously terrible times that she needed a bathroom stop, did not remove them the entire drive here. I tried countless times over the journey to initiate conversation, only to get a few syllables in return. And after a while I just . . . gave up. I passed the rest of the trip in a self-induced haze. It felt like letting my vision blur, like trying to *un*focus on the text of everything happening, but going through the motions anyway. It's a trick I developed while being berated in my early days in high-end kitchens. You can still pick up the gist of what's being screamed at you that way, but you spare yourself the sharpness. I was trying to just *get here* while I avoided my anxiety in the present.

Now that we're evidently getting close, her anger keeps bubbling closer to the surface, too. But as much as I don't want to discourage her from sharing, I don't think agreeing with her would be productive, either.

"I think we both gotta try to remember that we're traveling across the country, not back in time," I drone. "Maybe we should aim for optimism." It sounds and tastes like bullshit leaving my mouth.

She scoffs and cuts me a glare in the rearview mirror, so I double down.

"Maybe Spunes isn't as bad or as small as we think. Archer said they had an Olympian come from there back in the nineties. Got on the podium, too." As far as fun facts go, it may seem bland, but these days I think Indy is most interested in a place's ability to produce greatness.

"What for?" she asks. "What'd they medal in, I mean?"

"Long-distance running, I think?"

She lets out a low, satisfied laugh. "You see the irony, right?" she says. "That even its denizens want nothing more than to run far away from it." And with that, Indy returns her earbuds to their places and curls herself toward her window.

Well, *now* I do. Fumbled that one, I guess. I sigh and check the directions on my phone. Still over eight hours to get to Spunes, which puts us getting in after midnight. I'd typically stop and get a hotel, but I think it's clear that we're both spent, and tonight's the first night my boss has us booked for the rental, anyway.

I pull the truck back out onto the highway, and my mind defaults to drifting across the years, continuously searching for when it all started to go wrong. Retracing the steps and missteps leading up to three months ago when, after a decade and a half of nothing but culinary hustle, I lost my job.

Sometimes I think that it started with that first bad review five years ago. When I'd skipped a trip home for the holidays because I'd gotten word that a certain food blogger was coming into Marrow, all for her to ultimately declare my beef cheek "uninspired."

Maybe something splintered when I'd gone out with mono the year before last and came back to a kitchen that had felt noticeably happier without me.

Maybe keeping that level of intensity for that long, where every second counts and every detail is preeminent, simply isn't sustainable.

Whatever it was, I continue dragging myself through it, because I think reflection is the thing I'm supposed to do. I'm trying to feel something again, whether it's longing for my career or anger over its demise . . . but I've got next to nothing. There's the aftertaste of shame, the slight bitterness of embarrassment, but not much I can seem to build on.

All I know for certain is that it mostly stopped mattering after my sister's car accident, three years ago.

An *accident*. What a harmless-sounding word to describe something that wiped away someone's existence and changed the trajectory of all her loved ones' lives. A regular errand run on a regular day, a mere moment of carelessness or distraction or . . . I don't know what it was. I wish I knew. I don't know why I wish I knew. It's not as if that would change anything. Not anything that matters, anyway. It wouldn't have brought the guardrail closer or prevented Freya from flipping down that embankment. It wouldn't bring her back, nor would it change the fact that, after running away from my parents' home two months ago, my orphaned teenage niece is now in my back seat—righteously angry at the world, and just as rightfully angry at me.

I do my best to get a grip on my thoughts, trying to take in the greens and golds of the scenery around me as I chew over the restaurant quest I've been sent on.

Don't people always say that all big things happen in threes? Or is it only *bad* things? Either way, it tracks. Three months ago, I was fired. Two months ago, Indy showed up on my doorstep, and one month ago, I came home from my daily self-pity walk around Central Park to find three people in my living room. . . .

I'd found my former boss's face first, looking up at me with unnerving, irritating gentleness. Carlie Viscontti is the harsh, fearsome matriarch of a half-French, half-Italian family made up of restaurateurs, many of whom are synonymous with culinary royalty . . . and she was looking at me with thinly veiled concern, no matter that I lost her restaurant one of its stars.

By her side sat my former sous chef, newly promoted chef de cuisine, Archer. "Chef." He greeted me with a nod.

Across from them both, Indy slouched in a chair, a bored scowl on her face.

"I'm not here to talk about the review, the star, or any of it," Carlie announced.

"Then why—"

"But you knew better than to let that bastard get to you, Fisher," she added, frustration outlining her features and tone. It was the same thing she'd already said to me a hundred times. The same thing I'd told myself, too. "Roth is a miserable prick who's great at writing casually dramatic, negative shit because it's what sells. Even peppered in between the pithy complaints, he managed to recognize your talent."

"Thought you weren't gonna talk about it?" I lifelessly replied.

"I'm not talking about it," she said.

I gestured around the room. "Then why are we all *here*, Carl?"

"Because your mom called me," she said.

"*Jesus Christ*," I groaned, letting out a dark laugh and tossing my keys onto the nearby counter. "I'm thirty-one, Carlie. Why is my mother calling my boss?" Archer became preoccupied by something on his shoe.

"I like to think of myself more as your partner than your boss. We were a little more collaborative than that, don't you think?" she said, not without hurt. I swallowed, my own eyes going to my feet. I couldn't—still can't—bring myself to regret the outburst that got me fired, even if the backlash from my actions was regrettable. Richard Roth was the one who approached me while I'd been trying to enjoy a quiet meal, who thought he could joke with me about the way he'd disparaged my career, along with the hard work of my staff. He deserved my pie in his face.

I guess I deserved to be fired for it, too.

"It was obvious she had no idea that you weren't at the restaurant anymore, Fisher," she continued. "You'll have to come clean on that with her soon."

"Carlie," I started, wincing at the pain in my voice. I hate that I've disappointed her, too. Work was my pseudofamily at one point, until my *incident* left her hands tied. It's not as if she wanted to fire me.

When my parents and Indy would visit out here for holidays over the years, joining Carlie's family festivities had always been the perfect buffer. She and Mom sparked up a friendship of sorts, and it had always been nice to think of them as pals. My feelings were a little more mixed at the moment, though.

"Since it seems you are in denial about this," Carlie pressed on, "given that you won't even share with the people who care about you, let me just put this plainly: You are not doing well. And clearly, neither is Indy."

Indy sat up in outrage. "Why am I getting dragged into this?!"

I shook my head at Carlie. "Let's leave Indy out of it," I said. I might be good with the repeat rundown on my own down-fall, but I didn't think it would be productive at that point to go through Indy's again. She ran away from my parents' place already, for the third time in as many years, so I was hesitant to push her too hard and risk giving her any reason to try taking off again. Carlie's lips twitched into a frown, and she ran a hand over the white streak in her hair, contemplating a new approach.

"Let me ask you this," she said after a quiet pause. "You wanna get it back?"

I almost replied with something sarcastic. Something like, "*Which 'it'? My dignity, my job, the star I lost, or my life as I knew it?*" . . . but I stopped myself, because I knew she meant it all.

"Of course I do," I said instead, voice hoarse. I dragged my-self across the room to the remaining open chair and let my body fall into it.

She blew out a long sigh and looked over to Archer before she launched into her pitch, recapping one of her investment projects that had been in the works for nearly a year: a restaurant on the Oregon coast. I'd been moderately embarrassed to realize that despite her tirelessly championing me in both my work and per-sonal life over the last decade, I'd been too insular to pay much mind to hers outside of where it related to me.

She told me they'd been running into delays at nearly every step, that the town had been giving her trouble, and that she needed to get representatives on the ground to see it through the rest of the way. She told me she'd be sending Frankie, a general contractor we've worked with for projects in New York before, the same general who oversaw construction on Marrow, and that his objective would be to push through the remaining build.

"Where do I come into this?" I asked quizzically. "And Archer?"

Archer cleared his throat. "I want the job," he said. "Want the CDC gig there when it's done. Spunes isn't too far from home for me."

People auto-referring to wherever they grew up as "home" will never cease to amaze me.

"But," Carlie interjected, "I need him here for the time being. Otherwise I'm without a chef. I can't have you back yet, not until things cool off."

I covered a flinch. And waited for them to finish their explanation.

"Help me with Starhopper," Carlie said. "Come up with a menu like you did when we started Marrow. Figure out what that area needs and what people will want, what will work for that whole immersive experience. All that artsy, atmospheric stuff I know you're great with." She leaned forward and gave me a hard stare. "Show me you've got your head on straight and I'll bring you back here, back to Marrow, when it's done. I don't care if I get shit for it. We'll work together and we'll get that star back plus another one if you want."

It was like gas to flame, the feeling that sparked to life in me. It flickered weakly, but it was there. The notion of a comeback was something I could set my sights on, even if it would only be pride or vanity motivating me.

Indy snorted from her seat to my right and looked up from her phone. "You're telling me I just ditched one shitty town, and you're immediately gonna cart me off to another?" she said. Then added, "Whatever," before she stalked away, slamming the door to the guest room behind her.

"I'm trying, Carl," I explained to Carlie's worried gaze. I just

also felt like I was trying to breathe through a straw while simultaneously running uphill all the time. "I don't know why she
wants to be here or why the hell she wants to live with me, but I
guess she does so I'm . . . I'm trying." I shrugged.

"Seems obvious to me," Archer supplied, earning a sharp look
from Carlie and me. "I mean, Chef, you're a legend. You know
you are. And she saw *you* make it here, right?" he said. "You're
probably her hero, in a way."

I find that laughable and think Indy would, too. Maybe that
was partially true for the old versions of ourselves but not anymore.

I do understand why she'd want to get away from her home,
at least, and can only conclude that she got desperate enough to
get out of there that she ran here. Without Freya, I imagine that
shitty town back in Nebraska lost any shred of appeal.

"And you don't mind that you wouldn't have a hand in this
part of things?" I asked Archer. I think we're as close as I am to
anyone, which is to say, not very. The guy is a great chef, though,
and does deserve his own kitchen.

"I just wanna cook, Chef. You know me," he nonchalantly
replied. "Once I'm there I'll have the freedom to do what I want,
but I trust that you'll set things up all right, at least," he added
with a cocky grin. *Good*, I thought. You need an ego if you expect to successfully run a place.

Carlie got up and gathered her purse onto her shoulder. "You
can give it a think, but I know this could be good, Fisher. It'd be
good for you and Indy to get a reset, at least."

A reset.

The thought of being in a kitchen again still fills me with
palpable angst, swiftly followed by self-disgust. I'm so sick of this
thing I can't shake or name. It feels paramount that I figure it

out, though. Now that someone else's happiness could be affected by mine. And since nothing else I'd been doing was working, I knew I needed to agree.

"I'd need to be back by the end of summer," I said to my guests' retreating forms. "So Indy can start school in the fall."

Later, I was certain to thank Carlie for her relentless faith in me, for wanting to give me another chance. I took a recommendation from her for a therapist that Indy and I started having weekly video appointments with, and have been generally doing my best to get us on our feet since.

The minutes and miles drag on, set to the dulcet sounds of the truck, and eventually, Indy's quiet snores.

It's exactly midnight when the headlights shine on the town's welcome sign, which states:

SPUNES, OREGON
(Not to be confused with Forks, Washington)

I'm just glad that Indy isn't awake to sneer at it.

By the time we get to the rental house, the moon is high in a foggy, blue-black sky, but I'm too depleted to unpack anything other than myself, or to take in any of the details of the place. I blearily pull up the lockbox code and let Indy and me inside, before we both slog up the stairs to the first bedrooms we find. Her door slams, and I toe off my shoes, letting myself collapse into bed.

CHAPTER 3

FISHER

"*Fisher!*"

I swat at the hiss in my ear and try to burrow back into the bed.

"Fisher, wake up. *Please!*"

Awareness creeps over me as I start to make out my niece's face in the low-lit room. "What is it?" The glow from a monitor in the corner casts her in blue fear, and I try to clear the rest of the fog. "What, Indy?!"

"Something's in the house," she whispers. She's terrified, the edges of her voice shaky.

A thud and a bang clatter from downstairs, followed by a low, scraping growl.

"Do you think it's a bear?!" Her panic instantly catapults mine because how the hell should I know? This rental *is* in a more rural tip of an already dismal-sized town, but still, fucking *bears* being prevalent enough to bust into the house is not something I accounted for here. Where I come from the only real predators are the people.

Shit, I don't know my way around this house yet, let alone anything about the wildlife. I didn't even change before I let myself fall into a dreamless sleep.

More noises. A muffled sort of hiss.

My heart kicks off to a gallop, blood rushing in my ears as I slip out of bed and start looking around for something that vaguely resembles some sort of weapon. Indy's nails dig at my arm.

"*Ohmygodohmygod*, was that a *voice?!*" she squeaks.

Christ, I don't know, I want to screech back. *It might've been?!* I suddenly can't hear over my own adrenaline, and my mind is still trying to catch up. The chemicals blend and peak into consolidated extremes: Something or someone is in this house. Indy is terrified. She knows—*we* know, by experience—that both bad and random shit can and does happen. And I know that it's now my job to show her that she'll be okay, that she can trust me to make us okay. Keep us safe. I lunge for my phone on the nightstand and call 911, an eerie calm plummeting through me as I fire off the facts in measured tones.

"Stay here," I tell her when I hang up. Her head quivers in a nod.

I pad as quietly as I can into the other upstairs rooms until I come across an old wooden baseball bat. Between it and a rolled-up yoga mat, it'll have to do.

The rattling sound gets louder, like whatever it is is rifling through things, searching for something. *Jesus*, I know home invasions happen but has one ever happened in this place?! How fitting that this would happen to *us*, mere hours after arriving.

The gears in my brain feel like they're moving through Jell-O. *Jesus, don't think of Jell-O.* I physically shake my head to toss away the thought. *Jell-O makes you remember the funeral. The gelatinous*

thing in the shape of a Bundt cake and your former high school principal's
powdery face asking you if you'd made the food.

That growling sound again.

It *can't* be a person. It must be an animal of some kind, rummaging through the pantry. The sounds it's emitting are somehow . . . rhythmic? It *has* to be an animal. I just need to get down there and be loud, scare it off before it gets any bolder and considers coming upstairs. Maybe . . . maybe it's just a raccoon or an opossum and maybe it's not something massive and/or deadly. Fuck it, I can't keep thinking on this. I have got to man up and fucking handle this.

Be loud. Be big. It's more afraid of you than you are of it, dammit.

I glance back at Indy one more time, tears glimmering on her cheeks, and determination steels my spine.

I step off the landing and the wooden stair creaks beneath me. Another thud and more dragging sounds from below.

This feels like the part in the horror movie where the moron tiptoes down the haunted hallway, some monster crouched and waiting around the bend.

Be loud. Be big. It's more afraid of you than you are of it! I internally chant again.

It could also be a bridge for Indy and me—my chance to prove to her that we can make it through hard things. That yes, her mom is gone, and I know I wasn't there for her before . . . that yes, this is all so fucking scary, but even when something is unfamiliar and frightening we can tackle it and be okay. *Be loud. Be big. It's more afraid of you than you are of it.* I'm going to prove to her that she can count on me. That even though she's been robbed of her mom, even though I've been a lackluster uncle at best, I'm determined and committed to keeping her safe now.

I suck in a breath and leap down the last steps, letting out a forceful bellow as I pivot into the kitchen, bat wielded and ready.

The war cry dies a rapid, pitiful death. The energy deflates from the room.

The scene takes a moment to process. The thing is half-stuck on a corner of what looks like an apron and partially on a plastic bag. It thuds and spins against a twenty-four pack of soda on the ground in the pantry before it tries to redirect, whirrs, and bangs into the doorframe. It twirls around the wrong way again and bumps into more boxes it's presumably knocked down in its foraging.

"*Fisher?!* Fisher, what is it?!" Indy shrieks.

It's my new low, is what it is.

Is this rock bottom? I know if I considered each of the events over the last few years, I wouldn't think so. But if I began with Freya's death and then collected every shitty thing along the way like stones in my pockets, letting them sink me further and further down this spiral, then . . . maybe this is finally it? The thought is oddly optimistic.

"Come look," I yell back, because it bears seeing more than explaining. Then I remember that I already called 911. "*Shit.* Hey, bring my phone with you, please!" I shout.

She scrambles down the steps on shaky legs and passes me my phone before she stares down at the thing. She groans and sighs, hands balling into fists before she searches the ceiling. "Who has a vacuum set for four A.M.?"

I shake my head in silent, irritated shame before I try to call 911 back.

Maybe rock bottom is just above sea level, in a rental house in some nowhere town, staring down at a robot vacuum. Maybe things can only go up after this.

"Nine-one-one, what's your emergency?"

"Hi, uh, I just called in and reported an animal or a burglar in our house. It turns out it's not that," I say. "It's not either of those." I try to laugh, then silently curse under my breath when I see the lights flashing outside. I want to sob. Stomp my feet. Punch something.

"Never mind, they're here," I say. I hang up and bolt for the front door.

It's dark beyond the porch light, but I can make out an officer emerging from his cruiser. A fire truck comes burning in behind it, sirens blaring. I suppress the urge to groan again.

"Officer, I'm sorry." I hold up my palms before I step out onto the deck, set on getting everything out as quickly as possible. "Hey, listen, everything is all right here. There was just some—some confusion, and I'm sorry. I'm staying here for the summer, I got in super late last night but I guess the owners have their vacuum set up on a four A.M. timer and I swear to god, the thing sounds like an animal from a distance, but I apologize for bothering you and—"

The cop steps into the light and cocks his head to the side. "I'll still need to have a look around, sir. It's protocol." He plants his feet wide and sets his hands on his holster. His gaze narrows as he studies me from head to toe, like he's sizing me up for some sort of takedown. I have to fight against rolling my eyes. I'm six-foot-five and I probably have twenty pounds on him, but even with that in mind, I am categorically not threatening right now. I'm recovering from an existential crisis over a vacuum.

"Honestly, sir, everything is fine," I insist, just as Indy comes through the door at my back.

"He's telling the truth, Officer," Indy says. "Whoever owns this place has their vacuum set at a deeply ridiculous time," she adds, her tone both cutting and sullen in the way that only a teenager can master. My head whips in her direction in shock, the tiny show of solidarity washing over me like renewed hope. Like maybe this might finally shake Indy and me out of the deadlock we've been stuck in.

The cop—Officer Carver, according to his uniform tag—balks when he notices whatever my face is still doing in light of Indy's corroboration. I don't cover the hopeful grin quickly enough.

"Is this a *joke* to you?" he asks me.

I swipe my palms through the air like erasers. "No, no. I'm sorry."

"Because here's the thing, *sir*," he sneers. "You could be coerced into saying that things are fine. This could be a hostage situation. That is why I still need to have a look around." Indy laughs through her nose, but I nudge her with my shoulder.

"All right, yeah. Of course." I scrub a palm down my face and dig the heel of it into an eye.

"What's going on?" another man asks when he steps up onto the porch, this one a firefighter. More bodies exit the trucks behind them.

"A rabid vacuum, apparently," Officer Carver drawls. I clamp my teeth together, anxious to get this over with so I can wither away in private.

And now, yet another man walks onto the porch, judgment rolling off all three of them in waves while the rest hang back by the vehicles. The newest firefighter to join this trifling party gives me a look so wide-eyed it's painfully sarcastic, before he slowly lifts an ax into the air. Ready to save me from my robotic foe, I gather.

Maybe I could walk out into the dark night and lie behind the truck tires until they leave. Let them end it for me.

Instead, I gesture once more for them all to come inside.

CHAPTER 4

FISHER

Officer Carver takes Indy aside first to ask her some questions while one of the firefighters starts with me.

"What's your name?" the tallest one asks, fixing me with a hard glare.

"Fisher?" I reply, still not getting the need for the intensity.

"Fisher what?"

"Fisher Lange."

We go through the rigamarole of them checking my ID and verifying that I am Indy's legal guardian, with a few cursory questions about how that came to be.

"This says that it went into effect three years ago?" one asks.

"Uh, yeah," I manage to eke out. I dart a furtive glance around for Indy, hoping she didn't hear from the other room.

I expect them to leave once they're satisfied and have returned my documentation, but they only appear to make themselves more comfortable.

"What do you do?" the other firefighter asks me when he

joins, coming back from the direction of the kitchen. Suddenly I can't help but think that this part of the inquiry feels . . . unrelated to the issue at hand. And come to think of it, *why* are these guys asking me anything in the first place? I'm not an expert, but I don't think that's part of their job description. I'm also exhausted, though, and it's plain that I need to cooperate if I'd like this to be over as quickly as possible. So, even though the question is more complicated than he realizes, in an effort to wrap this all up I answer, "I'm a chef."

"Hmm," the second one hums. "The earrings made me think yoga instructor."

The first one turns to him. "That sounds judgmental, Silas. Maybe he just brews his own patchouli cologne, or dabbles in hemp jewelry." He swings back to me before looking down at his notepad. "Sorry about my brother. Where do you cook?" I notice that both have the name Byrd on their uniforms. This one appears to be older, his hair graying around the temples.

"I—don't? Currently," I respond, ignoring the jabs.

"So you're not actually a chef, then," the older-looking one says, dubiously. His gaze stays on his paper.

"Uh, I am. I'm just—"

"What is it that brings you to Spunes?"

"I'm consulting."

"That sounds like a made-up job," the younger-looking one—Silas, his brother called him—pipes up this time.

"Why would a chef not cook?" Now it's Officer Carver chiming in, finished up with Indy but apparently not satisfied with his interrogation.

"Because I'm *consulting.*" *And that is a long story that I prefer to keep between me and my therapist, jackass.*

"On what?" One of the brothers again.

I stand up and frown at the three grown men trying to nose into my business like *Gossip Girl* parodies. "Listen, is any of this pertinent to your—I don't know, *incident* report or whatever it is you need before you'll be done here?"

They share a look among themselves before the cop pivots back to me. I don't miss the way the brothers' gazes narrow on him when he turns, though. *Interesting.*

Carver blows out a breath. "It's clear that you're more accustomed to a city, so this concept might be lost on you, but it's a waste of our town's more modest resources, not to mention our time, for us to haul ass out here for a *vacuum*," he says.

The oldest-looking Byrd huffs out a sound and waves an irritated hand at him. "Misunderstandings happen, but he's *kinda* right. You got something to make you feel"—his shoulders bounce up—"protected? Maybe a bit less jumpy?" At least he has the decency to look like he doesn't *want* to say it, as opposed to the cop obviously reveling in my humility.

Before I can respond, the side door to the kitchen opens with a slap, and in walks a woman.

A woman in a shiny, cow-printed robe. It's wildly short in the front, longer in the back, and trimmed in whatever they make those boa things out of for bachelorette parties or Elton John concerts. It billows around her as she stomps into the room in big green rain boots, sparing everyone else a stern glance.

"Sage, dammit, what are you doing over here?" the younger Byrd complains.

"This could be an active crime scene for all you know," the older one adds with a worn-out sigh.

Sage rolls her eyes. "Pretty clear that it's not, since I spotted

Silas munching on their snacks through the window as I was
walking up," she states firmly. The youngest Byrd brother tosses
me a guilty look.

"And," she continues, "you two are the ones who decided to
cut through and fly down *my* frontage road, spooking all my animals awake early, and now Legoless is missing." She points a finger between the Byrds before she turns gray eyes on me. "I hope
you don't mind me barging in here. I knew my idiot brothers
were on shift tonight, and when I saw them through the window
I figured they were lingering. They're notorious for overstaying
their welcome."

She's suntanned like her brothers, with hair that's something between brown and blond, something between wavy and
straight. Freckles pepper her face and thighs.

"They're still right, Sagey," Carver adds. The way his voice
changes with her reminds me of balloons rubbing together,
and I hate it in a way that is immediate and bewildering. "You
shouldn't just barge in here, even so. You had no way to know if
it was safe or not." Both Byrd men rapidly turn on him and say,
"*Shut up, Ian,*" in unison, the rebuke dripping with venom.

Aha. A corner of this puzzle slots together and I'm oddly relieved that *some* instinct in me was correct for prickling at that
dynamic, even if every other instinct has been a monumental let-
down tonight. I chuckle before I can stop myself though, and all
three men rear on me.

"He's the one who prank called nine-one-one!" *Ian* whines.

"I didn't *prank call* you. I thought we . . ." It sounds brainless
and more embarrassing in front of a new audience member. "I
thought we had an intruder." Really, *I'm* the intruder here, aren't
I? I glance out the window and see the sun coming up and painting the morning pink. For some reason, I find the woman's eyes

next, a mixture of sympathy and wariness there. She turns back on the other three.

"Well, it's clear he doesn't!" she declares, looking between them. "If it'd been a woman that called, would you hover around and lecture *her* at all?" They respond with silence. "I didn't think so. Now beat it. And watch out for my cat."

There are a few low grumbles as they start to make their way toward the door. I snatch a cookie from Silas's grubby paw when he passes me, and he snatches it right back. Both brothers give Sage a side hug on their way out, but Ian lingers for a moment, a few feet from her. She holds herself rigidly, shoulders tilting away.

"You want some help looking for him?" he asks her quietly. There's a familiarity in his tone that only makes her stiffen more.

"Nope," she says with a close-lipped smile.

"Come on, then. I'll walk you back."

Her chin rears back a little before she shakes her head. "Just leave, Ian," she replies.

The cop turns around and gives me a final hard look I can't decipher. I'm still too mortified to do anything more than give him a bored glare in return.

When everyone else leaves and the cars all start to rumble outside, I glance around and notice that we're alone.

"*Shit*, where's Indy?" I say to myself. "*Indy?!*" I call back up the stairs.

"That's actually why I came in," she says, wincing. "Well, the cat thing is real, too, except I have a fairly good idea where he is. But . . . I saw your daughter climbing down the lattice from the upstairs window, before she pulled down a bike from your truck bed and looked like she was going to take off." She looks uncomfortable saying it, like she didn't want to rat her out, and for some reason that makes me respect that she did.

"*Fuck*," I hiss under my breath, closing my eyes.

"No, no, it's all right," she continues. "I ran over and distracted her. She's just on the porch."

My chest drops with relief. "Wait. How'd you distract her?"

"I handed her my goose." She says this like it's in any way a normal sentence. "And then I spotted you through the window and you already looked a bit like you wanted to die, or like you were at the end of the longest day even though it only just started, so I figured I'd, uh, help you disperse the crowd." She wrinkles her nose. "People can be a bit meddlesome around here."

"Ah, yes, the customary small-town welcome. Spying on their neighbors." I mean for it to sound light and teasing, but it comes out with an aggravated edge instead, like I'm too socially rusty.

She purses her lips and lifts a brow. "When there's only one other house around for miles and you're woken up by sirens, wouldn't you?" she says, flipping out her palms with a smile. "For the record, that's not a small-town thing. That's an anywhere thing."

She's got a point. "Touché. Sorry." I take a few steps and look out the window. Indy stands at the edge of the porch, frowning at the fat, white bird in her arms. He plucks at her hair with his bill and lets out a low honk that makes her flinch. "She runs away a lot," I admit out loud. "It's . . . been a thing." I figure I owe the woman the quid pro quo. Some vulnerability for her trying to spare me some embarrassment. I blow out a long breath and scratch at my jaw again. "Hopefully I won't have to call the Power Rangers again to help me find her sometime this summer." I try to make my mouth smile. I think one corner slants up.

She only nods before she reaches out a hand. "Sage Byrd," she says. I look at it a moment before I realize we weren't ever actually introduced. Lavender-colored nails, rings on every finger.

"Fisher," I reply, taking her palm. My calluses skate against hers, her hand tiny in mine and her grip surprisingly strong.

"If it helps, there's not much trouble to get into around here. At least not if you don't know where to look for it," she says, shrugging. "And I can show you how to detach the lattice, if you want. It's attached to a separate board because the Andersens once had a teenage daughter, too." She lets out a small laugh. "You mind if I check for my cat first, though?"

"N-no, not at all," I say, even though she's already pushing past me in a flourish of spotted, feathery robe.

"So," I try to make small talk as I trail down the hallway after her. I'm half wondering if I should clarify that Indy is my niece or if I should tell her anything else, but she hasn't asked, and this is the first semi-upbeat interaction I've had in so long that I find myself a little desperate to keep it going. I've also got the oddest urge to see what that robe feels like, something that I find perplexing and mildly annoying since I have no intention of actually reaching out for it. Must be a tactile sensory thing—used to working with my hands all the time. "Why does your cat come here? And where does he get in?" I ask.

"Dog door in the laundry room." She grins over her shoulder. "And, Nina—one of the homeowners—puts out tuna for him so he assumes he's got free rein. Her cat passed some years back so I've sort of let her share custody."

She opens the door to what I guess is the laundry room and flutters down into a crouch, propping open a cupboard. Sure enough, she's met with a bright yowl.

"There you are. Come on, old man," she coos, pulling the gray bundle of fur into her chest. When she turns around with him cradled in her arms, big gold eyes stare back at me, unimpressed. *Me either, pal*, I think blandly. He presses his head under her chin and curls in contentment. "He's in pretty good shape for fourteen, huh?" Sage says.

I find myself trying to return her smile, but something about it feels too bright, like I can't look at it full-on. My lips twitch before I squint away instead. I reach out and give the cat a scratch so I have somewhere else to focus, and suddenly his name makes sense. "Aside from the missing leg, it seems like he is," I reply, my smile not feeling quite as forced. "Clever name."

Our eyes catch again and snag for a moment too long. And I should just tear mine away from her, but there's so much to look at and I . . . I get a little bit stuck, I think. There are so many contradictions here. The wild robe and muck-covered boots, creamy, sun-kissed skin with freckles like little collections of fireworks. Pillowy, full rosy mouth in a square face. The moment stretches into three before we finally fumble to move at the same time. She steps toward me and I step toward her and we get tangled in a weird little dance of "Ope, sorry, yeah, let me just, here—" until I practically pick her up and switch our places. And though the contact lasts less than a second, the satiny robe leaves my fingertips feeling strangely cool, the sensation lingering like they'd slid against something damp. I have half a mind to look down and inspect them.

"SO," she shouts, blatantly trying to bulldoze past the awkwardness as we make our way back toward the kitchen. "Uh, some places I'd recommend checking out while you're in town . . . Start at the Magic Bean and Savvy's Bakery. If you go today you'll get to experience their Earl-Grey-and-blackberry scones. They only have them on Sundays. They're basically our town's form of religion."

I chuckle even as a pang of something cuts through me. People once worshiped my food, too. "Thanks," I say. And even though she's given me no reason to, I still feel the need to defend Indy. "She's not . . . she's not a bad kid, just so you know. She's just fifteen and has had to deal with a lot of change lately."

Sage just lifts a shoulder. "That age feels like being an adult stuck in a kid's body. Or, I guess the other way around too." She pauses, massaging the cat while she considers her next words. "My nephew's sixteen, going on seventeen. He's taking extra classes over summer before he starts his senior year, but I could ask him to show her around."

It's such a forward, earnest response that it takes me a moment to reply. "Indy's doing summer school here, too," I say. Has to, or she won't move on to her sophomore year. She skipped out on three months of school, and there are limitations to what the education system will put up with, apparently, even if you've lost a mom.

"Even better. Sam could maybe drive her, if you wanted. If you're comfortable with that, of course." She shrugs, jostling the cat in her arms, and her mouth kicks into a smile. "My advice when it comes to teens is to always know their friends. I teach high school social studies."

I find myself genuinely chuckling. Another contradiction. "*Not* a wealthy widow three times over, then?" I nod at the robe.

Her eyes flash and her smile opens wider in delight. "Not yet, but haven't you heard of manifesting? Dress for the job you want, they say," she replies playfully, dragging the back of her hand down the robe with a flick.

"I'll be honest, you could be an astronaut for all I care, I'll still take all the sage advice you've got." *Jesus, Fisher, that's enough of that.* I cringe at my own corniness. As if I needed to embarrass myself any more this early in the day. I recall the welcome sign and wonder if this place is already seeping into my psyche— osmosis via proximity, or something.

But then Sage laughs heartily, and the sound nearly makes me miss a step. It's a throaty, husky thing. A catch and a hitch at the beginning, crackling warmth in the middle. "I'm full of advice, Fisher, even if I'm not great at taking it myself. Don't let Mrs. Gale hold on to your mail for long down at the post office. She *will* find an excuse to read it. Don't go to Founder's Point unless it's low tide. Don't order anything at Walter's diner unless you want it *exactly* how it comes."

"I meant in regards to teenagers—to Indy," I clarify. "But consider that all noted, too." *Even though I'll be avoiding mingling in this town as much as humanly possible after this,* I don't say. I try for my most charming grin.

She blushes over her shoulder at me, eyes rounding. "Oh! Um . . . I think that's it! For now, at least." She takes a few more steps, almost to the exit. "Indy's a pretty name, by the way," she adds.

There's an opening there. I could explain where the name came from, that it's not from a wife and that it came from my sister, and therefore Indy is not my daughter. Maybe it'd lead to me telling her why we're here, too, sparking up some friendly rapport. But I get the sense that she won't push, and I'm rapidly wearing out, like even though it's surprising in a way that feels nice, this friendliness is also physically exerting. And I'm ready to hide away and try to forget this morning ever happened. Blips of everything keep trying to replay in my head, surging up like acid reflux. "Thank you. For earlier, too. For the rescue. Helping me clear them out of here and all," I tell her.

Silver eyes blink at me and away just as quickly. "I might have an idea what it's like to not want your humiliation dragged out for longer than necessary. Or rubbed in your face," she says.

I make a vague sound of assent. "Well, I appreciate it."

She smiles softly and opens the door, so I decide to blurt one more thing. "Let me know if I can return the favor ever."

She turns back with a frown, a single line between her brows, full bottom lip pushed out slightly. But then her smile lifts again, and this time, the curve of it hooks on something low in my gut and tugs. "Thanks. I just might."

CHAPTER 5

SAGE

"*You walked into his house in your robe?!*" is the first thing Wren says when I open my front door. She pushes past me and heads for my kitchen, pink box tucked beneath her arm.

"I had clothes on under it, Wren."

"It wasn't the cow print one, was it?"

"What's wrong with my cow print one?!"

Her mouth flattens into a line. "Nothing." And then she passes me a scone, and I forget what I was about to be upset over. Lemon glaze melts on my tongue, hints of Earl Grey and pops of berry—floral, bright, decadent. I could weep. A moan slips out of me instead.

"Who's helping your mom out if you're here?" I ask when I eventually swallow. "And who told you? It's been, like, four hours."

"Sam's working. He's trying to earn gas money, anyway." She nibbles off a corner of her own scone and stares out the window over the sink. "And Silas was already waiting at the bakery when

I opened today. Said he'd been up all morning and proceeded to tell me why. Said the renter's a consultant of some kind but wouldn't say what? Said he seems *fishy*."

I roll my eyes. "Silas would," I reply. "But I don't know. I didn't ask."

She turns on me with a frown that morphs into something conspiratorial. "He also said you stayed after to talk to him?"

"I stayed to get Legs out of their laundry room," I laugh. "And, once again, I didn't ask."

She flaps a hand at me in disappointment. "Aside from their description skills, your brothers are all shamefully better gossipers than you. It's the thing I miss most about being married to one."

I have a hard time imagining Ellis gossiping intentionally, but don't say as much. He is, however, excellent with recall. We both know that what Wren is referring to is less about juicy news and more utilitarian for Ellis. Silas and Micah are altogether another story. We're lucky Micah's off playing baseball in California. He'd undoubtedly already have the whole town looped in. Probably would have some elaborate backstory made up about the guy to embellish things, too.

"So, what's he look like?" She tips her head toward the Andersens' place.

Hot in a way that made me feel unsettled. Scruffy, unkempt, dark hair. Strong nose and sharp jaw, eyes that also looked dark from a distance but are actually more green up close. One side of his brow lifts more than the other when he talks, like he couldn't possibly waste the energy on a full expression. His looks sent a zap of surprise coursing through me, but his voice had been a shock, too. Deep and smoky and full of grit—a velvety thrill rolling down my spine.

"I don't know. Tall." I shrug.

Her posture falls in frustration. "Do better, Sage."

"Very tall? Taller than Ellis, I think, but maybe not as tall as Micah?"

She perks up. "Micah's a freak, so that's fine. Ellis is six three so that is still, like, *tall* tall."

"Yes. He's *tall* tall."

She somersaults her palms over one another for me to continue.

"Do you not even care to know the man's name, you dolly-mop?" I ask with mock outrage.

She stabs a finger at me. "That's your one allowance for the day, Sage Astoria Byrd. I'm trying to decide if he has the potential to be your summer flame. And Silas told me his full name. Fisher Lange."

There's something vaguely familiar about it when she says it that way, alongside his surname like that. But I can't call up anything specific in my mind, and I suppose it's just because they're not entirely *un*familiar words, when they're separated.

"Fine." I think about what details I can share without sounding too eager. "He had two tiny little hoop earrings. Broad but not bulky . . . brunette. Longish hair." He'd raked some behind an ear when he was looking out at his daughter on the porch, self-conscious in a way that'd been oddly endearing.

Her eyes round into saucers. "Oh my god. Like a hot pirate?"

"First of all, I never said he was hot. Second of all, don't you dare."

"Isn't that, like, your very exact dream man?"

My head falls back, and my shoulders droop. "You promised you'd stop using that information against me." I shove half a scone into my mouth when she fully squeals. I'll never live down the night when, immediately post-breakup, I'd guzzled a box of wine and babbled about all my relationship woes. How I hadn't had an orgasm for over eighteen months with Ian and how I'd since fallen down a blissful (if not overly specific) rabbit hole of pirate smut and fan fiction.

She bounces back to the window giddily. "Fine, fine. But *oooh*, this is exciting! Do you have binoculars?"

"Jeehus, 'En." I groan around the mouthful, crumbs scattering. "What happened to you worrying he was a weirdo?"

I jump when her hands slap against the counter. "You can-*NOT* be serious!" she yelps.

I swallow the pastry with force. "What is it?!"

"Serena Lindhagen just pulled down his driveway!"

"You're kidding me." I laugh incredulously. "That was quick!" I peer out the window, and sure enough, Serena adjusts the straps on the pretty blue dress I complimented her on last week, right before she grabs a pink box off the hood of her sedan and marches up the Andersen porch steps.

"*She brought him my cheese danishes!*" Wren says, scandalized like Serena's actually stripped naked and jumped him.

I briefly consider feigning ambivalence, but . . . screw it. I grab my binoculars from my miscellaneous junk drawer instead.

"You're better at reading lips," I say, passing them off to her. She suctions them to her eyes with shocking ferocity.

"Okay," she begins. "He just looks confused. Looks like just your basic introductions happening. He's now doing that mannish, back-of-the-neck-scratch thing they do when they're uncomfortable. Now the compulsive hand-through-the-hair thing. . . . Another awkward pause. A thank-you. And now Serena's turning to leave."

"Already? Interesting."

Wren glares at me icily for what feels like a full minute before she backhands me across the arm. "Ouch! What was that for?!"

"He is *stupid* good-looking, you ninny." She shoves the binoculars away and gives me an exasperated look. "That should be you over there acting like a frillybroom or whatever that ridiculous word was. Very sit-able nose."

I take my binoculars back. "She brought him and his daughter some baked goods, Wren," I say through a laugh. "She didn't proposition the man. And *Jesus*, good for her if she did!" I'm certainly not judging her for it.

"She's his niece, not his daughter."

"I—wait, what?"

Her eyes soften. "The girl. Silas told me she's his niece. Fisher's her guardian. I guess her mom died a while back."

Sadness drops like a stone through my chest. I knew he'd been embarrassed, but that explains why he seemed more than that. More . . . despondent. Like hitching a smile felt heavy, attached to some invisible anchor. Explains why his relief had been so palpable, too. Grief is exhausting.

"That reminds me," I rasp. "She—his niece, Indy, also starts summer school next week. I may have suggested that Sam would take her and show her around."

Wren nods heartily. "Absolutely. He's a good kid. You know he won't mind."

"I know," I reply quietly. That plumb line of sorrow vibrates in me still, like hearing about theirs strummed on a chord of my own.

"So I was thinking," Wren hedges, holding up a hand before she starts counting off with her fingers. "He's here for the whole summer. The mystery building. *He's* a chef. . . . He's definitely got to have something to do with it, right?"

"He's a chef?"

She sighs through her nose. "Once again, your sleuthing skills leave much to be desired. Your brothers got all this information." She lifts her arms, palms facing the ceiling. "So? Athena had to be right, yeah? It's got to be a restaurant, like she thought, and he has to have something to do with it."

"I guess we'll see."

She lets out an uneasy sound. "You know people won't be thrilled."

I snort. "But *why*? We need more than just Walter's diner, Wren. People leave and don't come back. August is great, but if this place keeps aging out of its citizens, not even the festival is going to be enough financially." I don't need to remind her that we are otherwise limited on tourism and that things like restaurants or breweries are the perfect draw—a great way to infuse money into our local economy.

"I agree with you, babe. But it's Walter's last year before retirement, and I'm just stating the facts," she says. "You know everyone wants him to get one more good tourist season before he retires."

"This is the third year in a row he's said it was his last, Wren," I say. "And he still won't say which nephew or niece gets to run the place when he goes. In other words, he's bluffing again."

"I'm not arguing with you. I think it's great," she says with a laugh. "Maybe with something else coming in, he'd have to actually mean it this time."

I cut my eyes across the meadow, curiosity sprouting like the dahlias I'm determined to grow this year. "I guess we'll see," I say again.

Ordinarily, I'd consider myself the ideal neighbor. I typically keep to myself, for the most part, and I make sure the property around my place stays tidy. No junk piles, no collections of weird gnomes or random sculptures cluttering up the lawn. But I'm also happy to check in on things when needed. I'm always obliged to help out the renters when the Andersens are away, and I'm forever available for a cup of sugar, while I'm not so overly friendly that they'd feel obligated to make small talk anytime we orbit one another. I'd sooner stay hidden and would go out of my way to avoid making anyone else uncomfortable. Plus, I do give a solid effort toward not perpetuating the small-town stereotypes. Therefore, *ordinarily*, I do not make it a habit to spy. I certainly don't bring out binoculars to do so in the first place, let alone anytime curiosity strikes.

But, not long after Serena Lindhagen leaves Fisher's place (and after Wren has left mine), I spot Bea Marshall—gorgeous red-headed hairstylist and skilled extractor-slash-purveyor of secrets—sashay up my neighbor's steps, too. She manages to make it inside the house, but leaves less than ten minutes later, a smug look on her face and a mildly confused expression on Fisher's.

Later that same night, I wake up when my plate slips off my lap and clatters to the floor, apparently having dozed off on the couch during my (very sad, girl-meal charcuterie board (adult Lunchable)) dinner. When I carry it over to the sink and start rinsing, a light catches my eye in the distance. I look up to see that it's the motion-activated light from the Andersens' garage, just as it shines down on the unmistakable silhouette of a teenage girl—sneaking out.

After that, it feels like I can't *stop* spying. Legoless frequently mewls his annoyance at me over the following days, and Sable bounces around at my side even more than usual, both of them agitated by the same frenetic energy, I'm sure. And *agitated* is precisely the right way to describe this. I am without a doubt intrigued by what they're doing here, but I'm equally as irritated with my inability to let it go and mind my own damn business.

"Maybe I do need cable," I repeatedly mutter to myself before I inevitably find more reasons to hover around my window. "Maybe this is like my reality TV."

Maybe you need to get another hobby, my dog's expression conveys.

Or get laid, the cat's mildly disgusted glare suggests.

Instead, I spend even more time in my garden than usual, or over by the redwoods that partially line the fence between our properties, "weeding." Which consists of me aimlessly plucking at the ground on my hands and knees while I steal glances and strain to overhear any conversations.

Basically: I'm a caricature of myself. Small-town girl enraptured by handsome stranger and his plight. It's pathetic, really, and I make exactly zero attempts to rein it in.

All I can determine through my fledgling investigations is that there's a distinct sense of melancholy between Fisher and Indy. They're never in the same area of the house, and when they are, one of them disappears almost immediately. Whenever Fisher wanders onto the porch, he studies his hands like the solution for something might magically appear there. Each time Indy stomps out, she clings to the railing and searches out in the distance.

Two days after the first visitors stop by, I catch sight of O'Doyle's truck creeping down the drive. An amazed laugh bubbles out of me as I practically skip over to grab the binoculars again. I know we're a fairly *direct* bunch in this town, but the poor man has already been forced through more than his fair share of awkward exchanges in the few days he's been here, and this is just plain ridiculous.

It's also (shamefully) entertaining.

I quickly find O'Doyle's pinched face through the lenses, even more wasplike than normal as she rounds the front of her car and makes her way to the door. Indy opens it for her, and O'Doyle shoves past, but within a minute, Fisher's showing her out again, his expression smoothed into something downright sardonic. O'Doyle, however, is red-faced and sputtering.

"Aunt Sage?"

"Gah!" I bark out a startled sound and toss the binoculars away with a thud just as Sam and Ellis duck into my kitchen.

"I have a doorbell, you know. Even your mother uses it," I inform Sam while I try to catch my breath, though it's clear from his derpy grin he doesn't buy the stern tone for a second. He traipses over to me and traps me in his long, coltish limbs.

"It's nice to see you, too, Auntie."

I pat him on his knobby back before he breaks away. Looking up at the kid's face is a bit like looking into a mirror. Same square jaw and big gray eyes, even has my freckles. He, however, inherited his dad's dark hair and his mother's curls rather than my wet-sand-colored waves.

"What are you guys doing here?" I ask Ellis, then flinch when Sable leaps onto Sam before he deftly starts marching her through a waltz with her paws on his shoulders.

"Mom told me you pimped me out to your neighbor," Sam says.

"She told him he needed to come introduce himself to the girl and show her around," Ellis clarifies.

"She's your age, Samuel, and cute to boot," I say.

"Yeah, yeah, yeah. I'm on my way. Just wanted to say hi

first." He tries to shove off Sable in vain, and she nails him with a sloppy kiss across the length of his face. "*Ugh*, and to drop off those from Mom." He points to a basket on the table.

I scoff when I see about ten of her infamous scones.

"Wait! How the hell does she expect me to eat all these?!" I call after Sam, who's hurrying for the door with Sable hot on his heels. "It's not even Sunday!" Which means she went out of her way to make them.

"No idea!" He skids through the exit before he peeks his head back in—at the cost of one more slobbery lick from my ill-mannered dog. "All I know is I was specifically told not to take *any* back!" And with that, he leaves.

Sable's whine echoes my own thoughts. Wren knows I can't stand wasting food, most especially pastries, and that I'll find someone to give the rest to. It's as good as shoving me over to the neighbors'.

Ellis plops himself down at my kitchen table. "Here, you help me eat these." I urge the basket toward him.

His face creases into a frown. "You know I don't eat those anymore."

I whistle out a long sigh. Ellis deals in absolutes. Dad's death was caused by a heart attack, which was caused by a fire in our barn, so Ellis became a firefighter. Our parents were gone by the time he was eighteen, so he became the one who took care of us. He took on the financial burden for us all and then didn't bat an eye when he also became a father to Sam in the same year.

Sometimes I think that he decided Wren was his forever when she became his first real friend in kindergarten. But now . . . Now, enjoying Wren's scones is no longer something he'll allow himself to do, because he no longer shares a life with her. It makes no sense to me, but in his labyrinthine mind, it's all purely logical.

"And what are you here for, then?" I ask lightly.

"Bud's due. Figured you could take me home after I'm done, if Sam's still got the Jeep."

Bud. His ex-wife's beloved dream horse that they couldn't hold on to when they divorced, who now lives with me, but gets ridden frequently by Wren and has his hooves trimmed and shod every four to six weeks by Ellis. I once thought having him here in a safe, neutral zone would somehow bring them back together, but it's been four years, and they've only grown more comfortable with their space, it seems.

My eyes drift back to the scones, and I decide that I won't be giving in and taking them to Fisher's. No more spying or inserting myself into other people's affairs, either. Ellis has unwittingly brought me a reminder that my feelings always get too tangled up in the end.

CHAPTER 6

FISHER

It's been a total of about eight weeks since Indy first showed up on my doorstep. A whopping two months in this new role plus a few days in this town is all it took for me to fuck up in the most fundamental way possible. It seems I've lost the kid.

Let me explain.

So far, in a mere matter of days, we've met not only Spunes's first responder force but also the town veterinarian—a younger woman who dropped off pastries and told me she'd happily stitch me up should I ever need her, despite my lack of fur—as well as a redheaded woman who ran her fingers through my hair unabashedly before she handed me a coupon for a free trim. She somehow managed to get me to tell her about the restaurant, that I was recently fired-slash-reassigned, that Indy is my niece, that I live in New York, and that I'm single and have never been married. I felt like I'd just filled out a loan application and left a therapy session in the span of ten minutes after she blustered back out of the house.

Indy slitted her eyes at me when the door clicked shut.

"What?!" I shrugged at her narrowed look.

"You can't be that clueless, truly," she sneered. "Don't give the townies fuel, Fisher. You know better." And then she trudged up the stairs with her arms still folded. And as much as I miss the kid that requested custom cakes in lieu of birthday presents and the one who called me Uncle Pishy, I was just happy this one finally spoke more than a few words to me.

Also, she was right. Clearly, I'm out of practice when it comes to playing things close to the chest, but I *do* know better.

This is exactly why, when the doorbell rang at 9:00 on the dot this morning, I immediately ducked behind the kitchen island and hoped that whoever it was would think we weren't home. The multiple large windows in this house should be charming, I'm sure, but make hiding inconvenient.

Still, I shouldn't have been surprised when, despite waving my arms around maniacally to grab her attention, shaking my head and hiss-whispering, "NO!" Indy simply tipped her chin into a grin and opened the front door anyway.

"Hello there!" Indy sang. "Uncle, I do believe you have a visitor!" But the smug look melted off her face when this particular visitor pushed past and let herself in. I straightened from behind my would-be hiding spot and reluctantly tried to plaster on a smile, tensing the closer this woman got. She reminded me of my elementary school principal with her pursed lips, severe frown, and short salt-and-pepper hair.

"Martha O'Doyle," she said, stabbing her hand out for me to shake.

"Fisher Lange," I echoed, flinching at her viselike grip.

"I thought it important for me to come and introduce myself

to you as head of the Main Street Businesses Coalition for Spunes."
She took her hand back and lifted a brow expectantly, like I
should've known what that implied.

"Uhh . . . thank you?"

She blinked rapidly, color heightening to the point that I was
fairly certain this was about to take a turn for the worse. "You *are*
responsible for the desecration of our once-beloved town community center, are you not?"

Oh. So this is one of those *people*, I thought. One of the people
making things difficult for Carlie, too.

I'm not sure what it says about me that I was glad she'd given
me an excuse to drop the friendly façade. I haven't been here for
a week, let alone long enough to desecrate anything, despite my
superb ability to fuck things up as of late.

"Nope. I'm not, actually," I replied with a sarcastic grin.

More rapid blinking. "But you're here for the new restaurant
it's being renovated into?"

Typical, tired small-town antics. Of course my business had
already been spread. "I am, but I don't own any part of it, and *I*
haven't actually touched the place," I told her.

She crossed her arms, her face squeezing like she'd sucked
on a lemon. "Then I'd like to get in touch with the person in
charge. Whoever's responsible for the design, particularly. We
have standards—"

"I'm sure a very resourceful person such as yourself will
have no problem doing so." I smiled with all my teeth, and color
splotches bled across her face once more.

"Are you not going to offer any more information than that?
If you're not in charge, what capacity are you here in?"

"I'm certain you'll be able to find that out on your own, too, seeing how much information you've already gathered. Now, I'm sorry to cut this visit short, but my niece and I have plans."

"We do?" Indy piped up before she noticed the daggers in my eyes and added, "Oh, right. We do."

I showed the woman out amid a slew of indignant, huffy noises before I swung the door closed at her back, probably harder than necessary.

"I don't want to go anywhere," Indy immediately snapped at me. I was about to hustle up the stairs to grab my wallet and keys so I could flee and get a moment to think, but then another knock rapped against the front door.

"You've gotta be fucking kidding me," I growled before I marched that way and ripped the door back open.

Only to find a stringy youth staring back at me this time.

"Who are you?" I bit out. I'm sure I was the paradigm of the grouchy old curmudgeon about to scream at this kid to get off my lawn, but then Indy skirted past me. Maybe she picked up the scent of Axe wafting through the air and recognized it as one of her own. Either way, introductions were made. This was Sam, the nephew Sage was telling me about.

"It would probably be smart if Sam showed me around town," Indy had said. Sam was visibly taken aback, and looked to me for confirmation. But I'd caught the slightest glimpse of an upward curve on Indy's lips—the smallest sprout of a smile—and had caved. I doubt she really needed my approval, anyway.

It is currently fourteen hours later; forty-seven minutes past 11:00 P.M., and I've texted and called about as many times with no word back from her.

It's at midnight that I finally decide I've had enough.

I don't care if that neighbor did help me out with the doom

patrol, *she's* the one who foisted her nephew on my niece, so she can be the one to help me track them down.

I've seen her fluttering around her property over the last few days. Always in some outrageous robe like an eccentric bird. Byrd. Ha! Hopefully a night owl because I'm about to wake her ass up and make her get a hold of her precious nephew. *God, more with the puns.* I need out of this place already.

I launch myself down the porch steps and into the dark meadow, worrying my nervousness into rage and accelerating my pace. I pound my fist against her front door and shift on my feet, trying to breathe through the anxiety. A dog barks from inside somewhere and I hear more commotion, and before I know it, she's there, opening her door and squinting a sleepy look up at me, clad in slippers and pajamas.

She's wearing a giant, baby-yellow T-shirt with a smiling snail on it—a smiling snail holding a tiny snail-sized baseball bat. Big, bubbly text above it says, GO GET 'EM, SLUGGER!

My indignation trips. How perfectly fucking irritating. How perfectly cliché. The ball of sunshine, wholesome girl next door.

"Fisher? Everything okay?" she asks, her voice husky with sleep in a way that shoots through my core. Of course she remembers my name and seems unbothered by the late hour, more concerned with me. She's so cute it's downright offensive.

"Sam," I sputter. *More syllables, man.* "Need you to call Sam, please. He has Indy."

"Oh, all right." Another bark from inside that makes me jump but neglects to faze her. "I could just check his location for you on my phone, too?"

"Yes. Yeah, I need you to do that," I say, trying and failing to sound adequately pissed.

She lets out one of those breathy laughs like she finds me amusing. "Would you like to come in for some tea or anything while you wait?"

"Tea?"

"Coffee, maybe?"

"*Coffee?*"

"Café au lait?"

My mind goes blank with white-hot annoyance. "No . . . I would not . . . like tea or coffee," I manage.

"All right," she says with a careless toss of her shoulders, and it's watching her little fuzzy slippers tremble when she steps away that tips me over the edge.

"No, I don't want tea or coffee," I repeat more firmly. "And while we're at it, I don't want your misfit townies banging down my door multiple times a day, either. I don't want to meet your banal, geriatric, ill-tempered but delightfully intrusive friends from the VA hall or nursing home you probably volunteer at. And I have zero interest in participating in your kissing booth to save some beloved town rock or pumpkin patch or whatever the fuck else you've got in mind. I need you to track down the nephew that is out with my niece, thanks to you. Otherwise, I'll—I'll call the police."

She *chuckles* at me. Chortles, even. That tempting, slinky sound. I feel deranged.

And then she stretches her face into something pleading, blinking big cow eyes up at me. "But that rock you're talking about is rich in history and sentiment!" she squalls. "That kissing booth paid for new grass on the soccer field at the elementary school, Fisher! My parents conceived me in that pumpkin patch!" She flutters her lashes dramatically.

I refuse to laugh. "Sarcasm doesn't suit you," I say.

"Really? Damn. Cranky and condescending works on you,"

she replies breezily, waving a flippant hand at me over her shoulder when she turns to grab her phone. "And I doubt you'd really want to jump to call the police, given that you already met, like, an entire quarter of the force in Ian the other night." Before I can come up with a rebuttal, she flips her phone out to me to show a location labeled "Sam" moving on the map. "They're almost home."

"Did he say what the hell they were out doing all this time?!"

She nudges the phone closer to my face as if in answer. "He didn't, but you'll get to ask them in mere moments, my friend," she says. I open my mouth to respond, but then her smile broadens—like she's *excited* for us to spar some more. It throws me off-balance. So I turn on my heel instead, just as I see the high beams cutting through the night in a car's approach.

It takes almost no time to confirm that it is indeed them under the glow of the vehicle's interior light, silhouetted against the surrounding dark. I'm not even halfway across the meadow when I see them dive for one another and begin aggressively making out. I grimace and mutter to myself when I cover the rest of the distance and she's *still* got her tongue down that Timothée Chalamet doppelgänger's throat, and they're still mauling each other like animals in a Nat Geo documentary.

I wait what has to be another four minutes, and they've yet to come up for air.

Another thirty seconds.

Fuck it. I'm already not winning points with her, and this little attempt at a coup d'état spiked my adrenaline so much that now that I see that she's safe, I'm crashing. I'm exhausted and pissed off.

I rip open my truck door and lay on the horn.

They spring apart in a gratifying shock before I feel her glare through the passenger window, horn still blaring. She slams out of the Jeep, Casanova hurrying out behind her. He slips on the gravel and rounds the back of his car before he continues tripping at her heels.

When I eventually let off the horn, Freya's dark eyes burn defiantly back at me from Indy's face. Chestnut hair bounces in a mussed-up halo around her head and shoulders. She doesn't slow down, just quirks her lips up in a phony, saccharine grin before she bolts into the house.

"B-bye, Indy," the sentient penis with a car calls after her, waving a sad hand through the air. The only response he gets is the slam of the front door.

He swallows and twitches my way. "Hi, Mr. Lange, I'm— I'm sorry if she was past curfew or something. She told me it was midnight and—sorry about that."

The kid is as tall as I am but looks like he's been put through a pasta maker to get that way. Lanky, thin, skinny wrists and sharp elbows—probably in some state of nicotine addiction. My saucier back at Marrow had a collage of bony-faced, droopy-eyed boys taped up in her work locker that looked just like him. *Jesus*, I think *I* might've looked similar at that age, too. The realization makes me feel even older and more tired.

But something also makes me doubt it was this knob's fault that she was back so late. I spare him one more look and wearily head up the porch.

When I make it inside, I find that Indy's already disappeared upstairs, and the temptation to scrap the day and go straight to bed so we can start over tomorrow is strong.

But that's what I've always done. If it wasn't perfect, I'd toss it aside. I didn't care if we were backed up and understaffed and dead on our feet, if I saw a sloppy plate, I didn't let it go to service.

Coffee tastes slightly off in the morning? Dump it down the sink.

Relationships that aren't convenient, comfortable, or easy? The ones that are never end up that way in the long run, so why get invested to begin with?

And I don't know if applying that culinary logic to this guardian role is ridiculous or not, but I do know that I've already been using it in other areas of my life, and it's not done me any good in those, either.

I steel myself before I make my way to her bedroom door and knock.

"Indy, come talk to me for one second, please," I say. I hear the creak of the bed and the shuffling of her feet before she opens the door in a manner equivalent to an eye roll. "I'm not trying to smother you here. But I do need to know where you are and that you're safe and what time you'll be home."

"I told you, he was showing me around." She jerks her shoulders up and shakes her head like I've just told her I expect her to wear a shock collar and not simply extend some common courtesy.

"You also left over half a day ago and—and hold on, showing you around *what*?! His oral cavity?! His upper respiratory system?! You know what—never mind." I inhale and exhale before I continue. "Let's not pretend you didn't take advantage of the fact that I'm not exactly practiced at this and wouldn't think to give you a curfew before you left. Your curfew is eleven, by the way." She breathes out an empty laugh at that, but I press on. "I'd like us to respect each other enough to get you through this summer in one piece, yeah? I won't make it harder than it has to be if you don't."

Her eyes harden and her cheeks redden before her face smooths itself back into indifference. "Didn't you pass on your chance to parent me, oh, three years ago or so?" she spits.

The blow lands like she intended. I grapple with my brain for a response and come up empty. I'm not sure how she even knows this. I wonder if it was something my parents revealed in a moment of frustration, or . . . It doesn't seem like something they'd ever do on purpose, though.

And—and I guess it's the truth, anyway.

This time when she shuts the door in my face, she does it softly, which is somehow worse. Like the punch didn't need emphasis to be justified.

I drag a hand through my hair and head to my unfamiliar room, asleep as soon as I hit the pillow.

CHAPTER 7

SAGE

The morning welcomes me with a metaphorical ice-water-bucket-dump of nerves from the moment I open my eyes. Warmer nights always make my dreams more vivid and insistent—living, breathing things that gnaw at me.

I may have promised I'd quit inserting myself into people's affairs, but of course, doing so has made my subconscious bristle, which is my only explanation for the back-to-back dreams I had last night after Fisher stormed off. The first one consisted of his niece falling out of her window while trying to sneak out, on a loop. The second: her tumbling down the cliff trail at the back of the property. The mouth of the trail is, technically, about three feet into the Andersens' property and not on mine, but as the path steeply zigzags its way down to our small, shared beach, it repeatedly crosses over, so I suppose I could be potentially liable for any injuries incurred there.

Still, I do my morning chores, and I try to shake the nightmares away. It's none of my business, especially after Fisher's fit last night. The last thing I want is to feel as though I'm some simpleton archetype in his eyes—some nosy busybody.

He'd been so polite and grateful that first night we met—almost charming, even. I suppose a few days of people knocking down his door may not have been the ideal welcome, but . . .

Bud lets out a low whicker as I run the brush down his sides, like he senses the turbulence in my thoughts. The sound brings my mind swiveling back to when he first came to live with me. He'd been warm enough at first, plied with sugar cubes and extra hay. But he fairly quickly grew testy with me, even worse with Wren and Ellis when they'd visit. He was dealing with big change and bigger uncertainty and trying to make sense of his surroundings. He didn't care for the judgmental cat roaming around, and the overlarge dog made him anxious. I had to learn to let Bud have *his* space first, and wait for his trust by showing him my own. I'd be sure to keep Legoless contained in my arms when Bud was around, and I'd make Sable sit and stay at a distance to show him I was somewhat in control, too.

Maybe it's similar with Fisher, in a way. Maybe instead of adding to all the new being thrown at him (even with good intentions like I had with Sam), I could help out with his environment first.

It is exactly the opposite of the promise I made to myself, but screw it. It's also in my best interest. Not just to protect myself from possible legal action with a potential Indy injury but to simply make the best of things in general. If they're going to be in Spunes all summer, we might as well make it a good one—especially since he'll have a hand in starting a business here that my compatriots and I will want to go on to enjoy. I could make his life easier *and* could act as the sartorial gatekeeper between him and Spunes, ensuring maximum success and comfort for all.

I'll just have to convince him somehow.

I decide to march over the meadow before I change my mind.

The marine layer is clingy today, but the warmth promises that the sun will burn it off soon. The scents coming from the flower garden are thick in the air; the last of the peonies were cut in May, but the mock orange, lavender, and sweet peas are more than making up for their absence.

I don't realize that I forgot to check the time until Indy opens the door with a squinted glower and obvious bed head. My face stretches into an immediate wince before I glance at my watch.

"Fisher's not here," she snarls.

"Ahh, shit. Sorry. Didn't realize it was only seven." *Off to a tremendous start with the comfortable-environment plan.* "Where'd he go?" *Doing even better with the subtle approach.* "I mean, you don't have to tell me. It's none of my business."

Her lip curls in annoyance, and she holds up a note in response. A single word written in an angry-looking scribble: *STORE.*

She raises her brows in a silent question. Probably something like, *"Are we done here?"*

And damn my brain for working how it does, but in this moment, I can't help but compare her to Legoless. He'd been fully grown when he'd shown up with a broken leg behind the local coffee shop, the Magic Bean. Serena Lindhagen's father, the senior Dr. Lindhagen, amputated the limb and recommended he go to a home that could care for him indoors. Somewhere he could maintain a cushy, relaxing life. Dad had just died, and Ellis was still malleable when it came to me, so he let me bring the cat home.

Legs was a terror. Growled, hissed, spit, scratched anything living to pieces, and pissed on half the house. He stubbornly kept trying to put weight on the missing leg, stumbling and yowling more every time he met the ground.

Until Silas and Micah had an all-out row that resulted in a broken screen door, which Legs promptly hurtled himself through at full speed. I was inconsolable, despite how rotten the beast had been to me.

I'd felt abandoned by so much back then, in that nonsensical way that kids do. Obviously my parents hadn't left me voluntarily, but I don't know that I understood it at the time. That damned cat felt like one more loss.

When Legs showed up a day later, bounding joyfully through the meadow with a dead rabbit in his maw, it all made sense. He'd dropped the thing at my feet like a sick and twisted offering, and I realized that having something to chase after had improved his gait *and* tamed him, in a way. Having a purpose had given him . . . well, *purpose*.

"You know what, I'm here for you, anyway," I tell Indy. A truth, even if it's newly born. "You think you could help me out with a few things?"

She blinks in slow motion, thrice. "*Who* even are you? Aside from the quirky neighbor, of course."

I lift a brow at the tone. This isn't one of my students I'm accustomed to, whose parents' addresses I could probably recite and who therefore show me a healthy amount of fear. "I'm *Sam's* aunt. Sage."

"Oh." She straightens in surprise, and bless Sam for having the ability to enchant someone, at least. "That's right. I, uh, I forgot," she says. "But—yeah, okay. Give me ten?"

"Sounds good. I'll meet you at the fence."

Fifteen minutes later, she approaches, her arms securely folded and her face scrunched with worry. "You're not gonna do the whole 'Sam's a good guy, and if you hurt him, I'll insert-bodily-threat-here' speech, are you?" she asks.

I laugh through my nose. "No, I actually just wanted to have a discussion with you about safe sex," I say dryly, and if fainting from mortification was a thing, I'm convinced it's what she'd be doing. "You see, when two people like each other very, very much, sometimes those feelings create these *urges*—"

"Ohmygod, no. *Please stop!* I don't need any of the talks, I swear." She flaps her hands like the embarrassment is so great it's causing her to vibrate.

I can't stop a full belly laugh from barreling out of me. "I'm kidding, Indy." *I couldn't resist being a shit back to you*, I don't say. *Let's get your hands busier and your mind idler (and more open) before we attempt too much sincerity.*

And that's exactly what we do. To her credit, she is an excellent hand with surprisingly few complaints. We make minimal small talk—the stock remarks about the weather and weekend plans as she helps me outline and dig a new hole for a small, shallow plaster pool I got for the geese. Once we get everything dug out to the right dimensions, we pack it down with decomposed granite before we install the liner and secure the edges with river rock.

Gary starts acting oddly attached, following her around and voicing his complaints when she's not nearby. When Gronk heedlessly gets closer to her, Gary has a meltdown unlike anything I've ever witnessed from him. He bites and jabs his beak at Gronk and positions himself between them, his neck curling into an aggressive hook.

"Uh-oh," I say aloud. I think I realize what's happening.

"What?" Indy asks, wiping some sweat from her brow after returning the wheelbarrow to its spot in the shed.

"Do me a favor. Go lie down over in that grass? I want to see something."

Surprisingly, she does it with only a small eye roll and little fanfare, and sure enough, Gary grabs the nearest twig and waddles over there as fast as his little legs will carry him. He places it by her head before he traipses off to grab feathers, more sticks, a bit of string, and even some clusters of moss. All of it he lovingly starts to pile around her frame.

"What's he doing?" she sneers.

A snort tears out of me helplessly. "He's building you a nest." And god, I wish she'd appreciate a melodramatic rendition of, "*YOU IMPRINTED ON MY SON?!*" and get the reference, but alas, I think the nuance would be lost on her. And I suppose it's not *her* doing, anyway. "He's decided you're his wife," I inform her through a sigh.

The corners of her mouth turn down when she levers up to a seated position and throws him an affronted glare. "Weird-ass bird."

"Aren't we all," I declare laconically. In truth, this could present a small problem. Geese need to be in pairs. Gary and Gronk were never mated before, but they'd been amicable partners, at least. Now Gary would pluck Gronk clean if he thought it'd make Indy happy.

I add that to the list of problems for future Sage and set us on a path for our next task, when something else occurs to me.

"It's been, like, almost three hours. You think Fisher's still at the store?"

She rolls her eyes. "Yes. The first time he went, he was out for nearly four."

"In *our* store? In Spunes? Why?"

She shrugs before she returns her arms to their standard crossed position. "Probably not. He always goes to multiple. But he's starting work on a menu, so I guess that means he looks for things locally. He never knows what he wants to make, I guess. Don't ask me," she adds when she sees that I'd like to ask more. "I don't get it, either."

"Hm," I say, frowning. Inexplicably sad at the mental image of a chef struggling inside a store, unsure what he wants to make.

"Oh *god*," Indy scoffs. I turn to find her looking at me with exasperation. "Don't feel *sorry* for him. He wouldn't accept the pity, and he doesn't deserve it, anyway."

I shake my head and smile. "And you think you're the authority on what's pitiful?"

There's a challenge in her double-edged grin. "Dead mom, so kinda. Yeah." She points to her chest. And this is one of my favorite things about teenagers, actually. Where adults require a foundation of small talk, followed by steps that build up before they're comfortable with the more revealing things, I find that teens are usually hoping to be perceived with minimal effort. Eager to be understood and seen.

Also, I recognize and appreciate some gallows humor—the brand of choice for this generation. "Orphaned at twelve." I point to myself.

"Dad didn't even want me in the first place." Her nose scrunches apologetically. "So, technically, I was also orphaned at twelve *and* left by choice well before that. Double whammy," she counters.

"Raised by adolescent brothers," I volley back. "Being forced to grow up too quickly into my emotional maturity means I surely missed developing some of it somewhere, which seems to manifest itself in me forever endeavoring to be important to someone or something." *Oof, hurt my own feelings a bit with that one.* "I say *yes* too easily to people for fear of abandonment if I'm not useful," I add, a bit disconcerted over the epiphany. "I . . . I think I keep my world small so I don't feel insignificant in it."

She blinks at me strangely before she says, "I want the opposite of that. I want my world big enough that I can't be cornered or stuck in it. Room to actually do big things, or at least have a chance to."

I nod and shrug in slow motion. "According to the holy trinity otherwise known as the Chicks, wide-open spaces give one room to make some big mistakes, too."

She chuckles in spite of herself. "I can see how that would be nice, too," she admits.

When Fisher gets home an hour later, Indy is moodily crouched at the ladder beneath me while I unfasten the lattice. He slides out of his truck and quickly marches over to her, starts speaking in clipped, muttered tones.

"You ready?" I call down to Indy.

"Yup!" comes her reply. I start lowering it, and I spy Fisher toss down his bags.

"You really think your neighbors would be happy about you dismantling their house and climbing their ladders?" he yells up at me.

I give him a beaming grin. "I do their Christmas lights every year!" I say before I make my way back down.

He mumbles more irritated sounds before he takes the lattice from Indy and holds it in place. I retract the ladder and turn to them both.

"That seems like a lawsuit waiting to happen," Fisher says, nodding to the ladder and me.

"Am I done here?" Indy asks.

"Speaking of lawsuits," I expertly pivot. "I need to show you the right path to the beach. It can be dangerous." I don't leave room for protests before I set aside the ladder and walk them over to the trail, showing them the markers for the safest way down.

I turn to find them standing in matching poses, arms crossed and mirrored, wrinkled brows.

When Indy reads the silence as an opening, she blurts out a rapid, "Okay, thanks," before she makes her escape back to the house. Fisher starts to walk away, too, but I stop him by telling him, "Hey, she was a great help today."

He swings back, frowning suspiciously. "She was?"

"Yep," I say. "If you're okay with it, I might ask her for other help this summer here and there. With other farm and garden stuff." I hastily add, "Paid, of course."

He cocks his head with a peculiar look. "You'd just offer her a job? What if she's a criminal?"

"I'd need more information," I say with a laugh. "And is she?"

He studies me like he's considering something. "No convictions." He sighs. "And thank you. That would be really great. I'd like for her to be included in something." His eyes skate away after he says it, like he's unsure if it was okay for him to agree. The last of the clouds have evaporated in the afternoon sun, making him the lone dark spot with the golden meadow at his back. A bee buzzes past him in a lazy whir, and he doesn't flinch, lost in thought again. I recall what Indy said about him not ever knowing what he wants to make, and wonder what's got him so uncertain.

"You're welcome," I say, pulling his gaze back to mine. "In

more ways than one," I add. And then, because that didn't sound quite as weird in my head until I spoke it aloud just now, "I mean, you are welcome for offering, and you are both welcome, like, here." I make a circular motion with my hands.

He chuffs a small laugh, and *oh*, his face is so warm when he laughs, even just barely that way. I enjoy a brooding pout as much as the next person, but I've always thought there were faces that look the most like themselves when they smile. Something in me shouts, *Again! Do it again!*

"Thanks," he says, mood and shoulders visibly lifted.

Yep, I'm gonna say it again. "You're welcome."

His responding chuckle has a little more sound behind it this time, deep and rumbly in a way that makes my returning smile so wide I have to bite my lip, nowhere else for it to go.

He swallows and swings a look back at the house. "Uh, I'd better go get my groceries put away," he says, waving a thumb over his shoulder.

"Oh shit, that's right," I reply. "Sorry. I've gotta grab my ladder, too."

We hastily head back, and I automatically reach into his truck and begin grabbing bags to help.

"You don't have to do that," Fisher says, awkwardly flustered as I use my elbow to open his front door. "You've done enough." I can't tell if he's annoyed or only thrown off-kilter by me. Likely both.

"You can help me carry the ladder back if that'll ease your masculine guilt," I joke back.

He snorts, an eyebrow jumping up his face. But he stops a retort when he sees me trying to figure out the collection of items I've unpacked. Things like caviar and cuts of meat I don't recognize, and freshly sealed bags of salmon he must've purchased down by the docks.

"Not a chicken-and-rice kind of guy, I take it?" I say.

He glares at me from the other side of the island. "I don't look down on chicken and rice," he says. "Don't judge me for fish eggs."

I put my hands up innocently. "Believe it or not, it wasn't the caviar itself that threw me," I say. "More that I didn't know it was even sold here. You're most likely the only person to buy that from the market this year." It was probably some special request item put in from one of the tourists last summer, I don't say.

He goes back to putting things away. "I'm working on designing a menu for the new restaurant being built in town. Star-hopper, they're calling it."

"It's gonna be a no-star-flopper if you try to put caviar on the menu," I laugh, cutting it short when he gives me a dirty look. "Listen, I'm sorry for the god-awful joke—truly, that was one of my worst—but . . . no one will eat that here. And I'm not trying to be insulting, I promise, but you might want to consider something more approachable."

He makes a tired sound. "More sage advice, huh?"

He's right. I cannot seem to stop myself. He must find me insufferable already.

"We really only have an influx of tourist business in August," I gently explain. "The rest of the year, your patrons would be us."

He nods woodenly. "I'll help you with the ladder," he says, effectively cutting the discussion short.

We each take an end of the ladder when we get back outside, quietly carrying it across the properties and into my garage. When I spin around to bid him a short farewell, I find him with his hands on his hips, shifting on his feet like he's got something to say.

"Maybe I could get your take on menu things as I go, or something," he says with a grimace that threatens to make me yelp out another laugh. Clearly, the idea of my help in this respect is agonizing to him.

"I'd love to," I say. He only bobs another nod, a dark lock of hair flopping forward in the motion, then leaves without saying anything more. I watch him walk off, rolling his shoulders and rubbing his neck like he's trying to break a knot away.

CHAPTER 8

FISHER

I'm trying to run down a gravel driveway, but the pebbles keep slipping away beneath my feet, sand through an hourglass that's trying to take me with it. Freya stands by her old car and waves at me, and I'm trying to reach her. I need to warn her not to go. I'm shouting without a voice; no sound will come out. My feet keep scrabbling away at these fucking rocks, but she just keeps getting farther and farther away until I fall, and now the ground is slipping away under my hands, too. And then I notice my parents on the porch, somber and benevolent as always.

"Can't you get to her?" my mom asks.

"I can't," I try to say, but the words never come, only a choked sob.

When I turn back to Freya, she's gone, and Indy's there instead, climbing into a Jeep with a scowl. I try again to get my feet under me, to yell, but nothing comes. It's hopeless, and I'm just uselessly falling farther and farther away. And now there's—wait, what the fuck—a goose? The thing lets out a honk, and I—

I lurch up from bed, sweat-drenched and panting. I reach up to my face and find tears that I wipe away, slapping at my phone to stifle off the alarm and trying to catch my breath. It's already light outside, still overcast like it seems to be more often than not here.

Here, in Spunes, Oregon. Where I am stationed for the summer while I try to prove my worth again, to both my niece, my boss . . . and to myself, too, I guess.

I focus on trying to steady my breathing while I untangle my legs from the sheets, throw on jeans, and go about my morning business. But I can't seem to shake the jittery, hollow feeling the dream left in me. Without being conscious of doing it, I make my way to the kitchen and start pulling things out of places, putting them back in others. It's not my home or my restaurant, but I still move the flatware to a drawer that makes more sense to me. I do the same to the knives. I stare into the refrigerator, which might as well be a black hole to another dimension.

I'm a chef that can't cook, I finally admit to myself. Or doesn't want to, at least.

I can go through the motions, I can make the things I've made a thousand times before. . . . But I sure as hell can't think up anything new, and I can't even seem to force the gears in my mind to turn quickly enough to mix up some of the conventional classics. I keep thinking about what Carlie said to me about a reset and getting back to basics, and I want to, but I don't think I know how. Doubtlessly I could make Marrow's stinging nettle agnolotti with white truffle butter and black trumpet mushrooms, but why can't I remember what Freya's favorite breakfast was or what Indy's used to be? I'd been paralyzed at the store yesterday, too. Just remembering the produce staring back at me has my heart racing again and my palms numbing. Everything had felt like it was anthropomorphizing in front of my eyes, mocking me.

The doorbell cuts through the din of my deafening brain, and I seize up more, if possible.

Between the nightmare and—and whatever else this is, I absolutely cannot deal with meeting another new person today. I won't do it. I refuse. But if I try to escape back to my room, I'll be discovered through those damn windows. I can't get to the stairs without passing too many of them to get away with it.

A flicker of gold catches my eye through the window above the sink, and I watch the grass sway slightly in the meadow. The stuff is dense and tall. Not tall enough for me to crouch inconspicuously in, but maybe if I were to lie down, it could hide me?

I don't give it long, my brain still misfiring and failing to help me get my bearings. I drop low and sneak out the side door like I'm on a SWAT mission. I tiptoe down the side porch, then skulk and weave around the truck. When I make it to the edge of the grass, I crawl underneath the fence slats and don't turn back.

Tossing humiliation and overstimulation on top of my dark emotional state has just made this all feel like too fucking much. I don't want to do this song and dance. *Or this crawl*, I think idly.

I want to find the ability to do my job again—even if this is just the rehearsal for the real thing, I want that chance to get it all back, to identify with that version of myself again. Which means I still need to do *this* job, however temporary, well enough that I not only prove myself but also might carve out some splinter of self-esteem again.

And fuck, I want to be done with this, whatever this is that episodically sends my blood rushing and my breath thinning over innocuous things these last few years. I want to be done with this never-ending nightmare parade. I want to fix this, and the only

way I know how is by finding something to work toward, which
I've got now with this summer gig. And yet I still can't figure out
where to fucking start.

But instead of pushing myself to remedy this, I'm hiding in
a fucking meadow just for a moment of solace. Hiding to avoid
talking to another human being.

Jesus. I ran a Michelin-starred kitchen once. I *reveled* in
attention—preened in it, even. What am I doing here?

I put an arm over my closed eyes to add another layer between me and the sun while I try to practice the breathing exer-
cises Dr. Deb assigned me. Rather than settling me, though, my
mind takes this opportunity to recall the same bullshit it always
does, replaying it without my permission. . . .

"*Has something ever been so good that you wanted to push it away?
Maybe you've seen a film, read a book, or even had a vacation that was so
incredible, you didn't want it to end. You wanted to hit Pause and stave off
the inevitable.*" I'd kill for a shred of that fire again.

I once had the most feared food critics in the world fawning
over me. I was in the top percentage of a career field that is notoriously hard to succeed in, and I loved every second of it. I craved
it—thrived in that environment. It was passion and heat and a con-
stant, wild adrenaline pumping through my veins. The problem is
that when I let go of the numb and remind myself to be present,
when I try to reach for that old me, all the bad shit manages to
sneak in first.

Which, again, is why I'm presently lying supine in a bug-
infested field, with scratchy weeds poking me through my shirt,
and . . . something walking toward me? The swish and scrape of
grass being stepped on gets louder. There's nothing I can do at
this point but try to come up with an explanation—

The three-legged cat from the other night pops through the

blades and appraises me with an impatient look. I wiggle my hand in a dull wave.

"Hi," I grunt.

I swear the cat sighs at me, his nostrils flaring and his whiskers twitching before he begrudgingly hobbles closer and steps onto my chest, where he proceeds to sink his weight, kneading against my pec with his only front paw.

"Ouch—*hey*. Shit." He purrs loudly, claws pressing against me like tiny blades. I try in vain to unlatch him, which only makes him cling harder. I tug again, and I'm certain he draws blood. "I didn't consent to this!" I say into his furry face. He's got the nerve to look annoyed to be doing this, his ears pressed back and his eyes narrowed to slits.

"What are you doing to my cat?"

I squint up just as Sage walks into my line of sight, blocking out the sun. A faint glow circles her head like a halo, gray eyes glittering. I'm stunned for the briefest second, and I completely forget about my circumstances, about the misdirected anger I had toward her the other night and my irritation from yesterday. Forget to be embarrassed at all as I stare back at her.

"What am *I* doing?" I point to her feline friend. "*I'm* being assaulted. Thank god you're here to rescue me again." My voice remains flat and vaguely annoyed even though I mostly mean that last bit. She's not at fault for any of the chaotic shit that keeps happening. She just keeps showing up for it, it seems.

"Ah, I see," she says, nodding seriously. "The one-armed felon. He's notorious around here. He traps all his victims by convincing them to *lie down in a field*."

"My attacker has *three* arms," I say lamely.

"Of course. Big, sophisticated, worldly man such as yourself couldn't be brought down by just any old limb-different assailant."

I slide a palm beneath my head and feel my face smile at that. Something about this pattern of Sage repeatedly finding me in vulnerable positions has cracked me, I think. Her cat stays heedlessly at ease on my chest, like he obliterated any personal space boundary I had left. And whether it's from the little weight pressing me into the earth or Sage's bright expression, I can't help but give in under the ridiculousness of it all, blood returning to my limbs, muscles relaxing helplessly.

"No robe today, huh?" I ask her, which is when my grin falters because I realize I've just alluded to watching her like some sort of pervert over the last few days. She wasn't wearing one yesterday when I found her working with Indy. Christ, did I just try to *flirt* while plopped in a field like a cow patty? I quickly take my arm back from behind my head and try one last time to peel off the cat.

"I was hoping you'd forget my robe," she replies, scrunching her nose and biting her lip in a cringe, and I laugh in relief. She assumes I meant the one from the night we met.

"Here—" She shifts to her knees, the sun glaring back in the movement.

With a short growl of protest, the beast is dislodged. He scurries off into the brush, and as I sit and dust myself off, I try to think of some sort of story to explain what I'd been doing out here in the first place.

But before I can come up with anything that doesn't sound too eccentric, she says, "Try this," with a smile so warm it's like she trapped some of that sunshine. She grabs something from the basket she'd set down and holds out a scone between us. "I was only coming over to bring you and Indy these to say thank you both for yesterday."

I eye it warily. "I'm actually not huge on sweets."

"Don't be a baby. Just try it," she says. The bratty eye roll she does with it sends . . . something through me. Something that makes me want to tug on her ponytail. "I mean, unless you have an allergy of some kind, of course," she adds hastily.

Martha O'Doyle's sputtering glare surfaces in my mind. "Is it poisoned?"

She gives me a bemused smirk and takes a hearty bite. I try not to watch her mouth or her tongue when it licks at a crumb in the corner. "Satisfied?"

Not in a very long time. The thought and the quick zing of desire that follows it both startle me. Another feeling jumping up unexpectedly, though this one wasn't necessarily bad, just . . . surprising. I hold out my hand and take the scone back, biting over the part that she already has. It's tangy, sweet berry, cool lemon, bright floral, then rich and buttery at the end.

"Damn," I say in genuine surprise.

"Yep. And these are over a day old. Hey, do you have time to help me with something?" she says.

I sigh. I should've known the treat would come at a price.

Still, I think I'd like to make up some sort of ground after being caught at a disadvantage again. It'd ease my conscience to atone for some of my previously bad manners, too.

"Yeah, sure," I say, successful at keeping the ire out of my voice.

"And before I forget," she says, "I should probably get your number so I don't scare you into running away next time I ring your doorbell, huh?"

Shit. "Sage, I'm sorry," I say. "I didn't know it was you, genuinely. I wasn't thinking clearly, and I—"

"Stop," she says, lightly tapping my shoulder. "I get it. But"—she huffs out an airy sigh—"you did offer to return the favor, so

I think I need to take you up on that. It's my sacred duty to teach you a lesson about small towns."

I notice the shirt she's wearing now. It features a series of different-colored horse heads, some with braids, some with shaggy bangs, one with a mohawk. The scroll across the top says HAIRY STYLES. I am so certain this woman owns an entire line of punny tops. "That so?" I reply.

"Oh yeah. Lesson number one: Empty gestures don't exist around here. People will take you up on offers. Case in point." She flourishes her hands in the sky. Pink nails today, a big turquoise ring.

With that, she stands and nods over her shoulder before she turns and heads in the direction of her house. I pop the rest of the treat in my mouth and clumsily follow behind, letting myself take the rest of her in, starting at the fitted top, down to her denim shorts. Petite upper body, with strong little arms, shapely muscled thighs that meet generously curving hips and . . . "*Shit*," I hiss when my toe catches on a knot in the ground . . . I'm jarred away from staring at her ass by the jolting bark of her dog as it comes hopping over from the back porch. I've seen the thing lumbering around from a distance the last few days, but up close, I'm still taken aback by its size. It's got to be over six feet tall standing on its hindquarters.

"That thing friendly?" I ask.

"Yes," she says ruefully. "*Too* friendly, in fact. Sable flunked as a livestock guardian, so I took her in when her owners brought her to a shelter nearby. She's too big for most, so they called me." She gives the lovable giant some enthusiastic scratches before we continue on. Sable slathers a wet kiss against my forearm like a quick seal of approval. Maybe she'll relay her thoughts to the cat.

I'm then formally introduced to the geese, Gary and Gronk, and I meet about a dozen chickens whose names I will in no way ever remember. When we round the farthest corner of her house to the side of her property that can't be seen from the rental, we come to a shockingly large flower garden. Rows and rows of some sort of tarp-covered mounds take up most of it, with a big iron-and-glass greenhouse at the back, and flowering hedges lining the sides of the space. Hundreds of colorful flower heads nod along happily in the breeze, the smell pleasant and light.

Scents were always important to my mentor, stuffy albeit brilliant prick that he was. His kitchen brigade was never allowed to wear anything fragrant. Couldn't risk it clashing with his food. I recall him verbally dressing down a sous chef for his deodorant once. For the same reasons, he was highly specific about any flowers he'd let onto his dining floor, almost never permitting arrangements on tables. Still, even if my knowledge is comparatively limited, kitchen life has forced me to grow acquainted with plenty of florals. Things that are either edible or complementary. So as Sage takes me through a detailed tour, I recognize a variety even as she names them off: lavender, roses, and decorative buds that we'd use for plating, like pansies and violas and button flowers. I recognize the stalks of a sunflower patch—Sage says they'll be a white variety when they bloom. She proudly points out a section of ranunculus and anemones, and a whole plot dedicated to impending dahlias—she tells me they have been pesky for her to grow. Her hands float across everything as she passes it by, the touch loving and sweet. I imagine the plants all smiling at her adoringly as she goes.

She breaks away from the garden and points off in the distance to a fenced-in pasture over by a dilapidated barn. "And I may as well tell you now," she says, "Bud can be wary of most men, so I wouldn't go skipping over there to try to give him a carrot or anything."

It's only then that I notice the giant Clydesdale grazing lazily in the field. "Jesus. No normal, regular animals for you, huh?"

Her head cocks to the side. "What do you mean?"

"I mean, a three-legged cat, a dog the size of a MINI Cooper, and a horse the size of a dually?"

"*You* know what a dually is?" She laughs. "And listen, I have a dog, a cat, a horse, and some birds. Not exactly exotic. Plus, they were all sort of bestowed upon me. I didn't seek them out."

The same thing that happened the night we met materializes again. Gazes catch on each other's, and I think she's waiting for me to fill the silence, but I don't know what to say and I don't look away quickly enough. Instead, I watch her adjust her ponytail, twisting it into a complicated knot on her head, and I get hung up on a piece she missed. The end of it curls around the base of her throat and below her collarbone, just above one of her freckle constellations at her chest peeking out above her shirt. They remind me of cinnamon dusting the top of a dessert.

"What the hell was in that scone?" I wonder out loud.

A blush eats its way up her cheeks as she chuckles again, and the trance breaks mercifully. I clear my throat before I ask, "What'd you need my help with?"

"Come on," she says, walking back toward the barn.

She takes me to a separate garden, this one significantly smaller than her flower setup, but packed with vegetables and fruits spilling out of their boxes.

"It's overgrown, but there's not really enough to sell and too much of it would go bad before the next farmers market anyway," she tells me. "I could use some help picking it. Keep whatever you'd like in exchange."

Her casual indifference comes off a bit forced. I can't help but wonder if she's trying to help me by . . . by letting me help her?

I also can't deny that it works. I load up baskets with squash, beans, some early melons, a bushel of basil, and every variety of tomato. I remember picking up some burrata at one of the stores I popped into and think about some simple combinations with all of it. By the time I'm done I've mentally assembled a week's worth of semibasic meals and I don't find myself resenting the idea of putting together any of them. There's soil caked under my nails and in the lines of my palms, and my legs ache from squatting, but it's a welcome burn. I feel relaxed, somehow.

Sage stands and wipes her hands on her shorts. "Thanks for your help," she says.

"Thank *you*," I say. "Pretty sure you've got Indy and me covered for the week with all this."

"You know, I could use some help tomorrow, too?" she adds tentatively, a smudge of dirt on one cheek. This crafty woman has thoroughly managed me, hasn't she? Lured me into her garden and used her flowers and food to put me under her spell. I feel my mouth struggling not to smile.

"All right. I'll come by in the morning."

Her grin splits and she starts walking backwards toward her house. I start slowly backing away toward mine. "Great. Come by at eight? We'll take my truck and head out from there."

"Oh." I halt in my tracks. "You need me to *go* somewhere with you?"

She props her hands on her hips and kicks at something with her boot. "Would you mind? You can take your own car if you're more comfortable. It's just that they're short-staffed at O'Doyle's, and I need a few bigger things, so I'll inevitably need a hand.

I feel guilty whenever one of the older employees with various braces on various joints has to help me, and—"

"No, I'm not—I'm not worried about going somewhere with you like *that*. I'm not uncomfortable," I say. "As long as I don't make *you* uncomfortable," I clumsily add. "I mean, as long as you're not worried about me."

She hitches a brow and grins in a way that makes me feel like I should be in on the joke. "I'll take my chances."

CHAPTER 9

SAGE

As soon as I hear the knock at my door at 8:00 A.M., I dive for the bathroom and give myself a quick once-over in the mirror. And while, sadly, I have not transformed into an irresistible siren in the span of one night since I last saw Fisher, it is still me in the reflection. Maybe a bit more flushed than normal . . . with an obnoxious fluttering in my stomach.

"Come in!" I call, knowing the windows are open to let in the morning breeze. "I'll be right down!"

The novelty of making a new friend in him is exciting to me, even if circumstances for initiating this friendship haven't exactly been ideal. He was clearly struggling with something out there in the meadow yesterday, so I decided not to take it personally that I'd spotted him making a break for it. He'd been struggling every single time we'd interacted, I realized, and maybe he just needed a reprieve. I honestly planned to walk around him at a distance and to pretend to be unaware. But then I watched Legoless's tail cut through the grass like a shark fin parting waves and saw his form slightly bounce when he latched on to his prey. I approached slowly in case Fisher managed to free himself first, but eventually found him there at my feet, and I'd been struck again. The hem of his shirt was riding up thanks to Legs's claws, his eyes squinting in frustration while he tried to get free. He only needed to stand up, to move, and gravity would've done the rest, but he was so stuck in his turmoil, he couldn't abandon his plan. And every time we meet, I find myself stirred by a strange mix of familiarity and mystery in him, like he's a puzzle I'd love to solve.

I suppose I've never been good at stifling my curious side, and maybe I never will be.

I grab my keys and some money from my purse in the hallway before I head back out, but my steps falter when I reemerge. The sight of Fisher with his back to me in my kitchen stretches that fluttery feeling into something foreign and loopy—something equal parts excited and self-conscious in an illogical way. I *just* caught this man scurrying like a little bug into a field yesterday, and yet heat is blooming in my cheeks at the sight of him examining the eggs on my skelter. He takes a few steps and looks around the sunroom, and it flares brighter.

It's just a tiny addition, really, but it's paned glass on all sides and across the ceiling, with a pair of sliders that lead into the kitchen and a single French door for the exit. I've got an overstuffed, mustard-colored chair in the corner that belonged to my dad. A footstool stacked with paperbacks and notebooks next to it that belonged to my mom.

Ian always complained about the sunroom. The floors are tiled, so it was too cold in the winter. All the glass let in too much sun and got too hot in summer. He hated that I had it arranged as a sitting room right there because it was too small to be a *real* sitting room when only a few people could fit in it comfortably. He complained about the shelf Ellis built for me along one of the panes, because I keep it filled with tchotchkes and plants, funky vases made from mini disco balls or vintage tomato sauce cans mixed in between cherished mementos. But Ian hated anything resembling clutter and the plants brought gnats and *Who wants that near a kitchen?* he'd say. I always felt like all his problems with the sunroom were the same problems he had with me. I was also too impractical, too inane. Just like he thought it should be converted into an insulated, more useful mudroom, he always wanted to convert me into something he deemed better, too.

"You ready?" I ask, annoyed by how timid my voice sounds.

"This is nice," Fisher says, still looking around the glass.

I swallow thickly. "Yeah," I hoarsely say. I struggle to tamp down the part of me that immediately wants to tell him how pretty it is in the mornings when the meadow's still kissed by dew or how it fogs up during the holidays when everyone's here and being boisterous—like the house itself has a physical symptom of joy. But then I force myself to remember that this is a virtual stranger, someone here only temporarily, who I don't have to pitch the virtues of my sunroom to.

We quietly make our way to the truck and pull down the drive.

"What's Indy up to today?" I ask. Seems like it'd be a safe conversation opener.

"Indy's hanging out with your nephew again today," he grouses, but for some reason, the grumpy inflection makes me smile once more. I can't imagine a single person on planet Earth feeling anything less than adoration for Sam.

"What happened the other night?" I ask. "Were they out past curfew or something? You didn't exactly explain."

He twitches uncomfortably as I pull out of the drive. "I also didn't explicitly give Indy a curfew before she went out. And you don't have to say it—I know that was my first mistake." I notice he's quick to shift blame onto himself or to explain when it comes to Indy. I wonder if he even realizes he's protective.

"I'm scared to ask if that had anything to do with the horn," I say, changing gears and heading down the road. "Hopefully no one got pinned against the wheel while in flagrante."

He cuts me a miserable glare. "Surprisingly, no. That was me alerting them that I was being forced to witness their passion against my will."

A laugh slides out of me, and he turns away. "Glad you find it so amusing." He pouts, but I catch the corner of his mouth tick up when he shakes his head. "God, I'm so clueless. I don't know what I'm doing when it comes to that kid."

Probably it's not that he's sharing this out of comfort or trust, it's more likely because every time our paths cross, he's already been in some exposed state—first with his obvious embarrassment during the vacuum affair, then during his mini meltdown when Indy had stayed out too late, and again in the meadow . . . but this small admission makes something twinge in my chest nevertheless.

"If it makes you feel at all better," I say, "every parent I've ever spoken to feels the exact same way."

He hums and goes back to watching the road in silence. I keep catching whiffs of his mild scent in the cab. It's clean and yet warm, something minty and woody, too. It's addicting in its subtlety and makes me want to lean in and seek more of it out.

After a while, he interrupts the scent profile I've begun building in my head to say, "I assume everyone around this place already knows about the vacuum thing?"

I grimace and hold back a chuckle. "What if I share some of my embarrassing stories? Would they help put you at ease?"

"Doubtful. I have a feeling I'll just get secondhand embarrassment on top of mine," he says seriously, eyes landing on me with laser-sharp focus. "But it would be very noble of you."

I find I'm driving below the speed limit for once, delighted to have him engaging with me like this. "Well, to preface this, you should know that my mom passed away when I was young. I was only six or so, and then my dad died when I was twelve, which left me being raised by three brothers. Ellis was eighteen." A wistful smile tugs up my cheeks, remembering the pure chaos of the time. "But, suffice it to say, I was too embarrassed to talk to my brothers about needing to buy a bra when I started . . . budding. And I'd found this nudie magazine in Micah's room once that had women with those little pasties on." I mime an X shape on my own nipple as if he needs some sort of demonstration, then feel myself blush furiously when I catch him studying the movement. I shift back to the road and try to concentrate. "Anyway, I, um—I put duct tape on my nipples and ripped a piece of one off, and it was bad enough that I had to get stitches," I blurt out in a rush. Oh god, why did I tell that story?! Quick, recover with a different one! "Oh! Once, in eighth grade, I was reading aloud to the class and accidentally read *ejected* as *ejaculated*," I say, my voice gathering volume as I try to dig myself out of this mortifying pit. "There were only eleven kids in my grade, so it *still* gets brought up occasionally." *OH MY GOD.* I really did that, didn't I? I just talked about nipples and ejaculating back-to-back.

"Where are you from?!" I all but scream at him, trying to catapult this conversation into a future where I'm maybe not so tragic. I can feel the sweat slicking beneath my palms against the steering wheel.

When he doesn't answer right away, I tilt back, only to find that he's adjusted to one hip, his broad shoulders facing me, and his expression barely harnessed. He's giving it a gallant effort, I'll credit him that. "Thank you for—all of that," he eventually manages, but the words sigh out of him like he had to boil his laughter until it evaporated into steam. "I'm technically from the Netherlands. We moved to the US when I was two and my sister was four. I live in New York now."

"So you're a chef in New York, but you're working here for the summer?"

One side of his mouth jerks up in a wry grin. "I am a chef," he says. "And yes, my backer bought a building out here that they're converting into a restaurant with an observatory, and she asked me to consult on the kitchen layout and to develop the menu."

It's an oddly stiff and selectively worded reply, but I get hung up on the newest information he's shared. "An *observatory*!" I say. "*That's* what that is!"

He side-eyes me curiously. "What'd you think it was?"

I mimic his expression. "Listen, none of us knew what to think. We just knew what it looked like."

"Which is?"

"Don't do that. Don't make this be the car ride where I talk about nipples, ejaculation, *and* penis-shaped erections. I've already given you so much."

He rumbles out a laugh, and I let myself steal another glance. It's even better than when he told me my sunroom was nice. I like how he tosses his head back with it, how his hand clutches his chest like he's trying to hold on to the feeling. He turns his head to me, still leaned up against his seat, and says, "You should get bonus points for throwing *erection* in there, though."

I give a little bow and flourish my hand in reply.

We settle back into a comfortable silence for a bit after that. The sun is spotty again today, but strong enough that the skies are more blue than Oregonian gray. Spunes is mostly comprised of jagged edges, but right now is when it's lushest, with bright pops of lupines and wild irises peeking through sprawling green. I roll my window down and let the fresh air slip through my fingers, let the resistance blast against my palm. A laugh hiccups free when I see Fisher doing the same.

When we slow down and make the descending turn that puts the old town into view, I say, "So, not to freak you out or anything, but because I happen to help out the homeowners while they're away, I also happen to know you're here for the whole summer."

"I assume you know a whole lot more than that, Sage," he replies.

I cast him a confused pout. "What do you mean?" I ask.

He blows out a long sigh. "You're gonna tell me that you haven't heard anything else about me, then? That the Main Street Businesses Coalition isn't out there plotting my demise as we speak?" There's an edge to his words, like he's daring me to lie. A muscle twitches in his jaw.

I'm not sure I should push him with that bitter tone, so I reach for humor instead. "Was it Hallmark that put you on to small towns? They get some of it right, but I swear . . ."

He only raises a brow and waits for me to continue.

I press my lips together and take one of the last turns I make to get into town. "I promise, the only reason I knew anything to begin with was because of my nosy brothers." I don't address the fact that they're probably why other people in town know things, too. For some reason, I want him to know that *I* wasn't actively trying to poke into his business sneakily. Aside from the initial peeping, of course.

"I know that Indy's your niece, but I could've found that out directly from her yesterday, and not necessarily because of any local nosiness or oversharing."

A beat passes, and I worry I've overstepped, but then he says, "My sister died three years ago. Car accident."

I inhale sharply, but consider my reply. I don't want to have a reaction that makes him uncomfortable. Then again, I can't bring myself to repeat the same greeting card slogans I've heard a thousand times, either. I decide to give him my plainest, most unfiltered thoughts.

"That is a fucked-up thing to have happened. To her, to Indy, and to you" is what I go with eventually. "And it's not fair."

His eyes flare bright and intense, still burning against my temple when I turn back to the windshield.

"Thank you," he croaks, barely audible over the muffled sounds of the car. "And . . . and yeah. We're here through most of August."

Sensing his need to move on, I pivot with him. "Seems kinda long just to help with a kitchen plan and come up with a menu? Just—" I hesitate, worried I'm officially crossing the threshold into busybody territory.

"Just seems like those are things I could do remotely?" he supplies.

I nod.

He turns and watches the road ahead, contemplative for a moment. "I've been struggling . . . at work. Out of touch, I guess, and it shows. It's *been* showing," he says. "I think this is my boss's way of helping me reset, while also giving me an opportunity to prove myself again. And I suppose she knew Indy and I needed the reset, too."

"It's nice that your boss cares about you like that, I'd think?"

He shakes his head and snorts. "Sorry, no, you're right," he says. "Nicer than I deserve, that's for sure." He lets out a reluctant sigh. "Carlie's good people. And just because I've been a mess doesn't mean she should have to let me bring everyone else down just for the sake of who I used to be."

"Grief changes you," I reply with as much brevity as I can. "And on top of that, it's probably a little more difficult to focus on, like, foie gras, when you're also suddenly worried about someone else's entire well-being all the time, too."

His eyes go wide again for a moment, like he's shocked that I jumped right to the grief of things rather than vaguely dancing around it. But the expression shudders away just as quickly. "It's always foie gras whenever someone makes a chef analogy," he says. "Why is it always foie gras?"

"The more important question is, *what* is foie gras, Fisher?" I reply. I can follow his lead here and keep it fairly light for him.

His chuckle is relieved, one side of his face pulling higher than the other. "I took you for something of a cook?" he says.

"You were in my kitchen for thirty seconds!"

"Exactly."

I've seen bashful Fisher, self-deprecating Fisher . . . and now I'm getting glimpses of confident, flirtatious Fisher. It seems entirely genuine, not a mask he's slipping on, maybe more like a hat he was meant to wear. And lord help me, I like this version of him, too, even if it makes me feel like I'm trying to balance on the tips of my toes.

I'm forced to turn and keep my attention on the road as I pull us into the parking lot. "You're that much of an expert?" I say.

"Believe it or not, they don't hand out Michelin stars to just anyone." He flashes a full smile at me when I whip his way, and the combination of his statement and the force of his grin make me slam on the brakes harder than I intend.

"Sorry, but *what*?!" I level him with an incredulous look. "You got a Michelin star?!"

His color rises, and he spins away, his expression closing off entirely. "Technically, it's the restaurant that gets the star, but . . . yeah," he says before he wordlessly exits the cab.

I look around, still dazed. "*What?*" I whisper to myself. Good god, did I really tell him I would help him with a menu? How did he not laugh in my face?

I rigidly get out and walk to where he waits for me by the front bumper. When I take a step past him, he stops me by my elbow, the touch lancing warmth up the limb and across my chest.

"It wasn't just the grief," he says, blowing out a frustrated breath. "Before. When you said that grief changes people. And it wasn't even that I immediately had Indy to worry about. Things stopped working for me before then. They were already taking a dive prior to the accident." He takes his hand back and shoves it in his pocket. "I felt like I should clarify that. It's part of why I was sent here."

He looks like he's just offloaded a confession, like he's a little ashamed but a lot relieved. And somehow, I get the sense that there's more he's not ready to say.

I take a deep inhale, the smells of grass and brine mingling with Fisher's scent around me—that intoxicating something that is most likely just his deodorant and not the mythical aroma my hormones are building it up to be.

"I'm sorry you were unhappy," I say.

His entire body tenses, his eyes searching the ground around our feet. "I wasn't *unhappy*. I was just . . . failing."

That twinge in my chest again. "See, Fisher, I have it on good authority that they don't hand Michelin stars out to just anyone," I tell him, dipping my head meaningfully. "I seriously doubt you were *failing*."

He tries so hard to smile at that, his hand swiping across his jaw and his fingertips pushing on the corners of his mouth like he wants to tack them in place. The sound of his palm against the stubble on his jaw makes my skin tingle and my nipples pinch. "I'll have to show you some reviews sometime that indicated otherwise," he hollowly states.

"I don't think we can base our success *entirely* on someone else's opinions," I say, disproportionately vehement. I think I might be projecting.

He crosses his arms and leans up against the car, big body landing heavily. "I think when your success quite literally depends on someone else wanting what you've got—wanting to spend their money on it—it does." His voice is somehow both resolute and tired.

Is this an argument? It sort of feels like it right now, but he's looking at me with such unfiltered curiosity that I think he just wants to know what I have to say. It's a heady sensation, and it also makes me want to steer things back to safer territory.

"Listen, I'm a teacher." I put my palms up in surrender. "No one *wants* what I'm selling, I just find ways to trick them into absorbing it."

I watch a flicker of something spark across his features before he chuckles, then settles into a light smirk. "Maybe, in a way, that's what I did, too," he declares.

CHAPTER 10

SAGE

Whatever discomfort Fisher might've felt over our conversation seems to be quickly forgotten. He stays by my side while we wander through O'Doyle's, amusing himself by picking up various items and showing them to me as if I haven't already seen them a billion times before. Conversation flows easily this way, too. He seems happy to listen, relaxing more and more as we go along. I tell him about the labyrinth drawings in the sand when we come to a magnet display section full of them. I explain how they're raked into a maze and how they're meant to be walkable paths with no definitive beginning or end. I explain that the small group of artists (some years only one older gentleman named Amos, with whoever he recruits from the beach) work on donations only. I wax on about how even though they inevitably wash away and it seems like this great effort for something so fleeting, people find them soothing and fascinating nonetheless. I think I maybe get too animated when I talk about the array of people enjoying them together during the season or that I sound a little too sentimental over something silly, but he surprises me when he puts a twenty in their donation box.

He studies a small figurine of two otters carrying a canoe while he tells me about how he left home at seventeen and went to culinary school in New York. He tells me about spending two years in France early on in his career and credits those years for a large portion of his success.

"So, then, are your parents still in New York?" I ask at some point. We've wandered into the women's clothing section, I realize.

He frowns at a cow print negligee before he looks back at me with a frightened expression.

"Not a single cow spotted since I've been here and yet . ."

I decide to try to stay on subject, hungry for more information from him while he appears to be in this generous mood. "I refuse to believe they don't sell bovine-themed lingerie in a place so vast as New York. Where I presume your parents still live?"

"Smooth redirect."

"Thank you, I know," I sing.

He takes a step closer and blows out a long sigh, cocking his head with a smile. "I didn't grow up in New York, so no, my parents don't live there. I grew up in Nebraska, which is where they still reside. Where Freya and Indy lived also." He gives me a look that begs the question "Is that enough?" and I decide that it probably needs to be, for now.

"Nebraska. Oh boy, I bet you're well versed in corny jokes, then," I say. His eyes clench shut like that joke caused him physical pain. "You'll fit in nicely here."

He shakes his head with a woeful look. "You'll have to forgive me, but I don't hold small towns in the highest esteem. Puns notwithstanding."

"Again I ask, was it Hallmark? Lifetime? Who tainted us in your eyes?"

"Firsthand experience," he says.

Oh. "Well, maybe we're not all the same."

He huffs a humorless *ha*. "You mean Spunes isn't like all the other girls?" he says sarcastically, and I have to let out a genuine laugh in reply.

"Much to our everlasting chagrin, that's for sure," I say. "This whole place is built on failure after failure and very little, or short-lived, hidden charm. Failed as a logging town, failed as a fishing bay, even the founders themselves were a cautionary tale. We've got about one month a year where we get to play the part, though."

He hums an indifferent noise and nods, and I get the feeling he's not the least bit interested in my pitch, so I swivel us to another subject.

"Now onto serious business," I segue, grabbing the first item to my left. "Do I need this for my collection?" I hold the kimono-style robe up against my body. It's patterned with pairs of coconuts and bananas placed lewdly between them. "Oooh, look!" I squeal when I glance just beyond and see the coordinating men's shirt. I hand it to him, and he holds it six inches in front of himself like a good sport, the corner of his mouth rolling down in mock disgust.

"Yellow's not my color," he monotonously states.

I give him a considerate stare. "You're right. Plus it'd do nothing for that monkey on your back."

That pulls a hollow chuckle from him. "Cute."

"Thank you, I know. I—" I spot Patricia Munty beside Fisher's elbow. Or the tip of her, at least. She's seventy-seven this year, with the same bottle-dyed orange puff of hair she's had my entire life. She is also four foot eleven on her best days.

"Hi, Mrs. Munty," I call in an octave too high. "Um, Fisher, this is Patricia Munty. She *hand makes* everything in this section." I give him a wide-eyed look. *Please be nice*, I hope it conveys.

Cataracted eyes behind Coke-bottle lenses stare up at him coquettishly. Her little canoe earrings—the ones I know that Athena Cirillo's sister, Venus, made herself to sell at last year's festival—sway gently. I raptly watch the interaction like I might will it into slow motion and catch any judgment passing over his features. From the baubles to her cypress-printed dress, Mrs. Munty looks like the human embodiment of our town, and I find that I have to see how he reacts to her.

"Call me Patty, dear," she says, demurely extending her wrist.

He quickly looks from me to her, then hangs up the shirt so he can take her whorled hand into both of his. "Wonderful to meet you, Patty." And I swear she nearly swoons. Fisher leveling the full force of this charming version of himself on someone is a sight. *He thinks my sunroom's nice!* I'm tempted to tell her.

"Didn't take you long to find our little hidden treasure, I see," she purrs and nods my way.

He lets out a low laugh that makes my ears burn. "I'd say she found me, actually."

I know it's only a polite agreement and that it shouldn't affect me in such a way, but that doesn't stop my mouth from going dry or my cheeks from flooding with heat.

Patty proceeds to point out the shirts she thinks he'd look best in, which is damn near all of them, according to her. She talks about her Eddie and how much he loved his silly patterns. How she needed something to occupy her time while she was grieving him, so she set to making clothes. Robes were the easiest to tackle at first, and then she never stopped.

"Sagey here keeps me in business, she loves them so much!"

she declares proudly. The flush that had just subsided comes roaring back. "Gosh, Sagey, how many do you have now? Fifteen?"

"I'm not sure, Mrs. Munty." *Twenty-one.*

Patty eventually leaves us to finish up what we came for, at which point Fisher turns to me with his arms folded and an inscrutable expression on his face.

"What?" I ask him.

"I think I've got you pegged, that's all," he arrogantly says. "You're the too-nice one, aren't you? The town golden girl. That's your thing." He pins me with an arch look. "The rescued animals, the rescuing me, all the free advice. The compulsive robe buying."

Two incongruous things are happening inside of me. The first thing is the realization that as I've been trying to get to know pieces of him, he's also been trying to get a read on me, and while that feels a little bit exciting, it also feels like getting home after a great day only to see that you have a gigantic chunk of spinach stuck in your teeth or one of those mascara boogers pooling in the corner of your eye.

And the other thing is that I am immediately triggered.

You're too nice is exactly the kind of thing Ian would say to me and in nearly this same way that Fisher just has—where it's something you mean to be playfully teasing in the beginning of the relationship, but turns out to be a real issue later on. It's never meant to be something bad, but it still sort of is. Ian went on to follow it with other admonishments like, *You spend too much time/energy/money on things that don't matter instead of spending that on something worthwhile. You could go to school for something else. You could, you should.* He'd belittled me and the life I'd built like I was spineless, like I couldn't possibly be satisfied living the way I do. Maybe I don't save lives or travel, and maybe I do wear some

ridiculous clothes and spend too much of my time in my impractical sunroom painting my nails just to wreck them the next day,
but . . .

But screw that. Perhaps I am too nice. I'm sure there are parts
of my life where I need to prioritize myself more, but in this case,
I "compulsively" buy her clothes for a valid cause.

Patty and Eddie Munty would let my brothers and me walk
to their house after school when Ellis was busy with a job and
paramedic training. They'd feed us buttered toast and taught us
dominoes, and I don't give a shit if someone passing through this
place thinks my quail kimono is the weirdest thing they've ever
seen, because it makes *me* smile, and I love that it was made by
someone who cares for me. Novelty or not, the happiness I feel
is real enough.

"I'm not too nice," I say firmly. "I'm most definitely *not* anyone's golden girl, and I like the stuff she makes because . . ." I
look around in frustration. "Because life's too fucking short,
that's why."

He rears back a little, blatantly confused. "Sage, I didn't mean
to offend you or anything, really."

"I know you didn't, but wait a second and let me finish." I
suck in a deep breath. My heart drums rapidly in my chest. I can't
pinpoint why I find it so important that he sees the whole picture.
All I know is that it stung coming from him because I don't want
to be painted in some vapid, meaningless, small way again. Something about him being new and not having any preconceived
notions of me makes me desperate to be properly understood.
"When people say that life's too short, I know that philosophy
tends to be synonymous with indulgence or with hurrying to
accomplish or chase something. Like 'life's too short, so you gotta
make a name for yourself or see the world now' sort of thing. But

in my case, life's already reminded me enough times that it's fleeting." I feel him looking at me as I run my hand back and forth along one of the oars on the wall. "And I decided a long time ago that life being too short and too beyond my control meant that I'd let the small stuff feel big. To me, at least. If it's something that doesn't matter to most, I think that means someone's gotta care a little more, right? Discarded pets, pretty flowers"—I look pointedly toward Patty's clothing section—"some raggedy kid that won't go on to do anything that changes the world." Our gazes clash, and I don't let myself blink away. "So don't think I choose those things just because I'm *too nice*. I'm not. I'm fully capable of deciding I want to do something because of how it makes me feel."

His lips are parted, and he's stepped closer to me. His eyes bounce around my face like they're not sure where to look, like he's searching for a crack in my logic somewhere. The lines between his brows leave an imprint even though he's not still frowning.

"All right," he says in earnest. "You're right." My eyes leave his face and get stuck on his throat. Such a simple response makes me want to fill the space with more explanations.

"When you lose people," I begin, and I see him instantly tense. "When you lose people and you're forced to internalize how little control you actually have . . . I think in the face of that, it's easy for everything else to feel senseless, too. Like, what's the point of pretty clothes or a perfect night sky or any of those inconsequential things that bring us joy? Why should any of it matter when it's all so easily wiped away?" I brave finding his eyes again. "I believe it's either that, or . . . or you decide that *everything* matters. All of it, all that little shit. Everything in the present and how it makes you feel in those tiny moments, *because* you can't possibly know when it'll all go away. If the result of that sort of caring is what makes me too nice, then fine," I say. "But I'm not weak for that."

He's shaking his head, the same astonished, strained look on his face. "You're not, and while I didn't say that, I'll admit it was shitty of me to imply," he says. "But I've also known people like that who got taken advantage of for caring that way. Who never got anything in return. From life, or from the people in it." He looks away and back. "My own sister included." He massages his jaw. "And maybe that's because she didn't ask, but maybe because no one else ever offered." His hands slide into his pockets, and he pins me with hard green eyes. "Tell me something I can do for you," he suddenly says. I think I'm maybe imagining that it sounds like pleading.

But then he adds, "You said you wanted my help with getting some things." His eyes continue making laps around my face. "But there must be something else you want. Something else I could do for you."

"This doesn't have to be transactional," I say, a little bewildered at the flip in this exchange.

"I'm capable of deciding when I want to do something, too, Sage, and maybe I decided just now that I'd like to be kind and caring for the sake of it," he firmly states. "You don't have to answer right away, but give it a think. My first offer the night we met might've been made out of being polite, but I mean this one with my whole chest."

I clear my throat and point to one of the paddles higher up on the wall. "Can you reach that for me?" I ask. "They're what I recruited you for."

He deftly plucks it down and then looks at me like he's waiting for more directions.

"One more, please."

He grabs another. "What are these for?"

"Training."

"For what? For this thing?" He points up to one of the festival banners.

"Yeah." I leave it at that. It's probably the perfect opportunity for me to explain more about it, but I find that I simply can't just yet. I feel like an exposed nerve. Like I just became way too unguarded to someone who *should* feel like more of a stranger still. I've always been someone that prides herself on her ability to read people, always searching in the gaps for where I might fit in . . . and Fisher keeps managing to flummox me.

I do a better job of staying on task the rest of our time in the store, asking for his help with multiple bags of fertilizer and a concrete planter I'd like to use for an ornamental tree somewhere in the sunroom.

"So, I take what I said back about you being the golden girl," he says when we eventually make our way to the register. "Even though I maintain that I didn't mean it in a bad way." He nudges his shoulder into mine good-naturedly. "But this motherfucker thinks he's everyone's golden boy, doesn't he?"

I follow his eyes to the winner's wall of photos. "Who? Ian?"

"Yeah. The life-sized Ken-doll reject," he says, and I fail to stop a laugh.

"He doesn't just think he's everyone's golden boy," I tell him. "He just . . . *is*, unfortunately."

I feel him studying me as we make our way out to the car. "Couldn't help but notice the weird vibe at my house the other night. You have a history?"

"Hard not to have a history with everyone in a town whose population number is missing a comma," I reply.

"You know what I mean," he says, those sharp eyes unwavering.

But that too-raw feeling is brushed again, so I say, "Careful, Fisher. You're starting to be a bit nosy. You might just fit in here more quickly than you think." I finish the remark with a dry laugh.

He doesn't respond to that, his mouth twitching in a brief smile before he shakes his head.

"We were together for five years," I concede. "We broke up a little over a year ago, and he's already engaged to an old friend from high school who had just moved back shortly before he broke up with me." I hope I hide the bitterness when I say, "He always told me I was too nice, too. He made me feel like I was too silly all the time. I think I might've been a little too small-town even for him. Probably why I had such a strong reaction earlier."

He looks mollified and even sheepish at that, and I have to bite back the urge to say something self-deprecating in a more light-hearted way, something that'd make my candor seem glib and less true. But it feels good to speak plainly for once. To worry a little less about making my feelings smaller to spare someone else the discomfort. My previous monologue might've left me feeling a bit too wide open, but it also felt great to get it all out.

I wedge the flatbed away from Fisher and push it the remaining distance to the register. I quickly start making small talk with Ransom Phillips, one of Sam's friends working here for the season. He darts multiple glances Fisher's way, who seems too lost in thought for me to make introductions.

Fisher stays quiet as we make our way back to the truck and through loading all my newly acquired goods. But when I close the tailgate on the truck bed, he stops me with a palm on top of mine before he says, "Something tells me I couldn't have you pegged in a decade, let alone a few days, Sage. But even I can tell that you're vast."

Stupid, traitorous blood in my veins, blooming to the surface. "Th-thank you," I dully reply, like that wasn't the greatest compliment I've ever received.

"You're welcome," he says. His lips press into a smirk, and I wonder if he's recalling the way I clumsily tripped all over my *you're welcome* the other day, like I immediately do.

I laugh through my nose and remember the last errand I have on my list. "Hey, I have to return a few books to the library while we're here. If you don't mind," I say.

"No problem at all," he replies.

"You want to join me? The library is *almost* as interesting as O'Doyle's, I promise."

Maybe the library would help him quiet his mind, too, like the garden did yesterday. It always does for me. I want him to see the wall of windows that look out past the park and over the sea.

Not to mention I'd love to counteract his small-town jadedness with one of our only year-round charms.

He smiles softly, one of those tiny earrings catching the light. "Sure. I just need to try Indy again. Tell me where to meet you."

I leave him with directions and start the uphill march, feeling a bit like I'm walking on air in spite of the steep climb. The entire main section of Spunes's town is built on a slope, with homes standing in clusters on the flat fingers of cliffs that spread outward, or over beyond the main ridge like where mine and the Andersens' are. Everything is architecturally an eclectic mix of craftsman or Victorian, and the library is one of those that leans fully into the latter. It's the tallest building in town, with the tallest windows and the most stairs. I ascend the familiar front steps now, legs on fire and a happy anticipation in my veins. Everything in this place, from the railings to the moldings, down to the mishmash of art on the walls, is crowded with too much gaudy detail. I love it. There's something new to see no matter how many times I've been. I love that it smells perpetually damp, that one alcove could be ten degrees hotter or colder than the next because of some old window or door. I love thinking of the people who have touched the same old books and walked the same spiral stairs. I think maybe that's one of the only truly romantic things about this particular small town. The numbers are comprehendible. I *can* actually imagine this place before and after me.

The first floor of the library was renovated when I was in kindergarten. I remember the year because this was where I'd come after school when my mom was in her final stages. I'd sit with Venus's basset hound, Tucker, and try to soothe him with all the construction noise coming up from below. That dog howled at any errant noise, which made this probably the loudest library on the western coast that year. But one day that fall, when Dad and Ellis showed up early, Tucker only whimpered and licked my palm. I think on some subconscious level, I knew he was warning me that they were taking me to say goodbye.

Tucker is long since gone now, too, but Venus's regal Maine coon cat greets me when I step off the ornate stairs and onto the third floor. Cupid twitches her whiskers and flicks her tail to indicate her excitement.

I take down my hair to ease my aching scalp, and start unloading my books onto the polished counter, when Venus herself appears.

"Sage," she sings in her biggest librarian voice. "What are you doing here?" She glances around nervously, then makes like she plans to round the counter and hustle me back out.

I give her a confused pout. "Um, I'm returning these?"

"Sage?" I hear to my right. "Hey, Sage, how are you?"

A sickly cold washes over me when I turn to find Cassidy there, with Ian right behind her, coming out from one of the alcoves. I happen to know that there's a stained glass window above a small table in that one, colorful mermaids with haunted eyes. Cassidy smooths her perfect dark hair around her flawless face and plucks at her shirt like she's pulling it back into place. My thoughts flatline. I've obviously known about them this entire time, I've obviously imagined them together, but I've gotten away with not *seeing* it this whole year. I certainly never imagined them here, in this place that holds so much for me.

I've never had to actually watch Ian slide a hand around her waist and tuck her into his side. I'm having trouble processing how openly affectionate he is as he rests his head on hers and looks longingly back at their table.

I follow his line of sight, and my throat goes impossibly tight, like I tried to swallow a cup of cold honey. Copies of Spunes history records, old articles, and photos.

"Oh, look, baby!" Cassidy coos, and I jolt like I've been slapped. "She's returning that book you were looking for. We can check it out now!" She turns to me, and I hope I arrange my features into something resembling a smile, but I can feel the corners of my mouth trembling strangely. "Are you studying for the trivia stuff, too?" she asks. "That's exciting! Ian's hours are crazy, so I would love to have someone to train with for the race." God, she's so genuinely sweet that I hate that I can't justify being unfriendly back.

"Oh, um. Well—"

"Honey, I don't think Sage is doing the festival. Besides, we probably wouldn't want to give the opponents a leg up, right?"

Ian looks at Cassidy like she's a precious cherub and he's sad to burden her with the evils of competition.

"Stop," she chides. Her hand lightly slaps against his pec and stays there when his palm comes on top of it. "You know that's not the spirit of this thing, anyway." She looks back at me. "Sage, I'm so excited you're doing it this year." She's looking at me eagerly, and I suddenly can't remember if I said I was doing it. I didn't, right? Is she just assuming based on the books she sees me with and ignoring Ian, or did I black out somewhere? I hear footsteps on the stairs, and my panic surges at the thought of more witnesses to this humiliation. My brain feels like static and *ohmygod*, do I have to tell them that I couldn't find a partner?! I have to make something else up. I'll say I'm going to Europe. That's it. I'll say, *Oh,* shoot. *I wanted to do it, hence why you see me with all these books here related to topics surrounding the damn thing, but that was before I learned that those particular days in August are the best time of year for Cannes, and you see, Cannes can't wait. Big things to do in Cannes. Huge.*

A rough, warm hand slips under my hair, pressing between my shoulder blades, and I instantly melt back like I might disappear into it. My eyelids flutter when the hand glides up to the back of my neck, fingers lightly squeezing.

"There you are," Fisher's deep rumble says against my ear, and my knees wobble. I lean back into him and turn my head to the side. He's inches from me, and my eyes go from the green and brown in his to a darker patch in the scruff on his cheek that I'm just now realizing is a dimple. I could push up on my toes and dip my tongue into it if I wanted. His fingers squeeze below the base of my skull again, and I have to choke back a moan. That rational part of my brain that should step in and tell me to be more reserved has been entirely hip-checked aside by the part that keeps replaying him calling me vast and the other parts that want to curl into his heat or pool into the strong grip at my neck. *This,* this *is what you can do for me,* I want to tell him right now, in response to that offer from earlier. *You can rescue me and my pride.*

"I want to show you something" is what I breathily say instead.

He smiles, and I can feel the laugh roll through him before it ghosts across my lips. "I want to see it," he says, and with that rational part of my brain still nowhere to be found, it is somehow the most illicit thing anyone has ever said to me. My blood feels like it halts and changes direction, my pulse gathers somewhere low in my belly. "Where is it?" he asks.

What is it? is also a good question. "Over there." I point aimlessly.

A phony-sounding giggle escapes Cassidy, but I keep my eyes trained on Fisher. "I'm Cassidy. You must be that chef who's here for the summer," I hear her say.

"See you around, Officer," Fisher says, not bothering to tear his gaze from mine, either. There's a delighted, wicked gleam in his eye, and it eases something in me to think that he's having fun with this, even if it's just to piss off Ian. When he finally does look away, he hits them with the widest smile I've yet seen from him. "Nice to meet you, Chastity. Have a good day," he states before he takes me by the hand and hauls me away.

CHAPTER 11

FISHER

I try a few times to call Indy to check in, but only get a string of irritated texts in response.

Apparently, one of Sage's geese broke out, waddled over, and won't leave Indy and Sam alone. She tells me he's not unfriendly to her, but continues to attack Sam, and they're busy trying to herd him back to the house.

Since I'm not sure how I can advise on the goose state of affairs, I head in the direction that Sage pointed me in. I can see her off in the distance—already a hundred yards or so ahead uphill, so I try to pick up my pace.

My mind drifts back over the last hours and days. Sage's assertiveness—the way she took the reins with Indy, with me yesterday, and again today when she plied me with usefulness. While I still experience brief moments of uncomfortable aggravation at having someone insert themselves into my life uninvited—an old, defensive instinct in me that's probably heightened by being in a small town again—it's also that same quality about Sage that makes it impossible to be anything but fully present when she's around. Like when your sock slips down the inside of your shoe and it feels like your entire nervous system becomes focused there. I doubt I could let my consciousness go blurry around her if I tried.

I think maybe I should apologize again for earlier, though. Despite the sarcasm, it obviously upset her when I called her the town golden girl. After hearing more about her ex, it's clear that while the love between her and this place is reciprocal, she still feels some sort of otherness—something that separates her even though I think she *wants* to be in step with everyone around her. Probably the same reason why she seems to chafe at any of my small-town commentary, too.

Jesus, maybe I need to schedule another video call with Dr. Deb. I think therapy might be making me more in tune with other people's emotions instead of helping me sort out my own.

I have to catch my breath when I finally make it to the front of the library, bracing my hands on my knees before I look up, up, up at the castle-like building. It looks more like something that belongs in France rather than in some oblique Oregonian village.

I make my way inside and up the spiral stairs, until I catch sight of Sage through the metal railing when I'm somewhere between the second and third floor. The look on her face makes me pause midstep.

Lips ashen, shoulders hunched, and chin tucked. Her eyes dart rapidly back and forth between the people in front of her, and her cheeks keep pulling up in a smile but falling short, repeatedly. It's like watching a screen getting hung up on a glitch. This is also when I notice that it's the cop in front of her, purring over the woman he's got tucked into his side.

It hits me now that I definitely know why I recognize Sage's little fissure of insecurity, that strain of otherness that keeps her apart in spite of all she does to incorporate herself.

It's because it's the same brand of insecurity for me, much as I hate to admit it.

I'm also reminded, once again, why I despise small towns. You risk running into the same cycle of people around every corner, every day. The same ones who've cast you in the same tired roles.

I find myself hurrying up the remaining stairs and stepping in close to her back. I decide not to analyze it when my hand reaches out to press between her shoulder blades. I only know how tensed up she seems, and that I'd like to smooth it away.

The moment my hand glides up to the soft skin on the back of her neck, she softens into it, and I'm filled with something both sharp and tender. For this woman who has no reason to trust or find comfort in me with any amount of quick ease but is leaning into me nonetheless.

"There you are," I say. I squeeze her neck in reassurance.

"I want to show you something," she replies dazedly after a beat, and I'm relieved when I see the color rushing back to her face.

"I want to see it. Where is it?"

She points in the general direction of the rest of the library, and I keep smiling like a moron at her pretty face. The woman Ian's with introduces herself.

"See you around, Officer," I eventually say, not looking away from Sage.

When I eventually do look up again, I let my palm travel across as much of her exposed skin as I can, holding Ian's stare as I do it: my fingers along the slope of her shoulder, knuckles tracing her arm, then down to braid her hand with mine. "Nice to meet you, Chastity. Have a good day," I say to them before I lead us away.

I choose an aisle at random and pull her to my front, facing me.

"You all right?" I ask. Her face is stuck on a strange, confused frown.

"Yeah. I just—I don't want to talk to them again," she whispers, averting her eyes. The skin at the base of her throat thrums wildly, a blush smattered across her neck and cheeks.

"Of course you don't," I say as firmly as I can in a whisper. Even if I'm selfishly glad to be the one rescuing her in a low moment for a change, I hate that she's having the low moment in the first place. As little as I know her, I still know she shouldn't have to be uncomfortable anywhere in this whole tasteless town. Not someone like her—this interesting dichotomy of warm and fierce. Who gives her time, home, and energy to wounded creatures . . . even the unfamiliar ones on two legs, like me.

"I don't want to leave, either," she says. "I don't want to act like it's a big deal."

"Of course you don't. You shouldn't be forced to leave anywhere. Definitely not because of that prick." Guilt rears up once again and kicks me in the chest when I think of how snide I was to her the other night. How fucking condescending.

"*God*, that was mortifying," she murmurs. "I froze. I've never had to see them together up close like that." She groans and tries to bury her face in her hands. "I don't *want* him, so why should I care?!" she continues whispering rapidly. "And who even is he? He *hated* PDA. He didn't even like the library. Always said the dust aggravated his allergies."

We're both leaned up against a bookcase, huddled closer

somehow. "I think sometimes some people make us different versions of ourselves, whether we mean to let them or not."

She snorts. "Right. She's better, so she brings out a better version of him."

"No, sweetheart." I push a lock of her hair back behind one of her ears before I can consider it or consider why I'm comfortable doing it. "I'd wager he just knew you were too far above him, so he tried to bring you to his level. By making the things that light you up seem dim to him." Her lips part, and her gaze sharpens. "I don't know the guy, but I know his type," I say. "Besides, it looked to me like he was going out of his way to try to make you jealous."

She laughs through her nose, rolls her eyes. "It looked to me like it was just natural, Fisher. I don't think Ian would recognize jealousy if it hit him with a truck. I doubt anyone's ever made him jealous in his life."

Having this conversation in hushed tones makes my blood feel like it's being whisked into a frenzy. "Try me," I say, because I'm still not second-guessing and it's the most present and awake I've felt in forever.

"What?" Her whisper is barely a breath this time, and now the nerves start to crank.

"I mean, *we* could try. It might feel good to take something back. If you want."

Her thigh lightly bumps into mine. "How?" she asks, the blush deepening on her cheeks and her eyes like platinum.

I slant a nod behind her. "They're across the landing there. I could—I mean—" *How do I put this in the least lecherous way possible where she absolutely recognizes that I won't hold it against her if she declines, but also knows I'm willing and able?* "If I kiss you, you know they'll see."

Her throat catches on a swallow and—what am I doing? I'm watching my fingers reach out and lightly trace it. The tip of my thumb as it strokes along her collarbone. I choke back a sound when her cool palm reaches up to my jaw, and I nuzzle into it.

And then she pats me gently. "You're trouble," she whispers conspiratorially.

I think I might be. Trouble or *in* trouble—one of the two. But it does rankle a bit that it's so easy for her to turn me down.

Nah. I don't buy it. I don't buy that she's so virtuous that she doesn't want to do something selfish for a moment, that she doesn't need a little win.

"Come on. I thought you weren't always too nice?" I say it like a dare. "Tell me you don't want to hurt him back a little."

"Once again, you are assuming that he gives a shit." She says it indifferently, but I catch the hint of a question in it.

"Fine. Even if it's not just about him, don't you ever just want to take something for *you*? You said it yourself—this is *your* library."

"I mean, I don't *own* it."

"But you said he didn't even like coming here. Just mentioning the place earlier made your face go bright like it was Christmas morning. Come on, Byrd, wouldn't a small win feel nice?"

A little crease between her eyes. She's considering it. And then she quirks a dark brow in a challenge. "Explain how kissing you is a win for me."

God, I forgot how good flirting with a woman could feel. "I could probably explain better with a demonstration."

Her mouth and eyes go wide in a smile. "Trouble," she repeats.

"It'd also show him you can't be alienated." Plus, that lower lip has a spot in the middle that looks berry-stained, and I really want to know if it's just as sweet.

"Are you sure?" she then asks, teeth pressing into that spot. Something gives a hopeful lurch in my chest.

But, *am I sure*? I don't know when I was last sure about anything. My thoughts and emotions resemble shattered glass lately. Pieces of them everywhere, sharp, some fragments so tiny and hidden I'll never find them until I unavoidably slice myself on them later.

I am sure that for no logical reason I'd like to go punch that idiot Ian in the face, though. I'm pretty sure I'd wear an entire banana-and-coconut-printed jumpsuit to taste her mouth right now. I'm almost sure they're pumping something into the air here. "Yes."

And then I do. We do—or, most accurately, she does.

She presses up on the tips of her toes and sinks her hands through my hair in a way that makes me nearly gasp before she softens her mouth against mine. A gentle press, before I take each of her lips between my own, one at a time. She's smooth and cool, and the slightest eagerness in her makes it roar through me. I thumb her chin to part her rosy mouth wider, and when the tip of her tongue touches mine shyly, something in me fractures and heats. She's so *sweet*, coaxing my tongue with hers, angling her head to offer me more, to take more. She nibbles my lip, and a tight noise leaves her, something that makes me feel electrified and slightly frantic. I lick at that sound like I might find it again and see what it tastes like when her little fists curl against my scalp. Her back pushes up against the bookcase with a muted thud as she tugs me against her. Then her hands leave my head and scrape along my back, down until they reach my ass, and she hauls our hips together. Suddenly, none of this seems like it could be about anyone else anymore, nothing shy or vengeful or fake.

Shit. Shit. Shit. Too fast. Too much. I'm already stiffening, and she's pressing me against the softest parts of her, grinding. I tear myself away, groping for her hands and trying to regain control. I grab at her wrists and push them apart and above her head, and fuck, it's somehow both better and worse, so much worse, but I cannot come undone in a fucking *library*. My pride can't take that hit right now, but every breath presses her chest into mine, her nipples pebbled through her top—

A drawled-out yowl sounds from just above, jolting us apart.

I let out a distinctly unmanly yelp when I spot a pair of gargantuan gold eyes staring at me from the top shelf, huddling myself over her, my shoulder like a shield.

"*Jesus, what is that?!*" I hiss. I've dropped Sage's wrists and spot them pinned against her sides. She huffs out a small pant that lands against my Adam's apple.

"Well," she says, breathing heavily, gulping. "I am not able to turn around to see for sure, but I'm guessing it's Cupid—Cupid the cat."

I take a deep breath, but don't move. "Just—I need just one second," I say. I glance warily at the beast again. "Christ! That thing mixed with a tiger?" It's the biggest domestic cat I've ever seen. This place is like a carnival fun house of animals.

"No," she replies, still searching my face. "It's just . . . really big." And then she claps a palm over her mouth to cover a hysterical laugh. The way her body vibrates against mine with it sends a bolt of molten torture through me.

I push away but let my forehead fall to her shoulder to muffle my own laugh, even if I'm not sure I get what's funny.

"*Shh*, we'll get kicked out," she squeaks between another short bout. My eyes get tripped up on her lips—thoroughly kissed—and I have to make myself look away and focus on some title beside her ear. *Farts and Arts: The Craft of Lighthearted and Life-Changing Comedy* by Farley Jones.

When I meet Sage's gaze again, she darts a sidelong glance across the way and back. "I'm—I'm not sure if it worked or not. It looks like they moved."

"Oh, uh . . ."

"I don't think they even noticed," she says, frowning.

I noticed. I definitely took notice. I'm *still* too alert. "Shit. Sorry." I'm not sorry at all. Not in the slightest.

Another laugh through her nose and a smile that could guide a ship into safe harbor. "Don't be. It was fun. Let me show you my favorite section."

And then she pecks me on the cheek like a friendly relative before she ducks under the cage of my arms and starts walking away, leaving me wholly stupefied.

CHAPTER 12

FISHER

She's recovered more swiftly from that kiss than I did from that bite of berry scone this morning.

Maybe I don't like this library, either. What the hell is so interesting here that she was this easily diverted? And dammit, how did she *get* to me this quickly? How did I go from wanting to avoid the obnoxiously quaint, grating kitschiness of this place to following its veritable spokeswoman around like a wayward dog?

She walks me over a ways and around a hidden corner where we come to a recessed section lined on both sides with more shelves, with floor-to-ceiling iron windows at the back. Above them is a leaded-glass arch depicting a canoe filled with colorful flowers that looks like it's about to float off into the sea beyond. The light filtering through it shines a collection of jewel-toned hues across the ceiling, and my eyes catch on a square there with a rope pulley dangling from it.

"What's that?" I say.

"Patience," she chides with a saucy expression. "We'll get to that part of the tour another day."

I clamp my teeth together and give her a flat look, still too revved-up to play back.

"You'll have noticed the recurring theme of canoes around Spunes by now, I'm sure?" she primly asks.

I grunt a confirmation.

"Well, do you also recall when I mentioned that this place was built on failures?"

"Am I going to be tested on this later?"

"Ooh, good question! Only if you want to be!" I scowl in confusion as she presses on. "History states that a well-to-do couple named Edmund and Ida Lee-Hughes settled here with their families in 1870, with the intention of creating a logging town. The origins of their fortune are a mystery that has inspired many an urban legend, but what is certain is that even though the gold rush ended in 1855, they thought there was more wealth to be amassed in timber."

I step closer to her. "Sage, I barely got my GED, not for lack of intelligence but mostly because lectures make me want to start lighting things on fire."

"Fisher, I'll be happy to listen to your origin story later, but right now, we're discussing canoes."

I growl in annoyance and let my head fall back dramatically.

"I promise I'll make it quick," she says.

And because my pride is still a little wounded, I decide to do an experiment. "What if I don't like it quick, Sage?" I ask, rapt on her reaction. "What if I prefer to savor things. Want it good and slow and drawn out?"

Pupils dilate, a tiny wisp of a gasp. A red flush across her cheeks. *There*. She's not so unaffected after all. She swallows.

Blinks. Then firmly tucks her expression away. "The Lee-Hugheses came in too late to the game, though," she continues.

"*Oh my god,*" I complain. "You're worse than your cat."

"So now they found themselves broke, with almost no prospective business, because they didn't account for their harbor conditions not being adequate enough for appropriate transport ships. *And*—the important part—they found themselves with a shit ton of felled trees."

"I'm riveted."

"They'd brought all sorts of family and friends here with them, too. People who'd started various businesses of their own under the impression that there would be a big, prosperous mill centering this local economy and drawing more people to the area."

I'm doing my best to resist it, but just like earlier when she started talking about the mazes and paths people draw on the beach, she starts pulling me under her spell.

"They needed to figure out a way to recoup some money, and fast. They looked at what they did have and came up with a scheme."

"Let me guess. It involved canoes."

"Precisely. Look at you! Star student!" she exclaims, and I find myself eagerly thinking I could be an excellent and enthusiastic teacher if she'd let me, too. "The entire family made up these phony brochures that they dispersed up and down the Columbia River, not only advertising this place as some idyllic haven but tempting people to come try their luck in a canoe race. The prizes would be ten different plots of land."

She grins, pleased with herself when she notices my attention. I lift a brow in encouragement.

"They had to figure out how to just barely turn a profit on

each canoe, small enough that people would buy in, and established that as an entrance fee. Obviously, this figure still sounded like a bargain when the chances seemed decent enough to end up with land. And even though the Lee-Hugheses were chunking off their property, they had way more than they could use to begin with, anyway. Not only that, but of course they made sure the plots they were giving away were the worst, most hostile little corners that they had. Everyone else in town agreed to the scam since they knew that more people—the contestants and the attendees, plus all their families—would mean more business for them." She pulls out a dusty book and flips to a page full of grainy black-and-white photos of angry-looking people in canoes.

"So it worked, then?" I ask.

"It did. But of course there's more to the story over the years. Greed, danger, love . . ." She looks sideways up at me over the book. "I'll save the details for another time, but can I tell you one secret?" She chews her lip like she might be truly nervous. I nod.

"The way our whole festival plays out nowadays is different, of course. The prizes, the events themselves have all changed over time. No one has a canoe provided for them, and no one gets any land, but in the end, it's still the same. We do it for us."

"What do you mean?"

"We've yet to have anyone other than locals win. Ever. Even back when it all started and the prize was some seemingly garbage land—those people always found a way to make that lot work in the end, and they never left. Now we draw in outsiders for our businesses to profit from, charge them a large enough entrance fee to account for the prize money, *and* one of us, or rather, a pair of us, always wins that, too."

I can't smother a grin. "I don't know if that sounds all that sheisty, Sage. Most tourist traps have the same idea."

"Maybe not," she says with an innocent shrug. "But in theory, anyone can win. There are buy-in contests for points that determine a team's starting order for the race, and those have double-blind judges, and the trivia is technically all public record." She delicately returns a book to its rightful place on the shelf before she casts a cute grin my way again. "I just think it's interesting, that's all," she says.

I think it's interesting that the last twenty-four hours found me laid out in a field, mingling in a random nowhere shop, and listening to history in a library, and yet, have also proven to be the most interesting day I've had in a long while.

CHAPTER 13

SAGE

I've finally figured out the whole *heart skips a beat* expression. It doesn't *miss* a beat, it actually starts skipping like Dorothy down the yellow brick road, possibly on Red Bull. Mine is still thrashing around in my chest and trying to reset its rhythm the morning after kissing Fisher, and I am desperate to find purchase again.

I managed to play it cool on our way home from the library, shyly bidding him farewell when we pulled into the driveway. I've opened up and typed a weird thank-you text about ninety-seven times, but have wrangled myself away from hitting Send. Every time I think about it, I groan aloud and throw an arm over my eyes.

Reckless, that kiss. I'd been naively trying to behave as if I had the wherewithal to keep my composure and then nearly came undone on the spot. He was so *warm*, solid, firm, big. His mouth tasted sweet and minty and made me self-conscious about my own, but not inhibited enough to drown out everything else. I got too lost to the feel of him, the sounds of him. Thinking of that small, raspy hitch he made against my lips makes something clench tight in me again.

No. No, I was too quickly overwhelmed and needed to focus on something else, which is why I reached for the history material. I couldn't risk fawning over him like he probably assumed I would, either. Not when he might've only been trying to return a favor.

It's still the dark hours of morning, but sleep is a lost cause at this point. I pace around the house, secretly hoping to rouse at least one of the animals early. No such luck, though. What's the point of these companions if they can't support me with some *companionship* in my time of need? I reach for my phone and send a silent wish to the internet gods for the perfect algorithm to trap me with a doom scroll distraction, but, because technology has apparently become so advanced that it has mastered the ability to sync with my innermost psyche, the videos I come across all consist of things that send my thoughts cartwheeling back into unsafe territory—à la thirst traps and cooking videos. Sometimes a combination of the two.

It's when I swipe out that another tempting thought hits me, and I'm thumbing over to Google before I can talk myself out of it. If someone has a Michelin star, I imagine they have an online presence of some kind. I hover over the Enter key after I've typed in his name and pause, walking over to the kitchen to make myself consider it for a beat. I could tell that Fisher was hesitant to be open with me, almost defensively private or evasive about certain pieces of his information. This isn't me lurking around the trees and stealing glances across the property lines, and it's not me asking him directly, either. This is intentional snooping.

Then again, any woman would google a man before spending time with him, which is what I will presumably be doing if I help him with menu feedback and if I work up the nerve to ask him to do the festival with me. Most would argue this is prudent with him in proximity, regardless. It feels a little late, given our previous interactions, but I suppose it might be better late than never?

I dive for the chair in the sunroom and hit Enter.

Results are all positive, at first. An article online that accompanies a younger picture of him. His hair was a bit shorter here, but just as unruly, even with a bandanna tied around the top of his head to keep it out of his face. He's bent over and arranging something on a plate with an expression on his face that I think is meant to look doting or concentrated but only appears posed to me.

I come across a list of awards. Another article praising him for being one of the youngest chefs in the country to obtain a star at twenty-three. A James Beard Award, too. Some food critic blogs that are exuberant with their acclaim, followed by some that are more ambivalent and reserved, then a few that are downright hateful. The hateful ones read like they're trying to shame anyone who enjoyed his food into reconsidering or like they're accusing those people of lying. I find myself getting offended on his behalf and even more on the behalf of these other people who lauded him. So what if he made the same things for a few years in a row. Is that not the norm? Maybe that's what his patrons were coming back for. Maybe those dishes were someone's favorite and they would've been devastated to have them taken off the menu. Maybe he didn't have that kind of creative control. It's the restaurant that actually gets the star, after all. Maybe it's the ownership's decision on those things.

I come to another headline titled MARROW LOSES TWO STARS, AND ONLY ONE OF THEM IS MICHELIN. It details how their Michelin star was revoked earlier this year and the head chef subsequently fired. I frown at that. He didn't divulge that he was fired, but I suppose he didn't lie about it, either, and it's not exactly a fun icebreaker to share. There are very few details about why the restaurant lost the star to begin with, only a few remarks and quotes from anonymous customers stating that the price did not reflect the quality and that the service was not enthusiastic enough. Toward the end of the piece, the author speculates that they did not personally find Marrow deserving of the loss but that maybe Fisher had set too high a standard from the jump, that he'd shown all this promise and was "gifted" this renown for being something new and exciting in the culinary scene, and then proceeded to stop doing new or exciting things. A flash of indignance heats beneath my skin at the term *gifted*, as if it wasn't deserved or earned. She repeats again, though, that this wasn't grounds for rescinding the star in her opinion, that she thinks it's a shame he was fired, but she also invites everyone else's thoughts in the comments after watching the linked video at the bottom of the page. I scroll all the way down and spot it: *Michelin-Starred Chef Has Public Meltdown on Critic.*

I hold my breath and click. I'm taken to a grainy video, clearly taken from a phone in a dimly lit restaurant from a few tables' distance away. Fisher is seated at his own table, a lone candle illuminating the hard planes of his face as he stares down at some sort of dessert. He's got a fork held tightly in one hand, the muscles in his jaw clenching irritably. Another man stands at the edge of his table, shrugging and talking animatedly with his hands, cocking his head at him like a bird observing a worm. None of their dialogue is audible until Fisher abruptly stands and shoves the pie in the other guy's face, and even then it's mostly just the gasps and muttering from around the room that get picked up.

"You don't know me, and you don't get to act like you do," Fisher says, stabbing a finger into the man's pie-smothered face. "You're not just fucking with my livelihood but a lot of other people who work harder than you ever have sitting on your ass smacking your grubby fingers on some keys." He makes to walk away, but turns back and says, "And you interrupted my dessert."

I can't imagine the guy didn't say something to initiate the whole exchange, but I blow out a frustrated breath nonetheless. "He started it" seems like an unjustifiable response, and without the rest of the audio, the video could too easily be interpreted as a harmless, affable critic running into a chef in a public setting, interacting respectfully, and then being accosted.

I end up searching out the critic's blog, and quickly come to the review linked to the entire incident.

WRATH OF ROTH BLOG

CHEF FISHER LANGE: SAFE AND . . . SO VERY SORRY

Ten years ago I had the distinct pleasure of dining at the Michelin-starred Deelane, Chef Fisher Lange's maiden voyage as chef de cuisine. I'd heard whispers of a new revelatory chef, someone who'd cut his teeth in some of the greatest restaurants in the world and was widely being hailed as the latest best and brightest. I set out with wary expectations, with the admittedly negative intention of proving the "hype" wrong.

Instead, I was pleasantly surprised. Floored, even. Every single bite was a delight. Brave, edgy . . . dare I say sexy? Fisher Lange's food was the perfect mixture of comforting and bold. Our boy wasn't serving the same schlock that everyone in town was. No, instead of drowning everything in truffles—the big "movement" of the moment, if you can dub it that—Chef served up a spicy pumpkin gnocchi—the likes of which still frequent my dreams. Instead of some basic-bitchy-bisque, Lange was ladling a cauliflower pot de crème that was well ahead of its time.

But even shooting stars must burn out, I'm afraid.

I'll admit, I enjoyed the opening of Chef Lange's current restaurant, Marrow, nearly seven years ago, backed by the renowned Visconti family. Everything was technically sound; his dishes were curated and cooked to perfection. I like to think that my very enthusiastic support perhaps even played a role in he (and Marrow) getting the Michelin star here.

I'm devastated to report, though, that nearly seven years later, while the points on technical skill remain and the menu is all but the same, my enjoyment was *not*.

Now I'd like to make something clear. Upon seeing the menu this time, I did not preemptively make up my mind to be disappointed. After all, when something is wonderful, *of course* we want to experience it again, right? I decided that I'd stick around, that I'd see if anything exciting had been added to the old. Additionally, I myself said in my first piece on him that his food tasted "like something you recognize but know you've never experienced before. Like déjà vu, reimagined."

The *only* thing I experienced at Marrow most recently was bitter disappointment. This is not that beautiful, brave chef of old, ladies and gents.

My biggest issue? Every dish was <u>safe</u>. Not even a new spin on the old. I understand that food's purpose is, at its core, to sustain and please. But at the price one pays for a meal at Marrow, you've crossed over the realm of mere sustenance and into one of art on a higher plane.

"*What happened to bravery?!*" I cried. "*What happened to individuality?!*" I grieved. Just . . . WHAT THE HELL HAPPENED?!

I can only speculate that the rumors of Lange's iciness and lack of personality are less based on his chilly demeanor and more in reference to actual ice and its utter f*cking blandness.

2.5 stars

UPDATED: {Upon publication of this piece, I found out that Marrow will have lost one of its Michelin stars.

Color me SHOCKED.}

I close out the windows on the phone and set it aside, feelings expanding like water ripples through my chest. Of course Fisher has been struggling. On top of grieving a sister, he's also lost the thing he defined himself by, if all the awards and previous praise from earlier in his career are indicative of anything.

It's still early in the morning, but Sable's left her bed and joined me downstairs, so I take this as a sign that I can begin the day. I feed her first, then fill up Legs's dry food bowl on the porch, assuming he's off on his morning hunt. When I start the trek to the barn, I'm stopped in my tracks at a sight in the distance to my right.

Fisher is attempting to make his way across the meadow with a ladle in one hand, a bowl in the other, and a small cylinder container held tightly to his side. He has to pirouette to avoid a leaping Legoless, who immediately tries to launch himself at his leg again. Every maneuver sends various liquids sloshing and flying through the air. He has to pick up his heels in quick succession as Legs continuously tries to get him. Jesus, that cat is a menace.

"Living out your *Sound of Music* fantasies?!" I yell out after he does another spin.

"Can you call this damn cat?!" he hollers back.

"He's a cat! He doesn't respond to my commands!" As far as he's concerned, we are here to serve his every whim.

When Fisher's only a handful of yards away, Legoless finally lets up, darting off in another direction to find a different prey. Fisher looks down at himself, splattered in debris, and barely suppresses some sort of rage. I begin to applaud.

"Bravo!" I brightly cheer. "That was beautiful!"

"Fucking hell," he growls, but a snort loosens his tight expression into something only slightly overserious. "Wanted you to try some of this for me," he states.

"If you'd called, I would have come," I say with a laugh.

"I couldn't find my phone and was already to the fence before I thought of it," he explains. "This first." He puts the ladle out my way. I look down to find some bright orange liquid remaining, a few tiny persistent chives floating on top. I lean over and take a large slurp.

"*Shit,*" I say in awe, fingertips to my mouth. I'm not sure what I was expecting, but it's not the flavors I'm tasting. Mildly sweet with a spice redolent of some kind of pepper.

"My soup idea for the restaurant," he explains eagerly. "Carrot jalapeño. Something slightly different but not stuffy. Good year-round. Goes with summer flavors, and the spice is nice for colder months, too."

"Delicious" is all I can say. It's phenomenal, but it's surprisingly hard to come up with the words. And he seems to be all business at the moment, so I try to match that energy rather than telling him I'd drink this from a dirty boot just to get more of it.

"Here." He offers up the bowl next. A white ball of cheese lies in the middle, with a colorful medley of other bits chopped up around it. "Burrata from a local farm with green apples, honey, basil from you, and prosciutto, that I'd pair with a basic garlic crostini."

I take the spoon that's still miraculously in the bowl and scoop a bit of it into my mouth. My eyes roll back in my head. He's behaving as if these things are simple, but I've never tasted anything like them. Still, they *are* comprehendible and people will understand them on a menu and won't be intimidated by them. "Fu-uck" is the reply I come up with for that delight. Imagining it with a crusty slice of bread makes me hum a little moan. I peer up to find Fisher looking . . . smug? No, I think that's just a touch of pride I see. Pride, tinged with relief. Like he's a little proud and a lot relieved to find that he *could* still come up with the right kinds of things.

"Last item—for today, at least," he says. "You can't have a restaurant on the ocean and not have some seafood, so I've got steamed mussels in a spicy broth." His tone is almost defensive, like he thinks I'll argue with him on the point.

"I didn't say no seafood, Fisher. I just knew that caviar and sashimi-grade fish would not sell around here," I say. "I don't want you to think I was trying to insult you or act like I think I know the only way. I have no qualms about being the expert here; you are." I feel it's important to say, given all I know about him now.

His brows pinch in before he replies. "I know. But you are the expert on Spunes, and you are the target customer base." He looks at the things in his hands before his stare finds me again. "I want to make sure you like everything."

I feel shy under his expression, the memories that were slow to surface in the aftermath of his dance battle across the field roaring to life in my mind. I can still feel the spot where his stubble was rough against my chin yesterday. I clear my throat reflexively and grab the tub, pulling out a mussel with my fingers before I take a hearty sip of broth.

I need a vat of it. "Mmm, *perfect*," I declare.

He dips his head in a quick nod, then hands me the bowl with the burrata to go with the mussels tub in my other hand. "Have both as a thank-you," he says. "I'll bring by the soup, too, in a bit."

I'm not shy about accepting gifts of the edible variety, so I pull both things close and reply with a hearty "Thank you" before another thought occurs to me. "Hold on, it's like six A.M. What are you doing up making all of this?" I laugh.

"Not sure. Maybe too much excitement yesterday," he says with a shrug.

I can't stop myself from fishing. "Ah yes, the history of Spunes keeps me up at night, too."

One side of his mouth kicks up, his newly freed hand shoving into the pocket of his black sweats. His white shirt has to be ruined, with all the spots littered across it now. Even disheveled and dirty with a ladle in his hand, he makes me want to twirl my hair and giggle like a moron.

"That's my favorite one so far," he says. He points using his chin somewhere near my chest before he turns and starts back toward his place.

I look down at my robe and groan. It's covered in canoes, with an emblem on one side over the chest, two paddles crossed over each other, and text that states, HAPPIEST WHEN WET.

After I get the goods put away in the house and knock out the initial chores for the day, it's not even 7:00 A.M. and I'm still brimming with some sort of nervous-excited anxiety. Whether it's from yesterday's events, this morning's interaction, or a combination of it all, I decide I need to do something physical, something to channel and funnel all this surplus energy through, and

since I've got no other plans for the day, I settle on paddle boarding. Silas and Ellis have been too busy this fire season to help me
haul my little canoe down to our section of the estuary yet, and
I'm not foolish enough to lug that load by myself down the cliff
trail. The paddleboard will still be cumbersome, but not unman-
ageable for me on my own.

I shimmy, squeeze, and jump my way into my wet suit and
head out into the brisk twilight air, board and paddle balanced
on my head.

It's one of those magical mornings where the water seems
bluer, the mossy grass along the banks appears greener. A mist
hovers over everything with a hush, waiting for dawn to welcome the day. It makes me think of the book of advice my mom
made for me before she died. It's filled with her favorite famous
mottos and pieces of guidance that she felt rang true in her life
and wanted to pass along to me in her absence. One thing I always come back to is a note that says, "Whenever you think too
little of the world, try to remember that somewhere, something,
or someone is always waiting to be known." I think it might be
derivative of some more renowned line, but I love her version
most. It's one of those things that simultaneously brings me a
sense of peace and keeps me curious.

When I paddle past a pair of otters, I practically squeal with
joy, but then I catch myself reflexively looking around like I'm
searching for someone to corroborate my excitement, and the blip
of embarrassment this gives me turns the joy bitter. Like eating
something too sweet that leaves a filmy aftertaste in your mouth.

I search around with a confused frown, trying to decipher
why that just happened and why I find it so bothersome.

I think I blame Fisher. I think I blame him for why *alone* suddenly feels more like *lonely*, and why the contrast of being on my

own against having someone around is so stark all of a sudden. Having someone asking me for my opinions, and simply having a partner in the extraneous—like nonsense errands, or a kiss intended to make me feel powerful but instead made me feel too easy to overpower—had been nice. I think I forgot how nice that could be.

It's such a small thing that I did, that quick reflexive turn. Logically, I know I need to let it go. But there's also a low, sinister voice in my head that tells me this is dangerous and significant and should not be taken lightly. That a few days with someone by my side should not fundamentally create an auto-response like that.

I also think this must be why I didn't jump at his offer and ask him to partner with me for the festival right away. It's as if my subconscious had my best interests at heart by being hesitant to reach for more connection with him, knowing it would be temporary.

But I also keep replaying his compliment, the look on his face this morning when he had me try his food, and the fun I'd had with him. I even found his grumbling over my library lecture charming, because if anyone knows when a student isn't paying attention, it's me. He was engaged the entire time. And just like when he'd suggested a collaboration on the Starhopper menu and kissed me in the library, I recognize that the man made that open-ended offer of his own accord, too.

By the time I get back, it's warm enough that I know it'll be uncomfortably hot if I put off the garden chores until later, so I do my best to shake off this strangely eclipsed mood and head over that way now.

My bucket slips from my hand, and a gasp leaves my lips when I take in the sight before me.

"No," I whisper in horror. "No, no, *no*." I roar out a garbled scream when I watch one of my dahlia stems flop over into a pile of her other downed sisters. Another starts to tremble, and all I can do is helplessly watch what should've gone on to be a blush Break Out Dinnerplate bloom the size of my head as it crashes in slow motion, dropping to the ground like a fallen soldier.

And this is when I see it. Its hideous furry head and demonic black eyes. Gopher.

CHAPTER 14

FISHER

It could be too early to call, and the last thing I want to do is jinx it, but I think Indy and I seem to be having an easier time. Things have been less tense in general ever since I came home to her and Sage taking down the lattice on the side of the house a few nights back. I woke up feeling lighter today, too, though that's less easy to pinpoint or explain. All I know is it's the first time I woke up feeling excited by the prospect of cooking something, even had a few simple ideas I was keen to experiment with.

It was still dark outside when I made my way into the kitchen and started brewing things like a mad scientist. A few hours later, I'd seen Sage's silhouette in the distance and decided I needed her feedback right there and then, tripping out of the house with my arms loaded down.

I'm sure I'll need to be firmer with self-control as far as Sage is concerned. Between the kiss yesterday and the sounds she made a little bit ago trying some of my food, I'm in danger of growing addicted to being near.

Indy asked for Freya's favorite chicken satay last night, and this morning when she woke up, she asked if I'd make her a spinach-and-bacon omelet. Having specific requests was so refreshing that it was a struggle not to act overeager about it both times.

We've got a little over a week until I'm scheduled to start working with the contractors over at Starhopper, the same time Indy has to begin summer school, so it feels like I've got to make the most of it now.

"Anything you want to do today?" I ask her while I finish cleaning up the kitchen. Amazing how much day there's been this morning, when it's not even 9:00 A.M. Maybe this is another point for small towns and that whole slower-way-of-life thing.

Indy gives me a tense look as she pushes back from the breakfast bar. "I actually made plans with Sam and some of his friends," she tells me.

Something slips in my brain and lands flat on its imaginary ass.

"Oh—uh, all right," I say. Then, more uneasily, "Probably need to ask first, next time, right? I mean, you did pull that whole stunt the other night."

"Stunt?"

"Not communicating with me and staying out past your curfew?"

"I didn't know that was my curfew, and I *just* communicated my plans with you for today." She says this with all the inflection of the Addams Family girl.

"Indy—" My phone starts to ring, and when I see Carlie's name, I hold up a finger to ask Indy to wait. She shoves her cell in her pocket and starts heading toward the door in one swift movement, and I simply give up for the time being.

I answer, infusing the greeting with a dismal amount of cheer. "Hey, Carl."

"Who'd you piss off?" she asks.

I take a wild guess. "Uhhh, you? By the sound of it?" But also Indy, that Martha lady, myself.

She blows a staticky sigh through the phone.

"We just got notification that our permit has been suspended until September. Apparently, there was a *new* petition."

Martha. "What reason did they give?"

"They didn't. They said we didn't pass an inspection step, but now we can't move forward until we can get them back out to pass us, which of course they claim they won't do until September," she says. "I had to do my own digging and threatening to find out the real reason."

I rub at my temples. "What do you need me to do?" I ask.

"I need you," she says as gently as I know her to be capable of, "to please make nice. See if there is any way around it. I'm out a huge chunk of change on this one, Fisher. I've got a fucking stargazing tower there, for Chrissakes!" she huffs. "I don't want to lose two months of potential progress. I know you were supposed to have a few weeks to settle in and relax over there, but in light of this latest development, I'm hoping you can help sooner. I'd really love for this thing to be done before their festival so we can capitalize on that business."

If I fail at this, too, before I've even had the chance to begin . . . I can't. I can feel Indy just starting to get comfortable. She likes going next door to visit the animals, and we are finally making progress in our dynamic, too. I'm not going to let my shortcomings or some bored town on a power trip get in the way. I scrap the remaining fragment of my pride.

"I'll figure it out," I say. "I know who to ask for help."

I grab the rest of the soup from this morning and start the march over to Sage's, missing a step when I spot something odd in the distance. Along the pasture fence stand Bud the horse, Sable the dog, and Legoless the cat. The cat sits perched on the horse's back, the dog at his feet—all three staring in the same direction.

The closer I get, the more noise I hear coming from the area in question. I let out a surprised laugh when I overhear a string of curses so explicit they'd make a line cook blush.

"Sage?" I round the corner to find her half crouched and lunging around like Gollum. She whips in a circle, revealing a dust-covered, sweat-streaked face. A wet suit hangs down from the top half of her body, shoulders and chest an angry red. "What . . . is going on?"

I jump when Indy appears at my side from out of nowhere and says, "She's been like that since I got here."

"*Jesus.* What are you doing here?!"

"Waiting for Sam." One of the geese lets out a noise by her feet.

"That thing supposed to be out?" I ask.

She rolls her eyes slightly. "He doesn't go anywhere far from me. It's fine."

I turn back to Sage and find her chaotically hopping around, aggressively stomping down dirt in various holes. "Do you have any idea what's happening here?" I ask Indy.

"She just barked *gopher* at me and then went back to this," she says.

"*I'm gonna gas this motherfucker!*" Sage cries. "No. I'm going to lure it out and trap it live. Draw and quarter it and leave its body on display as a warning for the next ones!"

Indy and I share a commiserative, frightened look. "Ind, why don't you go wait for Sam on the front porch," I say warily.

"Good idea."

When Indy's a safe distance away, I approach a still-feral Sage. "Did I hear something about a gopher?"

"Yes," she snaps, but her voice warbles dangerously. She straightens with a palm to her forehead and surveys the ruined garden area. "I already put one of the gas bombs down that hole, but I don't think I put it in right, or maybe it wasn't deep enough, because the smoke just came right back up." Oh *no*. Her voice has that high, strained tightness in it that always signals crying. "You don't understand, Fisher. It got like—more than half of my tubers. It *annihilated* them. They were so hard to grow, and I was finally doing it!" Fuck. The first hiccupping sob breaks free, and her words all start to run together. "I want it *dead*!" The opening tear rolls down. "I want its whole family dead! I want them to suffer and I want *pain*, dammit. So much pain!"

My hands float around my sides, unsure what comfort to offer or how to make the crying ebb. But then she buries her face in her palms and steps into my chest, bumping against me right there in the center with her fingers squished between us, and an inexorable laugh tumbles out of me in surprise.

I've known plenty of people who wear their hearts on their sleeves, but a handful of interactions is all it's taken for me to determine that this woman carries hers in her fist, ready to hand it off at any given time.

I rub a few circles against her back and try to ignore the fact that it's practically bare other than her bikini string. "Shhh. Easy, killer," I say into the top of her hair. "I never would've guessed you were this bloodthirsty."

"*I don't feel great about it!*" she bawls.

"I couldn't tell." I smother a grin. "Still, before you resort to medieval torture and execution, could we maybe try something?"

She steps away with a sniffle and meets my eyes. The crying has turned hers a beryl blue.

"What did you have in mind?" she asks, swiping at a rogue tear, already back to business.

"Well, first . . . Shit."

CHAPTER 15

SAGE

"What do you mean, *shit*?" I ask.

"I mean, literal shit. Dog shit and horse shit would be best, I think," he explains. He's freshly shaved since this morning, with a light flush in his cheeks, dimples that are dimpling, and . . . a small wet spot where I probably snotted into his white T-shirt. In spite of the conversation topic, his crooked grin makes my simmering blood heat to a rolling boil for entirely different reasons.

"I went paddle boarding," I explain stupidly. "That's why I'm in the wet suit. I got back and came to start on the garden stuff and . . ." I make the mistake of looking at the turned-up earth and the broken piles of stems, and I choke back a fresh sob.

"And a red mist came over you, I know," he says, feigning sincerity. "Bloodlust. Savagery. Murder." My chin wobbles guiltily, and his face quickly folds into a laugh. "I'm kidding, Byrd. Come on." And then he wraps an arm around my shoulders and leads me away from the garden.

I end up changing out of my wet suit, and Sam and Indy end

up forgoing their plans so they can spend most of their morning shoveling manure into the gopher holes with Fisher and me. There is a large part of me that would like to point out to Fisher that this is nowhere near in line with the charming or wholesome activities he probably thought I'd drag him into, but I'm feeling a bit too hangdog about the whole ordeal to find it funny yet.

By the time Indy and Sam do take off, it's the afternoon, leaving Fisher and me to finish whatever this fortification process is on our own. He tells me we need the biggest speakers we can find, so after a cursory text for permission, we scrounge up the Andersens' from their garage and set them up with a multitude of extension cords.

"Music? Really?" I ask.

"You might have to fall back on more violence, but a lot of loud noise and some hard evidence of other animals around will make this area seem less appealing, at least," he says.

"All right." I shrug. I suppose it couldn't hurt to try. I grab my phone, but before I can get over to the music options, I see some messages—a surprising number of them from some semisurprising names.

An "Atta babe" from Bea Marshall?

A series of question marks and exclamation points from Wren.

One from my brother Micah with a meme of an open-mouthed lizard that just says, "Hehe. Nice."

And lastly, one from Athena Cirillo: a screenshot of a conversation between her and Venus that includes a zoomed-in picture of me walking out of the library aisle with my fingers against my lips, Fisher not far behind me, wearing an inscrutable frown.

My stomach does a loop as I put the pieces together. They assume I'm canoodling with Fisher, as in, something more regular than kissing in the library . . . as consenting adults are perfectly allowed to do. Clearly, these people have leaped forward five steps to their own conclusions, but god, why do I sort of *like* this feeling for me? As if they're proud and excited for me rather than sympathetic or worried or patronizing? Venus herself had looked horrified when I'd walked into that library at first, all because she knew I'd run into Ian and Cassidy. Which, fine, I guess she was right to be worried since my brain did fully seize up on me when it happened, but it was the first time I was confronted with it! Anyone would act awkwardly! Not to mention how strange it is that I hadn't seen them before then. This town is too small for that to be coincidental, I'm sure of it. There's the way Savannah and Wren almost didn't make their cake, too, and the way my brothers ended their friendship with him.

So, I guess it's nice to feel like they're all cheering me on or excited for me about something, even if it's overzealous.

My blood heats up another degree when I remember that Fisher himself is in front of me and waiting for me to turn on some music.

I let out a weird sighing laugh to fill the space and start scrolling through options. "What do you think gophers hate the most? Smooth jazz?" Maybe something like that will help my heart return to a healthy resting rate, too.

"Bear in mind that *we* also will be subjected to whatever you play."

"So definitely go with the Kenny G, then?"

He laughs noncommittally, and I land on a random instrumentals station before I gesture for him to follow me inside.

"Let me get you some lunch or something," I say when we're far enough away from something that sounds like the *Bridgerton* soundtrack to hear ourselves speak. "To thank you for helping me." And to maybe buy me time until I manage to come up with a way to warn him about this new story being spun around town.

I still expect him to fight me on it or turn me down altogether. But he surprises me by saying, "I could eat," and pulling out a chair at my kitchen table. He sits facing me, one forearm resting on the table and manspreading in a self-possessed way that makes me feel like I swallowed something fizzy. Or maybe more like a Mentos was dropped into the carbonated feeling I was already trying to flatten in my gut. He must see the look on my face because he says, "What? You're the one who told me there are no empty gestures here. I'm taking you up on your offer." And my mind chooses this very inconvenient moment to perform a floor routine set to him saying, *What if I want it good and slow and drawn out?*

Jesus, my heart is thumping in my throat. I need to redirect.

"So, how did you know anything about all—that?" I segue, pointing out to the garden before I turn back to my refrigerator. I've got absolutely no idea what to assemble for a Michelin-starred chef. I can't really feed his leftovers back to him.

"France," he explains. "When I was living with my mentor out there, I stayed on his farm. I'm not sure if they were gophers, precisely, but there were a whole variety of rodents. He made me carry a drum out there to bang on for a bit every night, which might've been just to entertain himself. Who knows?" He snorts and gets a far-off look on his face. "He was a miserable dick when it came to his garden."

I laugh. Probably too loudly and definitely unnaturally, but I'm still trying to regain my composure. "Hey. Don't judge him too harshly," I say. "Creation is a lot of hard work."

"He *also* had a god complex." He raises his brows pointedly.

I throw a cherry tomato at him, which he expertly catches in his mouth and chews with a cocky smile. It should not be as sexy as it is. "Yeah, yeah. I'd have smote the hell out of the little bastards if I could have," I admit, still vexed. "Those dahlias finally looked promising this year." I put out a medley of things for grazing before I join him at the table. Crackers, cheese, meats, fruits.

He hums a short, satisfied sound when he pops a marionberry into his mouth. He'd hummed when he tried the scone the other day, too, and I wonder if he even realizes that food has this effect on him. For some reason, the observation helps to settle the rest of my nerves. I can be comfortable with this person, I think. We've managed enough vulnerable moments with one another in our time for that. Even if he does still harbor resentful feelings for small towns, I don't think he'll hold the rumor mill against *me* or be angry in any way.

"You mind if I ask, why flowers?" he says, cutting through my thoughts.

I finish the bite I'm chewing. "What do you mean?"

He adjusts in his seat. "I mean . . . that's a pretty big setup out there for just a hobby. And most home gardeners go nuts about tomatoes and zucchinis. Growing things they can eat."

"So, what, because I can't eat them, it's a waste of my time to grow them?" Even I am surprised by the bite in my tone.

Now I get one brow lifted at me. Like I just exposed something I hadn't meant to reveal. "I didn't say that," he says. "I meant that they grow things that are more self-serving. I just like knowing how *your* mind works, that's all."

Oh. "Sorry. Think I'm still a bit . . ." I shake my arms in the air in lieu of an explanation. He only nods and waits for me to continue, and I guess since I'm in for a penny already—between kissing him in the library and crying into his shirt and the way

I've word-vomited so many other pieces of myself otherwise—I
might as well give him the most truthful answer.

"I started with a vegetable garden, actually," I tell him. "But
I'd read about how cucumbers grow best when they're planted
next to sunflowers. The stalks make a good structure for the
cucumber vines, and they protect them with their shade. There
were other things like that, too, like strawberries pair well with
borage because the flowers attract bees and other pollinators.
And it was really difficult for me at first. I had to learn not to
overwater, and I'd go buy every single kind of plant supplemen-
tal thing and really just overdid it." I laugh, then pause when I see
his smile quirk wide before settling. "But mostly, I think," I continue, "well, I *know* that the first time I successfully grew something was the first time I felt . . ." I try to find the right words.

"Powerful? Omnipotent?" Fisher supplies.

"That, too," I joke. "But also like I wasn't hopeless," I say honestly, and his smirk gives way to a frown. "I always felt like I was
never much of anything growing up. I wasn't incredibly smart
or dumb, athletic or clumsy, loud or shy. I think it manifested
physically, too," I laugh. "Am I blond or brunette? I'm something
between. I'm not tall, but I'm not short. I'm not curvy, but I'm
not thin. I'm a lot of nots." I feel his stare on me like a brand, but
I push on. "I never thought I'd ever do anything extraordinary.
My brothers and I were always just trying to get by and figure out
our dreams individually as we went. All I knew was that the few
memories I had of my parents—especially my mom—were here,
and I wanted to stay close to them." It's probably the same reason
none of my brothers wanted this place. I think their memories
are more vivid and make it more difficult, where mine are fewer
and make me want to cling harder. "But . . . the first time I grew

a silly little flower here was the first time I felt like I could contribute something really beautiful to the world, with what I had within my reach. Everything right here at my fingertips." I brave meeting his eyes. "I like thinking about where flowers can end up, too. Sometimes they're the small things of beauty at something sad and hard, like a funeral. Sometimes they're trying to express something that words feel inadequate for, in a bouquet." I force a laugh and reach for a piece of cheese. "Now, most of mine just end up in Spunes's businesses for free, or I sell them at the farmers markets here or in Yoos Bay."

"How come?" he asks. "Why shouldn't everyone pay you for all of them?"

I blink a few times. "I mean—it's not . . . It doesn't matter. I *like* giving them. I love growing them. It's not like the people I give them to around here *need* the flowers."

"Why? Because flowers can't sustain them like tomatoes and zucchinis might?" he challenges, throwing my own logic back at me. "Just because it's something you love doing doesn't mean you don't deserve to be honored or recognized for it, too. Sometimes that comes in the form of compensation."

I'm tempted to respond with something cliché about money not buying happiness or how maybe I enjoy doing it just for the sake of doing it and the pride it gives me, but I realize that in this particular case it would be somewhat disingenuous. I would *love* to make a career out of it—to grow flowers professionally if I could. I'd love to be great at this and successful enough to make a living for myself.

But this is where all my convictions immediately start to waver and where I start to consolidate and cut my daydreams down to size. Because who am I to want something bigger for myself when so often I've been made to feel like the things I love are frivolous, anyway? Even saying "I want to grow flowers professionally" feels inherently unprofessional, because I immediately default to the things people like Ian valued and measured competency by. I don't have a degree in horticulture or botany, and I don't know the first thing about starting or running a business. Faint echoes of Ian's declarations over me needing to do things that were more *worthwhile* flit through my mind.

Starting down that train of thought is dangerous for me, so I look for a way to pivot the subject instead.

"Maybe you're right. But *hey*, interesting news! Venus the librarian apparently caught you kissing me," I say. I looked for a subject turn and hopped off a topic cliff instead. He chokes on something and starts to cough, so I push his water closer to him and try to soft-pedal the rest. "I think you could consider it good news, actually. I'm sure you'll be free from having more visitors now," I explain. "The one good thing about being the town tragedy is that no one's gonna try to get between me and some fun."

He glares at me between another cough, but recovers. "And that's what *I* am in this scenario? *Some fun?*" He coughs into his fist one last time. "By the way, I seem to recall, with stunning clarity, you kissing me back." He braces a tanned hand on his jean-clad thigh and leans toward me with a stern expression, so I look away from the face and back at the hand. It's a great hand, really. Vascular, with thick fingers that end in blunt tips. Clean, short nails. Knuckles slightly darker than the rest of the skin, like they've been scrubbed raw countless times. I note a few faded scars.

"Sagebyrd," he says, like bluebird or blackbird or like I'm some exotic, rare species he's just discovered and named. Just like that, it's officially the only nickname I've ever loved.

"What?" I ask dully.

"You just disappeared for a second there." He shakes his head and scrapes his hair back from his face. "You're not upset that people think you've taken up with some out-of-towner?"

Oh shit. *I'm* not, but I didn't consider whether or not he'd be upset. "Wait, are you seeing anyone back home or anything? I didn't think about this cutting into any potential love life you might've had here, either, but I didn't confirm anything with anyone, I promise. I can absolutely set the record straight."

"*Jesus*, no, I do not have someone back in New York," he retorts. "But putting my tongue in your mouth would've made me a real shit significant other, if I had." His throat works on a swallow, and I feel mine mirror the same. "And no, as shocking as it is, I wasn't exactly hoping to score while on this little detour from my life, so I don't care about being off the Spunes market. In fact . . ." He bolts up from his chair and paces over to my fridge, ripping it open with the comfort of someone I've known all my life rather than a few weeks. "Do you have any beer?" He starts rearranging things in the door. *Fascinating.*

"Like any good Oregonian, yes. Toward the bottom," I tell him. He continues his tinkering, and I get up to take a closer look, but then he finishes and grabs one of the frosty glass bottles from a drawer. "Grab me one too, please."

He closes the door with a boot as he turns around to face me, a beer held aloft in each hand. "Opener?" he asks. I take one of the bottles and step closer to the counter, expecting him to move back. Instead, I feel the heat radiating off him everywhere at my side and see his chest rise in my peripheral when I use the counter as leverage to pop off the lid. I hand his beer back and take the other by the neck, my pinkie grazing his skin. I open mine, and we share a look before we each take a long drink.

"I was actually coming over earlier to see if you might help me with something else, too," he says. "I think . . . I think maybe this"—he gestures back and forth between us—"could potentially help matters." He takes another long swig.

I watch his green eyes travel across my face nervously, music playing lightly in the distance.

"Tell me more," I say as if I'm not already internally kicking my feet with poorly suppressed glee.

FISHER

I tell Sage everything Carlie told me on the phone, about the permit denial and the project delay. She listens quietly, occasionally picking her hair up off her neck and gathering it at the back of her head with a thoughtful nod.

She kicked off her boots and socks when we got into the house earlier, and as I look at her bright blue toes and watch her heel bounce, now I wonder if it's too late to ask if I should have, too? I'm also suddenly aware of just how easily I let myself slip in here and get comfortable, let her feed me, rifled through her damn refrigerator . . . *Jesus*. Now I've had the nerve to ask her for an entire summer of her time, too.

"This will be easy, Fisher. Don't worry," she says, slicing cleanly through the angst in my head.

"So you're okay helping me convince them to let us finish everything?" I say. "And really, just so you know, too—they're through all the tedious bits, from what I understand. All the framework, at least, and all the bones."

"The shrine to the male reproductive organ."

"The *observatory*," I correct with a laugh.

"I do think the hard part is done," she says.

"Another dick joke?" I ask, and she tosses her head back in

a delighted chuckle, the sound sending goose bumps along my arms.

"It truly wasn't," she says, "but god, what an endless treasure trove that place is bound to be." She smiles brightly again. "I meant that the *difficult* part is done, as in, you have an inside man now, being with me, because they already think we're together. I know what things you can offer and what'll carry weight in swaying them, and we don't have to have any sort of unnatural production to establish being together; all we need to do is perpetuate it a little bit, if you'd be okay with all that that would entail?"

She gets up and starts carrying the leftover food to the sink and putting things in bags before stowing them away. I collect our empty beer bottles and start to clean up alongside her.

"Like what?" I ask, turning on the faucet and washing a plate from off the counter. Something like nostalgia washes over me. I've had so many important conversations over a sink.

She shrugs slowly. "Not sure. I guess just being friendly with one another when we're out?" She looks back up at me, the tips of her ears scarlet. When she chews her bottom lip, one of the plates almost slips from my grip.

I go back to scrubbing and nod firmly. "I'm fine with that," I tell her. "What sort of things would help sway them to let Carlie's crew finish?"

"Making sure you hire locally as much as you can for the remainder of the job," she suggests. "All that construction during the first phase, and no one knew a single person working on the thing." Her grin curls up softly when she passes me the other plate. I like that she doesn't seem bothered by me doing her dishes. I like when I get to be useful. "And just being together will help your case," she continues. "It'll be like you're one of us by proxy." The more she says, the more I feel drunk with relief. I didn't realize how worried I was about mucking this up here, about not being able to come through for Carlie, maybe even for myself.

"I do have some terms, though," Sage adds. "And I'd like to ask for something in return. I know you're not supposed to give with expectation and all that, but . . ."

"But nothing," I laugh. "You don't need to *give* me anything, Sage. I'll be happy to help with whatever it is." I'll feel better about her helping me with my end of it, in fact. I finish drying the plate in my hand and return my full attention to her.

She starts fiddling with one of her rings. "I want to compete in this year's festival," she says, still looking at her palm. "I want you to be my partner."

"You mean the canoe race?" I say quizzically.

"Yes," she says. "But it's more than just a race. Remember how I told you about the buy-in competitions?"

"You mentioned them, yeah."

"Well, if we want the best possible starting position, we'd have to try to do well in both," she says. "One is trivia, and it's always going to be based on the history of the Pacific Northwest, with a subset of questions surrounding Spunes."

"And the other one?"

"The other one is . . . a cooking contest," she says, her face pulling into something between a wince and a smile. "A cooking competition that utilizes a specific Spunes resource every year. Like *Iron Chef* or *Chopped*, except they get one ingredient and have to use it in all three courses."

That sounds like it has the potential to be my nightmare right now. "Why?" I ask. "Why a cooking competition?"

"It started as a way for them to recoup more money," she says, lips twitching. "Make the ingredient a specific good that they needed to sell."

"Generate the demand and then offer to sell them the supply?" I laugh. Maybe Spunes is a little sheisty, after all.

"Basically."

This is more than I would have bargained for, but not for any of the reasons she seems to think. I'm certainly not going to say no over the one thing I already know how to do as far as the cooking competition goes, and I'm not at all scared of some hard work in terms of training for this race.

But an official partnership, presumably mixed with all that perpetuating a romantic attachment would entail, makes me deeply fucking anxious. Every time I'm with Sage, I find that I want to see her more, and every time I feel a little more fucked. It's like a squeeze of longing for the next time hits me even before that current one has a chance to end despite how much I try to fight it. I ran out after her when I spotted her across the field this morning. I know what her mouth tastes like and the fascinating things she can say.

I'm getting better at sorting through my emotions, and it is becoming clear that I couldn't let myself be numb to things again even if I wanted to. Putting myself in a position where I'd be subjected to more of this attraction might not be wise, given that there's nowhere for it to go in the end.

I suppose I could try to savor it until then, though. To have some fun in the interim.

"You said you know the ins and outs of this whole thing, yeah?" I ask after a few moments. "Like, any sneaky rules and everything else to expect?"

"Everything," she confirms.

"Good," I say. "If we're doing this, I sure as hell don't plan on losing."

She screams a happy cry and launches herself at me with a bouncy hug. "We're gonna have to come up with a training-and-studying schedule," she says excitedly, giving my shoulders a shake.

"Yeah, yeah," I say. Can't stop myself from smiling back, though. "I'm supposed to start my part of things over at Star-hopper next week. Er, at least I was, before we got the notice to delay. So, I guess the sooner we figure that out, the sooner I'll know my schedule."

"Oh, we'll get you back up and running on schedule, don't worry. I already know how we're managing that."

"Do you?"

"Yep. You're gonna hate it," she declares cheerfully.

No doubt she's right, and yet I'm still smiling.

CHAPTER 16

FISHER

"These things foster a sense of trust and community," Sage says at my side. Three days after making our deal, she managed to organize this town meeting we are currently strolling arm in arm to. "They provoke us into intelligent discussions that help us continue to thrive. They're not as hokey as you might think."

"Oh yeah? I guess that's why that man brought his guinea pig in his pocket," I say flatly, nodding toward the person in question waiting by the library doors.

"That's Walter. He owns the diner, but he's retiring after this year. Or so he says. He's been saying it for a few years."

"Gerbil guy works in *food service*?!" I cry.

"Shh, *Pegasus* is a chinchilla!" she says. "And it's not like she stays in his pocket while he works." I can't help but notice how she did *not* say that he leaves the rat at home, but I make the conscious decision not to ask.

We file into the de facto town hall—which is apparently just the bottom floor of the library—and find our seats at the front near the temporary podium. Today, Sage is wearing a black sundress with white flowers that drapes and swishes around her shape enticingly, her nails painted fire-engine red. Rings still decorate each of her fingers, but I think they're arranged differently today, or maybe she's switched them out for different ones from what I've seen before?

More people continue to trickle in. Some faces I recognize— the hairstylist, the veterinarian, a smug-looking Martha O'Doyle among them. I spot the brothers I'd met the night of the vacuum incident and lean over to whisper into Sage's ear.

"They're not gonna be weird about us, are they?" I ask with a nod their way.

My eyes fall to something shimmery on the skin of her collar-bone when she lets out one of those laughs again, the kind that sends liquid heat in a torrent down my spine, and I make myself twist away. Someone's *laugh* has never caused such a visceral re-action in me before.

"If they try to pull the overprotective act," she says, "I will gladly remind them how they used to strap me into a helmet and convince me to practice headbutting with the goats and therefore have no right to act like they have my best interest at heart when it comes to my well-being." She sighs, smiling. "They're absurd a lot of the time, but they're not misogynists. They don't control who I date."

A few more people I don't recognize begin to take their seats, followed by the cop and his fiancée. A woman I vaguely remember from the library steps to the front of the room, smiles, and winks at me—Venus, I think. On top of giving me specific talking points and advice, Sage has been trying to help me learn the names of the more regular characters in her life over the last few days.

"Okay, don't forget to talk about your plan to hire locally as much as you can for construction *and* the contingency plan if it's not ready before the festival," Sage whispers. "Athena will start the meeting and explain what's going on, and then they'll let O'Doyle go first."

"Got it."

"Don't be nervous."

"I'm not nervous," I say nervously.

"Just make them feel important and included, and they'll be happy to support you, too, I promise. I'm going to kiss you and show you affection now."

"*What?!*" I balk.

"I'm going to act like I've never been happier because of you. Win you some more points, you know? Like I'm having the time of my life. Like I'm up on my supply of orgasms."

Sweet fucking god, did she just whisper *orgasms* in my ear? She curls her hands around my biceps and leans into me.

Someone's begun talking at the front of the room, but I'm officially too distracted. "Are you not?" I ask hoarsely. I tilt my chin and watch her brow wrinkle in confusion.

"Not what?" she asks, all big eyes and dark lashes.

I feel a bit like some debaucher of a sweet innocent for pushing the question, but *she* brought it up first, so . . . "Not up on your supply of orgasms?" I should probably be a little shamefaced about the huskiness in my voice. She flushes red to her ears.

"I've been single for, like, a year."

"So, no, then?"

She makes a scandalized sound, but grins widely. "I'm giving it my best effort on my own, but I could probably stand to put in some more work."

Well, this backfired. Now I'm dumbfounded, my thoughts careening to the picture of her *putting in work* on herself.

A throaty chuckle before she lays a kiss against the underside of my jaw. I think the brat *knew* she tortured me just then. I squeeze her thigh above her knee and let my hand stay perched there as Martha O'Doyle takes the podium.

"Walter," she snarls.

The man looks up from his rodent and gives her a dim look.

"Remember?!" she says. "The projector!"

Walter lurches up from his chair and tosses Pegasus like a hot potato to someone nearby before he power-shuffles to the back of the room, his soles squeaking on the tile. He clumsily hustles back with the thing, wheezing out rattled, loud breaths the whole way. For the life of me, I can't contemplate this urgency.

"Did you plug it in?" O'Doyle asks Walter just as he starts to bend back down to his chair. His shoulders slump in answer.

"I've got it, Martha!" someone calls out. I turn to see that it's Officer Carver, of course. Fucking golden boy. When he makes eye contact, I smile with something I hope is both smug and antagonizing. He doesn't return it.

"Lights!" O'Doyle adds.

The lights flicker off as O'Doyle drags over a standing screen, but just as the first image burns to life on display, the main door bangs open again and floods the room with sunlight.

"Who is that?!" Martha yells, squinting against the intrusion. "Who is over ten minutes late?"

The perpetrator is a curvy woman in an apron, with a messy pile of blond curls atop her head.

"That's Wren," Sage whispers in my ear, sending the hair on the back of my neck standing on end. "My best friend and Sam's mom," she adds.

Surprising, I think. She doesn't look like she could be any older than I am. For some reason, I'd assumed Ellis was much older. Wren finds Sage at my side and waves conspiratorially.

"Nice of you to join us, Meridian," O'Doyle declares flatly. Wren appears to ignore her, but someone says something low from the corner of the room.

"Excuse me?" O'Doyle calls. "Did someone else have something to say before I begin?"

"*I said,*" the voice says louder this time, and every head in the room turns toward Ellis. "She's still a Byrd," he firmly states. Sage's fingers dig into my arm. Wren closes her eyes like she's stung.

Sage jumps up from her seat. "All right, people, let's move on!" she says, clapping and drawing the attention back onto her.

"Thank you, Sage," O'Doyle replies. Wren slips into the chair on the other side of Sage and gives her palm a quick wring in thanks, too.

A whipping *thwap* makes the room collectively twitch in shock as Martha smacks a long pointer against the projector screen.

The first slide is a fuzzy picture of a couple surrounded by aisles of canoes. Martha starts taking us through the entire history of Spunes, showing years and years of photography that specifically include the old brick warehouse that is being turned into Starhopper. When we are barely in the 1900s, I whisper to Sage, "Is she trying to bore everyone into submission? Why is *all* of this relevant?"

Someone snores loudly as if in answer.

"Fine!" Martha cries back in response. "Forgive me for wanting you to have a full, comprehensive outlook on the disaster that would await us if we did not go forward with delaying this project." She stabs at the remote for the next slide.

A recent photo, with the entire stretch of lawn filled with people and vendors under E-Z UPs.

"I'll skip right ahead to the main issue," she says. "In order to maintain our permit to accommodate this many people, we need to have adequate bathroom facilities." She levels her pointer at me. "This man took away our bathrooms, and he cut into our available space with that—that *observatory*."

"I practically *just* got here. I did not take away anything," I say helplessly. Sage pats me on the shoulder.

"Can you guarantee that the restroom facilities on either side of this building, with outdoor access, would be done in time?" Martha asks me directly with another wave of her pointer.

I take that as my cue to begin, and I tentatively stand. "Uh, hi, everyone," I say to the room. "I am only one small part of this project, but I do have permission to speak on the owner's behalf on a few items, at least."

More blank stares. Sage beams encouragingly.

"While I can't guarantee the new outdoor bathrooms would be done in time, I can guarantee that we would open up the outdoor patio for mobile bathrooms to be stationed on to make up for the space that the observatory cut into." I look at Sage again, and she nods. "Uhhh, Walter?" I look at the man and his chinchilla, staring back at me with matching expressions. "I heard you have a nephew in Gandon that owns a portables company?" I ask.

His brow lifts in surprise. "I do, yeah."

"Well, I know that the general contractor will be looking to have some on-site during the remaining construction. And for the inconvenience, they would like to foot the bill for some to be here for the festival as well, even if the building facilities are complete."

"That would . . . be great?" he says, but looks around for confirmation.

Sage makes a painting motion in the air to remind me of my next point.

"They've also asked me to inquire with you all about filling some of the other project roles, so anyone who has recommendations is welcome to pass them my way at the end of this meeting," I say. "The only caveat being that they need to be available to start right away." A thumbs-up from Sage.

"An additional hazard," O'Doyle bellows. She clicks to another slide and continues on. Pictures of cigarette butts on the ground, litter, nails. She steps out from behind the podium, coiling herself for her deadly blow, I imagine. "This"—another whip against the screen—"was all in a matter of three months! We do not need to be burdened with additional cleanup work on our hands while prepping for the festival. I spent countless nights cleaning up all that you see in these pictures, but I won't do it again."

"I believe," I rebut, "that involving the community as much as we can going forward, whether it's having a representative acting as the main point of contact"—I briefly pause to let that take effect for Martha—"or perhaps organizing a regular meeting schedule to have a discussion about progress, would serve to alleviate much of these issues." Sage wrote that one for me, and I'm proud to have memorized it. "I've been asked to apologize on the project management's behalf about the mess and to tell you that they promise to stay more on top of these things."

At everyone's silent, exchanged looks, I decide to present my closing argument. "In conclusion, if we are committed to making sure the bathroom situation is more than adequate, and we promise to keep the community more involved in the remaining phases, I've been asked to—out of respect for the town—politely request your permission for our permit suspension to be lifted. How should we vote?" I attempt a confident smile.

"Will there be a Taco Tuesday at the restaurant?" someone shouts from the back.

"Uhhh," I say, "I'm not quite sure."

"Someone said you were in charge of the menu," someone else calls out.

"I am, but—"

"I think there should be a Taco Tuesday."

I feebly lift my shoulders. "Any preferences on what kind of tacos?" I ask.

"You should change it up. No reason to keep it the same every week." I look over to find that it's Wren who's added this.

"Fine. Taco Tuesday is approved," I say. I assume I have this authority to make it official, anyway.

"What about desserts?" Now I recognize Venus the librarian asking this.

"What do you mean?" I say.

"Well, some of the desserts you serve should be provided by Savvy's Bakery, I think, out of town support," Athena says. Hearty sounds of agreement bubble throughout the room.

"Sure, yeah. That sounds great."

"What about brunch?!"

"*Ff*—" I bite down hard on my tongue to stop myself from responding how most chefs feel about brunch.

"Brunch is out, people!" Sage chimes in on my behalf. "We've got Savvy's for pastries and the Bean, anyway!" A small collective groan.

"I assume you will be ordering the furniture for this place soon as well?" O'Doyle asks, finally intrigued and off the warpath.

"I will," I say, smiling in relief. I mean, I think I will. I'll make sure I do if that's what helps keep this thing going.

"Let's talk tables and chairs, then. . . ."

SAGE

Leaving the library with Fisher's hand in mine is an intoxicating, precarious feeling. Bea and Serena may as well be fist-bumping me with how subtle their proud smiles are. O'Doyle still looks smug but appears to be satisfied for the time being. Even Walter and Pegasus nod like they're impressed. Wren is percolating with excitement in spite of the public awkwardness with Ellis.

"You still coming by the bakery this week?" she asks with a distinct look, eyes wide on mine.

I established no plan to come by the bakery, but I can take a hint. I've barely given her a rundown on things the last few days. "Yes. I'll call you later." She grips me in a quick hug before she bounces away.

I'm in a hurry to get Fisher out to the parking lot so I can quickly assess how pissed he is about all the extra promises he had to make in there, like giving Martha a say on décor and using one of her relatives for some of the furniture, or giving the town the ability to rent the space out for large events, but now I see Silas waiting to head us off. The moment he catches me trying to yank Fisher in another direction, he calls out to us.

"Shit," I whisper.

"What? I thought you didn't care what they think?" Fisher drawls, following my line of sight.

"I don't. I'm trying to spare you from more, I dunno, *intrusiveness*, I guess? Figured after all that you might already want to call it."

He laughs and shakes his head with a sigh. "It's all good, Byrd. Really."

He sounds sincere enough, but this already feels like I'm getting more out of this arrangement.

I'm prevented from saying anything more on the matter when a phone gets shoved in the space between us.

"Silas, what the hell?!" I say to the big buffoon wielding it.

"Micah wanted to see what he looks like," he explains.

"Micah's on FaceTime? That's nice. You can't be bothered to text me back, but you can get on FaceTime for Silas?" I whine at the back of the phone like it's my sweet puppy of a brother. Silas flips it my way, four inches from my face.

"At least he's objectively better than Ian" is Micah's greeting.

"*He* can still hear you, and you saw him for exactly two seconds, Micah." Silas swipes the phone back to himself and hangs up without a goodbye—zero manners and an extreme lack of tact, per usual.

"I can't wait to tell my nieces and nephews one day that I brought you two together," he says, smiling back and forth at Fisher and me.

Aaaand that'll be enough of that. "You're dead to me," I snarl, trying to tug Fisher toward the truck.

"I suppose it was more the vacuum's doing, though, wasn't it?" Silas adds.

I'm going to end him. I'll shave a line down the center of his head in his sleep like he did to Micah when he was thirteen. I'll—

Wait.

I look back at Fisher when he isn't budged by another yank on his hand, and he's . . . *laughing*. A full-out, crinkly eyed, dimpled guffaw. The last hour should have been the stuff of his nightmares. An actual town meeting. Negotiating with busybodies. Overbearing family members shoving themselves in his face. And yet, he doesn't seem to find this whole thing too annoying at all.

He gently slides his palm from mine and reaches out to shake Silas's. "Nice to see you again—Silas, right?"

"Right. And you're Fisher Lange. I googled you," Silas announces. Because he truly lives to see how uncomfortable he can make people, apparently.

Fisher is outwardly unstirred, but I still feel him stiffen at my side. "Anything interesting?" he asks. I know Silas feels my glare burning a hole through him, but he doesn't face me.

"You're kind of a big deal, actually. Definitely too big to hang around here long," Silas says.

Fisher continues shaking his hand, both of them squeezing hard enough for their knuckles to go white. "Thank you for letting me know," he replies casually.

Silas's expression hardens a notch. I feel like I'm watching a conversation in code.

"What is happening here?" I ask after another awkward beat.

Silas is the first to break away with one of his easy, familiar smiles. "Nothing at all, kiddo. Glad you've got someone to hang with this summer. It's shaping up to be a bad fire season with the drought, so I suspect you won't see much of Ell and me."

I inspect his face closely to try to figure out what I'm missing. He's the only one of us who got Dad's pale turquoise eyes, his wavy, dark blond hair styled in what I lovingly refer to as a modern mullet. He's by far the most beautiful, temperamental, and impulsive of us.

"Be safe," I tell him, like I always do. Normally, he humors me and says he will.

This time, he cocks a brow and firmly states, "You be safe, too, Sage."

We make it within reach of the truck without being detained by anyone else, but before I can launch into any of the apologies I've been doing a mental read-through on, Fisher asks, "Can I drive?"

I thunder out a weird, offended-sounding laugh. "Do you not like my driving?"

"No. I just prefer to keep my hands occupied," he says.

Is he trying to tease me? Every time he says something like this, it takes a herculean effort not to titter like an idiot. I apparently have the pent-up libido of a catcalling construction worker because my mind yells, *"I'll give ya something to occupy your hands with!"*

I jut the keys toward him and jangle them between us. He surprises a gasp out of me when he circles my wrist and pulls me flush against his front.

"Thanks," he says, grinning like the devil himself, and my gulp echoes in my ears. "May as well sell this as much as possible, right?"

"W-what?" I ask, but then he leans down and pecks me on the corner of my chin, his stubble grating against me, and this is when I spot Ian and Cassidy over his shoulder . . . right before he slips the keys from my hand and trots over to the driver's-side door.

I try to relax into a comfortable silence as we make our way back, but we barely pull out of the parking lot when I have to blurt, "I'm sorry about Silas. That was strange and unlike him. Well," I concede, "not the presumptuousness, that was definitely like him, but the weird posturing energy wasn't."

"This isn't gonna be any fun if you're constantly apologizing, Sage," he tells me.

I study his profile, limned by the craggy coastal view rushing past. "You're trying to have fun with it, then? You're not too up-set over the antics so far?" I ask hopefully. And then I realize he's expertly sidestepped the point once more, so I add, "And what *was* that silent exchange, exactly?"

His forearm flexes as he turns the wheel. "I think he just wanted to acknowledge the fact that he knows I'm here temporarily."

Oh. Must be why he'd seemed ominous with his warning to me, too.

"Can I tell you something, though?" Fisher asks, his voice hollow.

"Of course you can," I say.

"Seeing you bicker with him made me miss my sister. I regret that I sometimes ignored her FaceTime calls." He clears his throat.

A pendulum swings inside my chest for him. My fingers curl against my thighs with wanting to wrap him up and tuck him away. "She knew that you loved her. I'm certain she did, Fisher. Siblings just know, I think."

"I hope," he says, worn and weary. "I definitely wasn't always a great brother. Or uncle, for that matter. I have to do better."

The pendulum swings again because *this* is something I might be able to help with. A way to ensure the benefits in this arrangement are even, too. "I can help with Indy," I blurt. I try not to sound too desperate. "I mean, I'm not sure *specifically* how, but I know I can help as much as anyone could, at least. I don't know exactly what she's going through, but I at least know what it's like to be a young woman without a mom."

His mouth presses into a hint of a smile. "Thank you. I need all the sage advice I can get."

CHAPTER 17

FISHER

"For real?" Indy says. "We can't just drive to the next town? Or as far as it takes for us to find intelligent life *and* a Target?"

I turn off the ignition in the O'Doyle's parking lot and give Indy a pointed look in the rearview mirror. Sage spares me from replying first.

"While I'm sure you're safe in assuming those things are mutually exclusive, we've gotta get him a wet suit and get you school supplies. And this is the only place weird enough to have both," she explains, unbothered.

Indy just laughs, seemingly satisfied with this response, which makes me feel like I need a notebook. Last night, I asked Indy if Sam was her boyfriend, and by the nasal, disgusted, horrified scoff I received, you'd think I asked her something much more invasive. I make a mental note: *Teen responds well to sarcasm only.*

But of course I'm contradicted shortly thereafter. With Sage, it's not limited to sarcasm. Indy answers her earnest questions with equal frankness and ease. They banter without any acidity from Indy's end. They also team up to tease and bully me over a variety of things.

Still, even if their comfort level is not the case for Indy and me yet, watching them interact gives me hope.

After shopping, we end up grabbing burgers and fries from Walter's and take them with us over to the park by Starhopper, per Sage's recommendation. We fall into easy conversation divided between comfortable silences and slurping on our drinks.

When Indy starts asking Sage about her various ear piercings, I let my mind wander to more food, even though I'm full enough that I've had to sit back in my seat to be comfortable. I think I'll try to run by the store again for another batch of blackberries, since what I keep buying and trying just doesn't taste the same as the ones Sage had at her house. I've started playing with a chipotle blackberry sauce for a burger on the Starhopper menu, but I'm also mulling over a lemon pudding cake we used to make at Marrow. Instead of the rhubarb we typically used to accent it with, I think I'll do something with those blackberries whenever I find the right kind . . . maybe a white chocolate crémeux alongside.

I'm still mentally deconstructing when Sage asks me, "How long have you had your ears pierced?"

I blink a few times and pull myself out of the daydream. *When was the last time I daydreamed about making anything like that?* "Since I was fifteen," I laugh. "Why?"

Sage sets aside her soda and leans her elbows on the picnic table. "I guess it seems like a semispecific choice? Normally, there are tattoos that coincide and such, too."

"Oh yeah? Where are all your tattoos, then?" I ask, nodding to the four or five earrings she has per ear.

"Touché," Sage replies.

"Mom said you were picked on for your ears as a kid," Indy

adds. Her eyes go wide for a second after, like she feels bad for oversharing.

"Yep," I quickly respond, hoping she won't be discouraged. "My ears were this big when I was nine. Seems silly looking back, but I guess it was my idea of a fuck-you to those kids at the time."

"Can't let it get to you if you own it first," Sage connects. She fixes me with a look that tells me she sees right through me, too, maybe beyond me just being bullied for having big ears. I shift uncomfortably in my seat.

"And by the way, how do you know I don't have tattoos?" I hedge, hoping to evade the implications in that look. "Maybe they're just on parts of me you haven't seen."

Indy makes a noise from her sinuses. "Sick. Save the act for when I'm not around, please," she whines.

It was Sage's idea to bring Indy in on the jig yesterday when she'd asked us to help her harvest tulips. She'd leaned in my way over the tray we were putting her bulbs out on—a dirt smear on her cheek as she told me that *showing trust often earns some, too.*

Indy had seemed mostly indifferent to the whole thing. "*Whatever you gotta do for work, I guess,*" she'd said with a shrug.

"I'm gonna go say hi to Sam at Savvy's. That okay?" she asks me now.

"Sure. Yeah, of course. Definitely," I reply. In obvious shock that I was even asked. I catch Sage's smirk in the corner of my eye. "We'll meet back here, or something. Just check in with us in a bit?"

Indy rolls her lips and nods before she skips off toward the bakery.

I turn back to Sage's knowing face. "Walk?" she asks me.

"Sure."

We clear off our garbage from the picnic table, and I follow her over to the trail at the border of the park. Today, she's got half of her hair pinned back, but the wind keeps stealing pieces of it from her clip and blowing them across her face and around her tanned, freckled shoulders. She doesn't seem to mind, just keeps grinning to herself—entertained by her own subconscious. I have the distinct thought again: I wonder how she burrows into me this quickly, into my head and into other vital parts, and I can't help but wonder how the hell I can affect her like this, too. Guilt rides the thoughts, though, because what would be the point? I need to try not to forget that I'll be leaving at the end of this thing.

"You changed your nail color again," I observe. A harmless comment to fill the silence. She spreads a hand out in front of her as if to check. Today, they're a pale orange.

"You noticed?"

"You change them a lot, don't you?" I say with a shrug. But when her smile spreads wider, I think my chest expands to the same degree.

"I do," she says. "Wren thinks I'm nuts, but I probably change them three times a week. It relaxes me."

"Toes, too?" I ask.

"Foot fetish?" she replies, eyes narrowing in adorable mock suspicion.

Just a you fetish, I think. I thankfully stop the answer before it escapes me. "Just curious about you, is all." *Keep letting me in that mind. You make it look like it's a fun place to be.*

"Most of the time, yes," she says. "Toes, too." Her shoulder brushes against my arm, and the slightly sticky heat adds the smallest friction, sending my synapses into free fall. "I read, too," she continues. "Or journal. What do you do to unwind?"

I know what I would like to do more of. "Exercise, mostly. Watch TV. The usual."

"Cooking shows?" she asks.

I flinch like I've been gut-punched. "No," I say ruefully, suppressing a shiver.

"That bad, huh?" she chuckles. "Probably like surgeons watching medical dramas. Can't stand to watch other people do it wrong?"

We've come to the part of the loop that forks off toward the front of Starhopper, and I decide to veer off in that direction, suddenly eager to get inside and have a break from the wind and sun. I said I was curious about her, and she's managed again to flip things on me somehow. I pull out my keys as I clear my throat and try to explain.

"Sometimes that, but it's not that anyone does anything particularly unrealistic. And they're usually not doing something risky like it would be with some medical show. I just . . ." I frown and wipe at my brow. "I don't do anything especially important, so it sounds ridiculous to say that watching cooking shows gives me—anxiety." Metal scraping, loud voices, heat and smoke and steam. I'm as numb as I can be when I'm at work, so why would I want to experience it in my free time, too? I flinch when her cool fingers touch my forearm.

"What do you mean you don't do anything especially important?" she asks, her expression furrowed in concern.

I huff out a forced laugh as we step toward the door. "I'm not saving lives, Sage. I'm definitely not in any real danger, either. I'm usually making pretentious shit by overly complicated methods."

She looks devastated by that, and I can't decide if I'd like to say something sarcastic to brush it off or bury my face in her neck and let her comfort me.

"Literally every significant event in life is celebrated with food somehow," she says. "You really don't think that's important?"

"I don't make *food*. I—I don't make the stuff you need to *sustain* you."

"Maybe not, but at its core that's what it is! Plenty of people aren't looking to just eat. Some of us are trying to be *fed* something, I don't know, *more*, when we go to those places," she urges, emphatic. I open the door to Starhopper and hold it ajar for her, and she steps in close to me, ardently holding my gaze. "How can you say all that stuff to me about growing *flowers* and not feel the same about what you do? Especially when you've proven that you do it *well*. You've gotten awards for it, Fisher!"

I groan. "You googled me?" I worried she might after her brother brought it up the other day.

She blushes. "Screw it. You know what? Yes, of course I did. After that first day in the library." She stabs her hands out at her sides and lets them fall back to her thighs with a slap, and I try to reconcile the fact that she undoubtedly has known about all the other shit for a time, then, too. And she never held it against me? "*Food & Wine*'s most promising chef at twenty?!" she continues. "You couldn't even legally drink!"

"*Legally* being the operative word," I mutter.

"A James Beard Award at twenty-two?! And by the way, you have *three* fucking Michelin stars?!"

I march through the entrance even though I'm looking for an exit route away from this topic. "Exactly. And no."

"Exactly what?!" she's almost yelling now as she follows me and gently grabs my forearm again, turning me in a half circle her way. Her eyes are bright, and there's a prominent vein pulsing in her forehead. I feel adrift and confused. I started a conversation hoping to glean more about her, and she's got me raw and open instead. I have no clue how we got here, but my heart is racing with her a few inches from me, and I think that maybe I'm just going to say it. I'm going to say what I think and let myself sound as pathetic as I feel.

"I mean," I say, "that is *exactly* why I have no reason to be this goddamn miserable. I got what I wanted. I accomplished a dream, and it felt completely fucking empty. And then I went and fucked it up, anyway." I gulp back a few breaths before I add, "I'm not sure how much you found, but I take it you saw that I lost one of those stars, too."

The tension visibly unravels through her, everything softening. And then she does something I don't expect. She doesn't try to say something placating or dismissive, doesn't press for more information, and she doesn't tell me I'm right, either. Her scowl simply untethers and fades away before she moves closer and gathers me into a hug.

It's misery. It's agony. It's bliss. Why is it that someone hugging you and holding you together can make you feel like you're about to shatter?

Her arms come around my ribs and cross at my spine. I feel both of her hands ball into fists and push tightly against me, like some sort of reverse Heimlich maneuver.

I breathe out a long breath and give into it, let my cheek rest on the crown of her head. Her scent invades my senses—citrus and sweet, like these ridiculous fancy marshmallows we made for a whole s'mores series at my first sous gig. Orange-blossom marshmallow squares dipped in chocolate, rolled in crushed pistachios.

"Thank you," I say into her hair, voice gruff.

Her responding laugh vibrates against my core. "For what?"

"For the hug," I say. "And for not telling me I'm an ungrateful, whiny, privileged dickhead."

Her hair catches in my stubble as she pulls back to look up at me. "I don't think that. Not at all, Fisher."

My thumb smooths the crease between her brows playfully, and I'm tempted to touch her lower lip. Everything in my body is tempted to touch something. I stare at her mouth a tick too long, and I feel her hold her breath. I think about it—about kissing her for a moment, and it feels like that moment balloons . . . but no. She was comforting me, and I refuse to misread this or risk taking advantage of her. I gently extricate myself with a grateful smile before I can give in any more, and I rotate toward the rest of the room.

"Want to check this place out with me?" I ask, drawing a circle through the air.

A look I can't unravel flickers across her features. "Okay."

The main restaurant is still a blank slate. Framework and drywall are done, but Walter's nephew is a stonemason and is set to start working this week on the sections of exposed brick that need repair. Carlie hired one of Martha O'Doyle's brothers for the plumbing and her sister for all the interior painting.

Carlie had told me that the observatory dome was the only thing that was nearly complete, since that required a more specialized group.

"Apparently, there's a brewery over in Bend with one of these," I say to Sage, pointing out one of the window frames at the tower. "Carlie jokes that she might've been slipped psychedelic brownies when she visited it but that it was the ultimate immersive experience. 'Good food, friends, and a journey through time and space,'" I quote her.

"I like her. She sounds wise," Sage says.

"She'd love you, that's for sure," I say. Then I nod to the observatory. "You wanna go up? The elevator's not running yet, but we can take the stairs."

We head outside and scale our way up the spiral staircase that wraps around the outside of the tower, pausing when we make it to the second-story platform to take in the view. Sage smiles wide to herself again as she looks around. Like maybe where I see a nice ocean and a patch of green grass, she's seeing memories and more.

"And you tried to tell me that's not hidden charm?" I say, looking at her expression. *She* charms me beyond reason.

"Fine," she says. "Maybe there's some." She tucks a wisp of hair behind her ear. "Why is it you hate them?" she asks.

"Hate what? Small towns?"

"Yeah." She cants her head to the side and holds me with an owlish stare.

"*Hate*," I say, "is maybe a strong word." When I don't say more, she nods for me to continue, but I pat my jeans to find my phone, getting the key code for the door and letting us inside.

I let my eyes adjust to the indoor light. Shiny blue-black tiled floors lead up to walls painted to match, with labyrinthine shapes painted all around. "Maybe she *was* on psychedelics when she decided to do this," I mutter, hoping the attempt at a joke might buy me a distraction. I find Sage still giving me a shrewd look, and heave a sigh.

"I don't hate small towns," I say. "I just think they tend to have a dark side most don't consider."

"Care to elaborate?"

No. I almost tell her as much. But I've already cracked myself open, anyway. "I guess it started when I was younger and started noticing things, like . . . when I was still little, my parents opened up a sandwich shop in town, right? Not a chain restaurant of some kind, just a tiny family deli. My sister and I would make stroopwafel with my mom at home and bring fresh batches for sale every day." She's looking at me like she already knows where this is going, lips pinched sympathetically. I keep telling her anyway. "No one wanted to give their business to outsiders, though. Someone's teenager even vandalized it once." I let out a dark laugh. "My parents didn't set out to put anyone else's business under. They wanted to share something they loved doing and wanted to make a living for themselves doing it. They certainly weren't trying to monopolize milquetoast America. But you'd have thought they were, with how few customers they had. All because there was already one other family that owned a deli a few blocks down." I finger the protective sheet covering one of the telescopes. "It went under in less than a year.

"After that, I think I always felt apart, or something. I saw how stuck small places and small minds can get. Got bullied in school. Had a hard time making friends. I wasn't trying to be a corn-fed jock that peaked in high school, so suffice it to say, I never fit in much," I add bitterly. I bite my tongue before I tell Freya's story, too. How watching her mistreatment made me hate the place even more.

"That why you went to culinary school?" Sage asks.

"Probably," I say plainly. "There wasn't much in the way of fine dining, since even our casual options were limited." I've made my way around the circular room and back to Sage, face-to-face.

"I remember thinking," I say. "I remember thinking that if I was better than they were—someone *special*. I thought I'd be happier than they were, too."

A commotion from outside pulls our attention to the door just as Indy, Sam, and another friend step into the room. I make the assumption that Sam can track Sage's location like she did the night I was looking for them. Indy introduces me to Blake, whom Sage already knows as her former student.

"Can I hang out with them for the rest of the day?" Indy asks.

"Sure." I wish there were a way for me to tell her I'm proud of her for being open to making friends, but I can't imagine doing this and it not earning me one of her mortified scowls.

"Just don't be out late, all right?" I add. "We both start things early tomorrow morning and need the sleep."

"That's right," Sage says with a signature bright grin. "You guys start summer school, and we officially begin training."

CHAPTER 18

SAGE

In a shocking turn of events, I am once again up before dawn. Today, however, I think it's from excitement.

I cannot say the same for Fisher.

I'm sipping on my coffee when I see his silhouette making its way across the meadow, his wet suit dangling from his hand and his gait visibly sluggish. Sable's nails tap-dance against the tile in the sunroom when she spots him, too. I open the side door before he has a chance to knock, and he blinks like I've shined a flashlight in his face.

"Why aren't you dressed?" I mean to ask it softly, but in the quiet of the morning, my voice possesses all the subtlety of an air horn.

"Coffee?" is his only reply. I'm unsure if it's meant as a question or as a prerequisite for interacting. Either way, I lead him into the kitchen and pull down a mug, passing it to him while I try to slip on a mask of patience. I hover at the counter when he drags himself to my table and sits in a chair facing me.

I keep quiet until I think he's down to the dregs, and decide to gauge his mood by setting the stage for my own. "It's so beautiful out there in the mornings," I tell him, voice tight with exhilaration. "Everything looks like it's letting off steam, like dragons are just starting to wake up, too, or something." I sigh happily. "It's nearly silent and completely peaceful, and the water is . . . well, the water's like fucking ice needles, but it's also genuinely refreshing. There are harbor seals all over where we're headed today. Last time, I saw a pair of otters. It's gonna be amazing, Fisher."

He exhales a tired laugh and rakes both hands down his face before he grabs his empty mug and goes back to the coffeepot.

"Not much for chitchat this early, huh? Guessing that appetizer day was a fluke?" I sing. "That's fine. I'll wait. Another thing I'll have to win you over on."

He manages to maintain eye contact while he gulps down the entirety of his second cup. And it's almost unfair, how even puffy and tired work on him. How even his moody morning face is handsome. The light circles under his eyes only serve to make him more real, more *here*. Present and in the flesh, in my kitchen, with my dog's big head just below his ribs. Sable moons up at him as he scratches behind her ears, so much unfiltered adoration in her doggie expression it should probably embarrass us both. Her tongue lolls out the side of her mouth, and I suppress the urge to roll my eyes at her.

"What are you wearing under that?" he asks me, his sleep-hewn voice wiping chills across my skin in an instant. When he notes my perplexity, he lets out a drowsy growl and rubs at his eyes. "I mean, *just* a swimsuit?" he clarifies, lifting his bundle of neoprene in the air. "I didn't know what I was supposed to wear under this."

"Oh," I say. "Yes. Just wear as little as possible." And then, aggressively gesticulating with my arms, I add, "Like, so you're comfortable, I mean."

"Right," he says.

"Right," I chirp back.

Because miracles do exist, we manage to avoid any more awkward innuendo-laden exchanges and shuffle to the barn to collect the canoe once he's changed. It's cumbersome work, but we guide it down the trail with a few breaks.

"All right," I begin when we've got it shored. "This is Connie."

His forehead folds up in amusement. "The canoe?"

"Every vessel deserves a name," I say. "Connie will be our official race canoe, so let's treat her right."

"Aye, Captain," he says with irony, bringing the hot pirate comparison full circle. I swallow a nervous giggle.

The proximity to the water and the anticipation of finally getting to do this make my mind turn over into hyperfocus, so I launch into the instructions I've got mentally plotted. The sooner I can bring him up to speed, the sooner we can begin to seriously train.

"Today's going to be all the basics," I inform him. "Safety first, then where to put things, how to move, how to work with each other's rhythm and strokes, et cetera."

He gives me a long-suffering look before his shoulders lift in a helpless shrug. "Of course it is," he mutters, fiddling with his life vest, the orange sunrise at his back.

"Here," I say, reaching out and batting his hands away. I finish doing up my own vest before I reach for his, tugging down on the zipper where it's snagged and pulling it back up in one fluid motion. When his body goes rigid under my knuckles, I try to make quick work of the clasps, too, but end up pinching the tip of my finger in my haste.

"*Ouch.*" I wince, slipping it into my mouth. Fisher's throat bobs in the corner of my eye, but when I bring my gaze up to him, his darts away. Maybe his caffeine hasn't kicked in yet, or maybe it has and that's what's got him so jittery.

In any case, I press onward, too excited to linger. "Let's talk about the paddle first," I say. Slipping into my teacher voice is unavoidable. "I'm sure you've heard it referred to as an *oar* as well, but *this* is technically a paddle. Oars are attached to a canoe and propel it in the opposite direction from where the rower is facing—like what you see them doing in crew. *Our* race allows single-blade paddles only, so we will both face forward and we'll propel ourselves the same way. While the canoes themselves don't have to be entirely wood anymore, in honor of tradition, the paddles do."

I wait for his silent nod of confirmation before I continue, grabbing my paddle and holding it out between us.

"This handle here at the top is called the *grip*. You'll always have one hand on your grip and the other here, on the shaft."

His head falls back with a dark laugh, and he searches the sky. "Byrd, let's just go, please," he rasps. "I'm more of a hands-on learner, anyway."

If he thinks his ire will faze me, he's sorely mistaken. With three older brothers, I am well versed in being the source of annoyance and pushing on regardless.

I mentally set aside the rest of my lecture for now, though, and follow where he's already stomping away. I definitely do not stare at his firm (surprisingly thick) thighs, or his equally taut ass in that wet suit. "Okay, that's fine. I'm flexible," I sing.

"I'm sure you are," he grits.

We slide the rig in the water and get settled into our designated spots without any more tantrums or tipping it—and it's off to the races, figuratively speaking.

I start babbling on about the various parts of the canoe and explain how I've arranged the seats to face one another for this particular lesson only. Today, I'm rowing from the stern, while he sits on the seat at the bow. He's visibly prickling again about twenty minutes into my tutorial.

"We need to switch places or something," he suddenly blurts out, just as I'm demonstrating how hard and how far from the throat one should grip the paddle. "I feel like I need a parasol sitting here being towed along like this," he complains.

"A parasol?!" I sputter a laugh. "With that getup?!"

"You know what I mean," he snips. "*I* should be paddling you—*fuck*. I mean I should be the one paddling this canoe!" he shouts. He buries his face in his hands.

"All right, all right," I say. "Perfect timing for the flip lesson, anyway. First lesson is how to recover if we capsize."

His hands fall away with notable exasperation. "I suppose you're gonna say something about me flipping you now, aren't you?" he growls.

I frown and straighten a degree at his tone. "Well, I mean, you can if you want? Or I can flip you, or I guess we could do it together?"

"Oh, I'll do the flipping, Sage."

"Wonderful! Ready whenever y—"

The shock of the water never fails to take me by surprise. My breath freezes in my lungs, the frigid ocean bites at the bare skin on my cheeks. The initial trickle that makes its way into the suit jolts through me, too, but warms soon after.

I break the surface on a laugh and search for Fisher, but don't find him or his paddle floating alongside.

"Fisher?" I call out.

I hear a muffled knock from inside the overturned canoe and swim back toward it, scooping up my paddle on the way. Here in the estuary, the water is calm and probably only ten feet at its deepest. I push below the surface and under the gunwale of the canoe, and sure enough, I find him inside when I pop back up, his own paddle bobbing by his shoulder. He doesn't look surprised that I discovered him.

"Hiding from me?" I ask, my voice reverberating through the hull around us.

He smiles and shakes his head. "Just knew you'd find me."

His eyes dip to my mouth before they glance over the rest of my face in a way that would normally have me flustered but only makes awareness sizzle beneath my skin right now. My scalp burns hot in spite of the freezing water. Aside from the sounds of our breaths and the water gently lapping, the noise from the outside world is cut off here. It feels like its own pocket in the universe, like we can say what we want, do what we want, and we might be able to forget the rest of it. Forget all the noise—maybe even the internal clamor.

"I did find you," I say, just barely above a whisper. I don't say that I'm glad I found him that night he showed up here or that I'm glad he found me in the library that day, but something tells me he knows what I mean. We both can't seem to stop finding one another.

The damp makes the ends of his hair curl against his neck, his wet eyelashes like spikes around his dark eyes. My body's drifted closer to him without me being cognizant of it. When his gaze drops once more to my lips, I lick at a drop of salty water there.

"Sage," he whispers forcibly, eyes stuck on the same spot. Every tiny sound echoes in the enclosed space—my breath as it picks up tempo, the hitch when he swallows. The sucking thump of water against wood batters in time with my pulse. My life vest bumps up into his, and one of his big palms grasps at my hip beneath the surface, thumb pressing the soft spot just inside the jut of my bone. All my warmth becomes concentrated there, and the small disturbances of our movements send ripples crashing against the boat faster.

It's like the library all over again, where the safety I feel with him is somehow dangerous—impossibly tempting. The difference is there's nothing to excuse it this time, no one but us here now. I'm not comforting him, and I don't need some arbitrary win.

I just *want*. All I am is want. There are thoughts trying to rise in my mind, words I should say and—and I know I'll need to reflect later, but maybe I can actually take my own advice and live fully in the present. He *wants*, too. I can see it in that irresistible color high on his cheeks and in his expanding pupils. Can feel it in the way his treading rhythm gets unsteady and breaks. *Maybe I could do something like this*, I think. *Maybe I can have a casual fling.* We're already doing so much together as it is. Already on our own team in this arrangement, and maybe this could just be an added perk.

An added perk and nothing more, because it *can't* be anything more.

The moment I realize my internal noise is gaining volume, it's as if the want becomes a living thing, screaming above it. I press myself in closer, our noses brushing, and we both inhale sharply at the touch—or maybe it was just me and my echo. I breathe him in for one more beat, waiting for a loud enough reason not to or for him to turn me away. Instead, his air lands warm on my cheek and his hand clutches firmer on my hip, and I decide to drown out the rest of it, tipping my mouth to his.

He hums from the back of his throat—that same noise he makes when something is delicious—and wraps both my legs around his hips, sending the water sloshing in a frenzy around us.

"Put your arms around my neck," he tells me, reaching out to grip the edges of the canoe so he can keep us afloat.

I comply, caught in some sort of trance that has me dipping forward to flick my tongue into his dimple and run my teeth along his jaw. Somehow I know that from now on, the tang of him and salt water will be what I think of when I imagine summer's taste.

A whimper unspools out of me when he runs his lips back and forth along my neck, the cold water tickling me from his hair and his stubble scraping the sensitive skin.

"*Fuck*," he whispers below my ear. "So sweet, Sage."

I turn, and he captures my mouth again with his, nipping gently at my lips like he's savoring me. My hips roll of their own accord, needy and seeking, and I suck in a small gasp when his thrust up to meet them. I use my heels to crush myself closer, rubbing at the hard ridge of him trapped between us.

This is impossible—insane. This can't go anywhere like this. My impatient mind starts sprinting full force toward any plausible scenario where we can peel ourselves out of these suits and get to each other, and consequently stumbles on all the awkward logistics.

Something knocks hard and sudden against the top of my head, bright starbursts behind my eyelids. "Ow," I hiss. My fingers jam against the hard surface above me when I lean back to see.

Oh, fuck. I push off Fisher like I'm on fire and scramble around for my paddle in a panic. "The seal!" I quickly shout at him.

"A SEAL?! WHERE?" he roars, kicking up and slamming his head against one of the carrying yokes.

I'm sure I'll find that funny later, but right now, my heart is racing in my throat. "No—no, not a *seal*!" I yell. "I mean we have to *break* the seal and get this turned over before the canoe settles too deep under the water and we have to abandon it. We need to get out, and then I need you to use your paddle to try to get it wedged under this side, NOW."

He complies at once, and we both dart under the water and head toward the stern. When I emerge, it's already more swamped than I've ever had to recover it from before, but I refuse to admit defeat quite yet. We're not at risk for hypothermia, and we're both strong.

"Okay, once we break the seal, we've got to get this end lifted up and roll it to the side," I explain. "There's a bag hooked onto the seat at the bow. I'll need you to unhook that and start scooping out as much of the water as you can before we turn it all the way."

He nods and gets to work.

Between the two of us, we manage to break the suction and grunt our way through lifting one end. He hauls ass as soon as we maneuver it onto its side, grabbing the dry bag and rapidly scooping water out of the hull. I keep it steady with one hand and use my other arm to help fling it out, too. We're both wheezing and breathless by the time it's in an okay state to climb back in.

"Hang on," I gasp. "Need to catch my breath, and then—" I cough. "And then I'll show you how to get back in."

His breath saws in and out of him at my side. "You all right?" he asks, brow furrowed in concern.

I meet his gaze but quickly blink away. I need to not think about what we were just doing or we'll be stuck here even longer while I try to regain my equilibrium.

"Yeah, I'm good," I say, feigning composure and grinning stiffly. "You good?"

"Yeah, I'm good," he repeats.

I show him how to pull himself up and tuck himself to the

side as he gets in, not going to his knees since that would just make the canoe slip out from under him and send him right over the opposite side. When he's succeeded and stable, I reach up and let him help me in after. This time, I make sure he's set up at the bow, and I flip my seat forward at the stern to avoid being face-to-face. I toss him vague instructions over my shoulder, telling him to watch how I row and to try and mimic it as we make our way back home.

The disquiet comes howling back out here in the open, outside of the safety of our little inverted world. My strokes pick up speed alongside the anxiousness of my thoughts. What do I want from him? More importantly, what could I possibly expect from him? Other than his friendship and partnership this summer. I'm not so obtuse that I don't recognize that we're attracted to one another. But I'm also unable to lie to myself, and the truth of the matter is I've never once had a fling. I have never operated this way, and I don't know if I'm capable. I stab my paddle clumsily into the water at the thought.

Silly, soft, too-nice Sage. Why shouldn't I be able to just enjoy myself? To take something I want for what it is and have a hot summer full of healthy sex and fun?

If he's open to it, too, that is.

That's the only capacity I could let someone like Fisher in. Eventually, people like him always get bored with people like me. He'll flee at the end of August and sprint right back to his reality. Because that's what he once called this summer, isn't it? A *detour* from his life.

Maybe I'd like a detour of my own. The trick would be keeping those boundary lines firm, keeping things surface level. For how open we've already been with one another, pulling back on that might be difficult.

God, this is infuriating. The first new friend I've made in years, someone who is helping me finally do something I've wanted for *me*—and I had to go and have a devastating crush on him.

We paddle the rest of the way home in silence, this stupid suit and the twisting in my gut pulling tighter by the second. I practically leap out of the canoe when we finally make it back to our little half-moon strip of beach.

"We don't need to carry it back up the trail," I say, reaching in to grab one of the yokes and dragging it onto shore. I don't meet his eyes.

"Sage," he says.

"I've got a blind over there I store it behind. No one else comes here, so it's safe."

"*Sage*," he says again.

I close my eyes and summon my courage before I finally look at him. My mouth judders open when I find that he's peeled down the top half of his wet suit.

"Sorry," he says, bare-chested and glistening. "I was overheating, and it felt too tight," he explains, quickly adding, "We need to talk about that kiss, don't we?"

I look up at the sky to avoid staring at the chest. The smattering of hair dusting across his pecs and the junction down his abdomen. "It's all right, Fisher. We don't," I say. "It was probably a bad idea."

"It was *definitely* a bad idea," he agrees, and my eyes snap back down to his.

"Right," I agree angrily. "But out of curiosity, just so I know . . . why, exactly, do *you* think it's a bad idea?"

He rubs at the back of his neck, biceps bunching firm. "Because, Sage. I'm a fucking mess," he says.

Damn him for that. For shifting the onus on himself instead of making this easy and saying something along the lines of, *Because, you sweet summer bumpkin, I know you'll catch feelings, and I'm still a decent guy that doesn't want you hurt.*

"We're all a mess, Fisher," I reply. "But look—it's fine, really. You don't need to worry about me getting this"—I point back and forth between us—"mixed up again, okay? We're friends. I just got caught up in the moment. Small-town girl with stars in my eyes and whatnot."

"Don't do that," he says harshly. "'Can't let it get to you if you own it first,' right? That's what you said to me the other day." His expression softens. "As your *friend*, I don't like when you try to make yourself seem small. And I'm sorry I ever belittled you before, I was wrong." He huffs out a frustrated sound. "I don't know how to defend you from yourself, though, Sage."

I search his face in stunned silence, and he closes in on some of the distance between us. "I'm a mess because I'm fucking untethered. I've spent too much time white-knuckling my way through shit, and now I'm trying to figure out why. I'm questioning my career—something I no longer have, Sage. I should get that straight and make that clear. I was fired. I'm questioning *many* of my life choices, too, and to add pressure on top of everything, I've got a fifteen-year-old kid depending on me who I've already failed tremendously."

"Fisher—"

"I'm sorry, but I've gotta get this all out and lay my cards on the table before I lose the nerve again, okay?" he says, his mouth bracketed in pain. When I nod, he continues. "I'm her godfather, too. I was officially appointed to that role and everything. I was in a rush to get off the phone with my sister the day she called and asked. And it's not like I even remember *why* I was in a hurry, but I do remember every word she said to me during that conversation. And you know what I did when the time came and I was supposed to step up?" Emotion hardens itself across his features. "I fucking *abandoned* Indy." The break in his voice has me desperate to reach for him again. "My parents offered to step in, and I just let them. And not because I was struggling with something like addiction or because I couldn't carry the financial burden. It was all because I didn't know how I'd make it work with the career I was half out of love with, anyway. Because I didn't feel like I knew what I was doing and I was still gripping my life so tight that I was terrified of *anything* else that was out of my control. And guess what? None of those things have changed for me. I'm just finally facing the truth of them and *trying*, I guess. This is me trying, and I'm still this much of a mess." His eyes dart back and forth between mine. "Sometimes I get so lost in my head that I have to remember to breathe, Sage. I . . . Until I started spending time with you, it was like I forgot how to just be present." He lets out the saddest laugh. "But I think you make it hard to be anywhere else." I'm openly gaping at him, I'm sure, but he keeps going.

"So, it's not that it's a bad idea for us to become friends," he says. "I'm happy we've got each other, and I'm *glad* we're doing this. Criminally early mornings and all." A muscle ripples up his jaw, and he blows out a long breath through his nose. "And I won't lie, Sage. I want you. More than I should, I think, but it feels *good* to want." A look of raw longing drifts across his face. "I just don't know what I've got to offer beyond whatever we are to each other for a few months. Friends, teammates. Friends with benefits, for lack of a better term. And I'm so tired of letting people down, Sage—myself included." His eyes flick to my mouth and back up just as quickly. "I promise I wouldn't let you down in *some* ways." He smirks, and I bite the inside of my cheek to stop the butterflies trying to flutter up from my chest. His expression sobers. "I *know* I'd let you down if I led you on, though."

He's essentially confirmed what I already knew, but hearing him explain it, realizing he's just as unsure . . . it sounds like he's also as much at risk of getting hurt.

It's no wonder we keep finding each other. I'm learning that it's okay for me to want more for myself, to want the new and the unknown, and he's trying to learn how to hold on to less. How to let go. How to quit trying to hold on to control, to let go of regrets and shame.

"I think," I say. "I think that maybe we make ourselves wait. Just to make sure it's not a fluke thing brought on by the romantic setting." Because no matter what, it's bound to make things awkward the hypothetical morning after, if we take this step. We've got nearly a whole summer left to get through. I need to leave the romance at the door.

He fails to stop a grin. "I've always said that nothing screams romance like being submerged in the icy Pacific before seven A.M.," he says.

I snort. "That's an oddly specific motto."

He steps closer. "I don't think it was a fluke. Know why?" he asks.

"Why?"

"Because *that* was also at least a half hour ago now," he says, taking a dangerous step closer, so close the temperature changes at my front. "And I'm still hard for you."

Hunger sweeps low and licks back up my spine in a loop. I glance down to check if he's telling the truth, but the half-draped wet suit blocks my view where he's holding it. And he tips my chin back up to his face, anyway.

"You can talk that long and stay hard?!" I dumbly ask.

"Sweetheart, I'm finding when it comes to you, I don't know what I'm capable of, but I'm happy to test those limits." He breathes into a smile. "I'll follow your lead. And our deal stands no matter what you decide."

I try to swallow, though my throat feels bone-dry. "Okay," I tremulously agree before I spin and yank myself away.

CHAPTER 19

FISHER

I haven't heard from Sage for a full forty-eight hours since our first canoe lesson. I try not to get too spun out over it. Maybe I was too open, or maybe I offended her by even suggesting a friends-with-benefits arrangement?

It's probably for the best. I'm not sure it'd be smart for me to throw myself at her feet, either. I just knew that I wanted to.

But *wanting* isn't always the wisest reason to make a decision, so I wanted to acknowledge that at the same time.

Things with Indy are holding steady for the most part. I think she's annoyed that I picked her up from summer school today instead of letting her catch a ride home from Sam or Blake, but she hides it well. Despite the mildly sick feeling that I've carried through the day over the state of things with Sage, Indy and I manage a nice evening together. She works on schoolwork at the kitchen island while I throw together a panzanella and drink a jar of wine.

After dinner, we sit in the living room and watch *Friends* reruns on the couch, and just as my eyelids start to feel heavy, she asks, "Did Mom ever tell you about the carpool thing?"

I sit up and search my brain. "I don't think so," I say.

She shakes her head. "These stupid mom cliques were always such bitches to her," she tells me. "Even when I was little and playing soccer, they'd never let her be part of the carpool rotation."

Anger razes through my chest when I think about that town and those people again. "I'm sorry I wasn't around more, Ind. For both of you."

She scowls and tucks her feet farther under her on the couch. "It's not your fault they were ignorant shits."

"Am I supposed to ask you to watch the language, or . . . ?" I genuinely have no clue.

She only shrugs with her arms folded, hands hugging her sides. "You know, Sam's mom was sixteen when she had him, too," she says. "But it doesn't sound like they dealt *her* the scarlet letter around here."

The sadness that pierces through my chest hits me so strongly and severely I want to claw at it and rip it back out. How could those nothing people continue to treat Freya like they'd deserved the same air as my kind-to-a-fault sister, let alone like they were better than she was?

"Sam's mom was probably already one of them," I guess. "You know how townies protect their own."

After a few silent seconds, she says, "I think I'm still angry at her. I'll never understand why she kept us there."

The ache surges so deep I imagine it squeezing my bones.

"I wish I knew, too," I croak. "I don't know why Grandma and Grandpa are still hanging around that place, either." They were the original pariahs, after all. The ones that ended up having to find work two towns over.

"Probably because they've been indoctrinated now," she replies bitterly. "Nan has a bunco group and everything."

"You're kidding me."

"Nope," she says, the *p* popping in anger.

I don't know what to make of that, so I don't try to offer any explanation or commentary.

"Indy, I'm sorry," I say. I've tried to apologize in roundabout ways before, but they were stiff conversations that I always brought all my justifications to. *I thought it would be best. I thought Grandma and Grandpa would do a better job than me.* Now that we seem to be figuring things out as we go, I also feel sorry that I missed years where we could've been doing the same. "I should've been there for you. It's what your mom asked me to do, and I'm so sorry that I wasn't."

She only stares at me for a few beats. "I'm glad we're together now," she says.

"Me, too."

We do the *exact* same awkward Midwesterner-rolled-lips smile at each other in synchrony, before they both turn into a real laugh. And then we slip back into a comfortable silence in the glow of the television.

"Did you know," Indy says toward the end of another episode, "that Mom was coming home from one of those pyramid scheme MLM parties the day of the accident? Of all the stupid things in all the world, it's like she died trying to find her people. Still trying to find somewhere to fit in."

I watch a tear fall silently down her face, so much like Freya's it's unbearable. I shove down the urge to shy away from my own pain over this, something I defaulted to for far too long. If Indy can be brave like she's being right now, I can, too. I let the knot tighten in my throat, surrender to my tears as they quietly come.

"When I was smaller, I thought maybe one day we could move to New York, by you," she says. "I thought if she got out, you guys might end up like Ross and Monica or something. Like she'd go to a coffee shop and sit on a couch and miraculously find us a new life." She half laughs, like she doesn't want me to think she's serious or like she's telling me how ridiculous that dreamer is to her now. "And it wouldn't matter that I was the girl with the teen mom or that I didn't have a dad, because it would be a whole different world, you know? Not just the same people trying to fulfill their same parents' mediocre, empty, suburban dreams in the same fucking place all the time."

I'm not sure why it breaks my heart that this is her take on things when I've always had the same outlook. I'm also not certain that sharing my experience from here on the other side (with how that's going for me) will help her cynicism, though.

I think of Sage and her relentless determination to make something beautiful with all that she's had at her fingertips, in spite of her life's tragedies. If I can help Indy adopt that mindset, I think she'd be okay no matter where she ended up.

"I think finding the right people—finding *your* people—can be the thing that makes anywhere feel like home," I say.

She selects the next episode and doesn't look my way. "Or," she says, "you learn quickly that no other person has that kind of power, anyway. The kind to make you happy. So you figure out what *you* want and where *you* want it, and *you* go after it. Like you did." Another zap of pain before she adds, "And maybe anyone that fits into that is who your people are meant to be."

Long after she falls asleep, I find myself still thinking about that. About how even successfully ending up in New York and reaching what I'd thought was a dream didn't end up making me happy. Didn't really end with me finding my people, either. Carlie and her family are somewhat close, but I was always still an employee. I realize that I managed to let other people dictate my life's direction, in a way, even from the other side of the country.

The determination that etches itself into me now is a quieter kind, something seasoned and calm. Next time, I'll truly be doing it for me. To prove to myself that I can and to show Indy, too. I'll take the life I have at my fingertips and make something of it. I'll spend more time with people outside of work. I'll say yes when people invite me out for drinks, and I'll take Indy to some Broadway shows. I'll stop to listen to the musicians in the park for once. I'll emulate what Sage seems to employ, and I'll experience those small joys I too often ignored.

The following morning, Indy asks again if she can go with her friends after class, and this time, I oblige. The day stretches before me like a blank slate—or maybe a bit more like a chasm. I don't have work to take solace or find distraction in. There's not much else I can do for Starhopper until Frankie shows up tomorrow for us to begin on that stage of things. I've sketched out the changes I'd suggest for the kitchen layout already. And I think I'd like to do something other than work, anyway, so fiddling with menu ideas today doesn't interest me.

I pull out my phone and contemplate texting Sage. We can't avoid each other forever . . . unless she wants to now? Unless, as Indy would say, I "fucked up the vibe" and now she'd rather bail on the deal altogether. But I've already got my end of the bargain, really. Why wouldn't she want me to help her get hers?

Fuck. Unless I misread something somewhere along the way? It's not completely inconceivable.

I can't sit here and continue winding myself up about it, I

know that much is true. I do a mental scroll of anything else I can tackle to be productive. I could start studying for the trivia thing? But I've got no clue what to study, so I'd need her for that as well. I would rather not "practice" preparing three courses for me, myself, and I today for the cooking competition. Besides, we haven't quite gone over all those details yet, either. Are we limited on how we're supposed to prepare each meal? What are the time constraints, et cetera?

It's time to put into practice what I decided I would last night, to find some small joys for myself. It takes a disturbing amount of time for me to land on physical exertion. I figure it checks off multiple boxes, anyway. Even if it's not canoeing, it's still some kind of training, and endorphins never hurt when it comes to the mind.

CHAPTER 20

SAGE

I'm pacing back and forth across the tile in my sunroom three days after kissing Fisher (again), my mom's advice journal in one hand and my phone in the other, following the oscillating path of the fan I plugged in. I'm stuck on one of Mom's notes that says, *People can't follow your rules if you don't make them clear. This applies in all your relationships: parenting, love, and friendships alike. If you don't tell people what is and isn't okay with you, they have no way of knowing.*

I finally hit Send on the text that says, Maybe we need to establish some rules, and force myself to sit.

I bounce back up when I realize I need to elaborate. For us, I send prematurely, too, and utter a curse. For our . . . potential . . . beneficial . . . situation. There. That should be clear. I'm being respectful and completely chill about this.

I met Wren at the bakery yesterday morning before opening, to finally get her caught up in person on everything rather than some nondescriptive texts exchanged in something resembling a game of phone tag. We are both notoriously terrible at thorough, consistent conversations over text, and I wanted real-time advice.

"So, what is it you're afraid of, exactly?" she asked when I told her about his proposition.

"I mean, it couldn't go anywhere, anyway," I said. "He's here for a summer. It's temporary."

"So, I ask again," she said, pulling things down from the walk-in and sliding them into the display case. "What are you afraid of? Specifically."

I pushed up to sit on the counter. "Is it not obvious?" I asked, irritated with myself. "I'm afraid I'll catch feelings."

She nodded thoughtfully and came to lean beside me. "Did I ever tell you that Ellis is the one who helped me perfect the scones?" she asked.

I frowned and shook my head.

"For weeks, I fiddled with them. Sam was three, and we'd just moved out of your house and into the little basement apartment at my parents'. And I swear to you, Sage, I had to have made him eat hundreds of them with me. I wanted my own recipe and my own thing on the menu. It wasn't important, but it was important to me, you know?" She cleared her throat. "And you remember, it's not like we had any money back then or anything, but once I got the recipe cracked, Ellis went out and put the deposit down on the industrial mixer we've still got. You'd think he'd have been happy to not have to eat any more of them, but instead, he got me something to make huge batches at a time." She looked at me and quietly added, "Every single time I use that thing, I remember him carrying Sam around our insanely tiny kitchen, always shirtless and always eating my ingredients or sticking their fingers in whatever batter. And I remember how good it felt." She bunched her shoulders up. "Does it make shit hurt worse now? Sometimes. Most of the time." She sighed. "Always.

"But," she kept going, "I still wouldn't change any of it. It's cliché, but true."

She went on to say that if she were me, she would try to establish some guidelines to mitigate the potential pain. Like, avoid getting too personal too often or limit our benefits to once or twice a week. All of it sounded unnatural to me, but I figured I'd open up the conversation with Fisher, at least.

The only thing that does feel natural is wanting it.

I scream when there's a knock on the glass. "Shit!"

"Sorry," Fisher laughs, leaning against the doorframe. "I was coming back from the trail when I, uh, got your text, so just figured I'd pop by." He sounds out of breath.

"Why are you so sweaty?" my mouth asks without clearing it by my brain first. It comes out like an accusation.

He grins lopsidedly, and my stomach sharply dips. "I went running on the beach and did some push-ups and shit. But if you're asking why I did *that*, I dunno? I guess because I'm on a journey of self-discovery and healing, and it seems like that's the sort of thing one does during one of those expeditions."

My shocked bark of laughter dies when he lifts the end of his shirt up to wipe off his brow. I glimpse a light line of hair sweeping down his stomach, a vein trailing up from his shorts. I spin on the ball of my foot and occupy myself with putting down my phone and sliding the journal away.

"That's good," I say. "For the race, anyhow." I turn back to find him five feet closer, playing with the leaves on one of my peace lilies.

"Right," he agrees. "Still want to keep training this week?"

A shot of nerves and anticipation bleeds through me. "Yes. Why wouldn't I?"

He shrugs innocently. "Just checking. The only days that I can't are Wednesdays."

"How come?" I ask. Then—"Shit, ignore that. You don't need to explain yourself."

He crosses his arms before he reaches back to rub his neck. "It's just—"

"No, Fisher, it's fine. You don't need to explain. Really."

"I, uh . . . I have my standing appointment with a therapist Wednesday mornings. I started seeing her a few weeks after Indy showed up. She goes to her separately, too."

The sudden urge to leap on him has me gripping the nearest windowpane. The way that he's trying so hard to do everything right all the time with Indy and doesn't even comprehend that about himself has an amp plugged into my sex drive for some reason. He makes me feel like I've got some sort of nerve condition. Fluttering spasms all over. Maybe I *should* just leap on him and we don't actually have to talk all this out first.

"I keep telling people we need a therapist to set up shop here in Spunes," I say, voice rickety.

"*Sage*," he says, and oh no. He's coming closer. He's closer, and I can smell him. And of course he smells even better than usual, because even though he's sweaty, I am made of nothing logical right now, only hormones and a lust-filled haze. "You said you wanted to talk about rules?"

Rules. Yes, rules. No rules. The word starts to sound foreign in my mind the more I repeat it. There's a term for that, I think? Semantic satiation. I can remember *that*, but rules? I don't remember any of them.

I feel his stare land on my mouth. I lean into the glass at my back, feel my palms start to heat against it. His hand comes up beside my ear, and he braces himself onto it, tilting over me.

My chest lifts and falls almost comically, like I'm some distressed maiden trapped in a corset, but really I'm just trapped under my own skin and bones, desperate to fuse with his. His teeth meet his lower lip like he's trying not to smile.

"Must be a pretty sizable list," he says, his head and smile tilting.

"List?" I echo back dazedly.

"The rules you came up with," he explains. "If it took three days to assemble, I'm guessing it's big."

He slowly runs the backs of his fingers down my shirt over my waist, over my hip at the top of the peasant skirt I yanked on this morning.

"Tell me your first rule, Byrd," he says, voice low, and god, for the life of me, I still can't think of one. All remaining thought whirrs and flees when the tip of his finger hooks inside my waistband. His chest works hard enough to push into mine now. "Do I need to tease it out of you?" he asks, his voice shaking through my core. Before I can answer, he says, "No, I don't think you'd like to be teased."

"I wouldn't?" I struggle not to sound incredulous or to shout something brainless like, *Yes, huh!*

"No, Sage. I think you'd respond better to being very intentionally worked up," he tells me. "Should I tell you how?"

I hope my nodded reply is more understated than I feel.

"I'd start by asking if it was against a rule to tell you I've been thinking about what you taste like every day since the library," he says. He runs that same fingertip side to side in a path on my bare skin. I swallow with difficulty and bite my lip to stifle the noisy chuff of my breath. We both watch his hand continue to trace back and forth between us. "I'd have to see if there was a rule about me figuring out everywhere else you have freckles, too," he says. I suck in a gasp through my teeth when his erection grazes my hip. "Am I allowed to work out everything you like? What makes you turn that pretty color here?" His other hand comes down the glass, and his thumb glides under my collarbone like he's painting my blush with it himself. "What makes you wet?"

A mortifying noise whimpers up from my throat. But when my back bows and my hips lift against him, he looses a short, broken groan of his own.

"Kiss me," I say. It sounds like, *Please, please, please.*

He brings both his palms around my ribs and lowers down to me, painstakingly slowly. *Not teasing, my ass.*

We both hum when our lips finally meet. His tongue slips against mine, and I smile at the overwhelming relief, gripping him closer. The respite quickly burns off into wild need, and the skin on my upper back makes a rubbing squeal against the glass. His palms cup beneath my breasts, and I groan, trying to arch into him.

"Tell me what you want, Sage," he says. His teeth clip at a soft spot at my neck.

"*That*," I say. "You telling me what *you* want." I squeeze my thighs together at his responding sound. "I don't want to think," I add. I want to chase this pleasure until I feel like it's running through me.

He leans back to look at me, eyes glazed and pupils blown. I tip up and nip at his ear, my teeth toying with the metal. He pins me back into the wall of glass and rewards me with a searing kiss.

"Hold up your skirt," he says into my lips. He starts gathering it in fistfuls up my legs, his mouth still grazing mine.

When he reaches the tops of my thighs, I clutch the fabric in my trembling fingers, watch him settle down to his knees before me even as I feel like mine might give out.

"Oh, Sagebyrd," he says with a humorless laugh. "As much as I like your crazy robes, I think I love these more." His thumb slips inside the plain cotton thong.

I somehow flush hotter over him complimenting my robes. "Yes," I say, "but—" I hiss when he nuzzles and kisses my thigh, his palms running up and down in soothing motions. My fingers ache to drop the skirt and comb through his hair. "One can't grocery shop in panties alone."

He ignores my quip, centering all his focus on the rest of me. His rough hands knead my calves, his mouth finding a sensitive spot beside one of my knees that makes it nearly cave. I'm suddenly jealous of anyone who's ever watched him cook before, if his concentration looks anything nearly as devoted or passionate as it does right now.

The first warm press of his mouth through wet fabric makes me buck and tremble. His thumb follows his path and drags and circles. He gently tugs the material down my thighs, patiently and sweetly lifting both of my feet to step out of it.

"Okay?" he rasps.

No. I feel myself being irrevocably changed, I think. I'm more than or something other than okay. "Yes," I say.

"You'll tell me," he says, planting a sucking kiss at the juncture of my hip, "if you don't like something."

"Yes," I agree.

He parts me with his thumbs and sweeps his tongue through me in a hot lick that wrenches a sob from my chest. "You'll tell me if you do," he says as if the noises he's stealing from me aren't evidence enough.

There's nothing rushed or measured about how he savors

me after that. When I clumsily try to chase a certain rhythm, he hooks my leg over his shoulder and takes over. He hums that sound I love against me, and it feels like it's inside me. It's fucking euphoric. He laps at my nerve endings until I can't tell if I'm peaking or plummeting, until eventually it's both, until it's cresting over me and sweeping under me, until I'm wrung out and breathless and pulsing all over.

I've dropped the skirt at some point and gripped his hair, so I let my hands slacken and smooth along his scalp. He rests his forehead against my stomach and threads my languid limbs back into my underwear, rising up from his knees as he pulls them into place. Our chests press into a tight hug, and I realize he's just as breathless as I am, his heart pounding just as wildly. I softly kiss along his jaw and tentatively palm him through his shorts. He makes a ragged, splintered sound.

"I didn't expect this," he grits before he takes my lips with his. "It's almost time for Indy to get home. We don't . . ." Another kiss. "Don't have time."

Something pricks behind my breastbone, but I smile. "I didn't expect you today, either," I say. "Stay," I add before I think otherwise. I grind against his considerable length like I'm helpless against that, too. "Let me—"

"No," he gruffly whispers, but he smiles back. "No, I just mean it's okay. We'll have time, Sage." His throat bounces on a swallow. "I want to take my time."

In the effervescent aftermath of the orgasm, his words make me inexplicably sad. We have time, but how much of it?

"Still, stay or . . . come back for dinner?" I ask. "It's my monthly dinner with my brothers tonight. Sam's gonna be here, too, so Indy wouldn't be miserable." I'm not sure why asking *this* feels quite so vulnerable when he just had his tongue inside me.

A slash of white parts his face in a soft grin. "Okay," he says, then kisses me abruptly once more, like he can't help himself. "What are you making me?"

We end up making pizzas together on the grill using the store-bought dough I have in the fridge, topped with a mishmash of items from the garden that Fisher convinces me to combine.

"You sure you want pizza?" I ask him at some point while he helps me assemble. "I imagine you've had some of the best pizza in the world before. Doesn't it make the more basic stuff bland?"

He picks up my glass of cheap white wine and takes a hearty swig. He might've dealt me a release earlier, but he's the one who looks more relaxed, somehow. He moves around my kitchen with the ease of someone who's in control, more at home in one.

"I think the best pizza I ever had was my senior prom night in nowhere Nebraska," he says, his face tightening with a laugh. "The cheese was like rubber and the sauce was like acid and the crust was undercooked in the middle and burnt on the edge."

"That sounds disgusting."

"It was. *But* . . . there was this girl." He gives me a sly look. Sun-kissed brow, wet lips, five o'clock shadow, and a shiny earring make him look like a rogue buccaneer. I wonder if he actually does have some hidden tattoos.

"Of course there was," I say.

"My parents basically insisted I still go to prom even though I did not have a date. I—god, this is embarrassing—but I think my mom bought me a boutonniere and everything." He winces. "But this girl, she was a mean thing all through elementary and middle school and a real monster in high school, too. She was also the prom queen—Lauren Chilton. Made everyone call her

'LC.' Her prom king date was a special kind of prick, too, but long story short, she caught him making out with the captain of the girls' lacrosse team at the dance and started flirting with me."

"Aha, so you already had history with that whole make-the-ex-jealous thing, huh?" I playfully say.

"Anyway," he brushes past, "I tried to play it cool the whole night and not act like all my teenage dreams were coming true. She asked me to take her home and wanted me to run her by the local waffle house on the way. But without the dark gymnasium or the music or dancing, I was too nervous to eat in front of the girl. My stomach was in knots." He blows out a laugh. "She made out with me for a solid seven seconds when I got her to her driveway and touched me through my slacks for a nanosecond, until my stomach immediately played a whole orchestra of ominous noises, and she quickly lost interest." He pops a marionberry in his mouth. "I pulled into the first convenience store and ate a slice of pizza that'd probably been under a heat lamp for ten hours, and that there is the story of my first kiss."

So the terrible pizza was the best because of the memory with it. It's no wonder he puts so much of his own value on how good he is at his career. Food once related to experiences for him.

"Hey, before I forget to ask, where do you get these?" he says when he eats another berry. "Mine don't taste the same."

"Those," I tell him, "grow right here at the back of our properties. They're marionberries. You're probably buying regular blackberries."

He frowns and gives the thing a dirty look like it's made him feel stupid, and I laugh and kiss his chin.

Silas, Ellis, Sam, and Indy show up not long after. We sit in the evening sun, eating and drinking and laughing. Silas and Ellis overshare more of my embarrassing tales, and I counterattack with a lifetime's arsenal of my own. Indy and Sam eventually leave us and go for a walk down the trail. As the sun fades, the sky turns pink.

"That boy's in trouble," Silas says with a nod toward Sam in the distance.

Ellis levels a severe frown his way.

"Why do you say that?" I ask. I move to collect the empty beer bottles on the table, but Fisher presses me back into my chair by my shoulder and starts grabbing them himself.

"Anyone else want anything?" he asks.

"Yeah," Silas says to him. "I want *you* to cook for us. I want some crazy shit, too. Something with foam and sugar bubbles and dry ice or something."

"*Jesus*, Silas," I groan.

Fisher gives him a passive response and carries the detritus inside.

"Why'd you say that about Sam?" I ask Silas again, back-handing him across the shoulder for good measure.

"Because," he replies, "he looks just like Ell did with Wren. Look where that landed him."

"Shut the fuck up, Silas," Ellis says, but there's no burn in it.

"According to Indy, they're just friends," I say. It's none of our business what they do behind the scenes. "Wren and Ellis were in love."

"Can we talk about literally anything else?" Ellis says.

"I'm just saying," Silas urges, "it's been four years. It's time to get back out there."

And this is where the conversation always dies. Because not all hearts break, or *heal*, the same. Ellis braided his life with Wren's in too many ways not to still be frayed.

Fisher squeezes the back of my neck once when he rejoins us

outside. There's a far-off voice in a distant room of my mind that whispers to me again, *Danger! You're capsized and in over your head! Don't get so comfortable in your inverted world that you can't turn yourself to rights!*

Another one of Mom's phrases chases it at its heels: *Don't worry so much about the clouds that you miss the flowers at your feet.*

Flowers might fade, but I think I'll enjoy them while they're here.

CHAPTER 21

FISHER

The day Frankie gets into town, it feels like time starts trying to gather speed.

The work at Starhopper itself is nothing I've got any sort of experience in. I'm more like a ringleader/middleman for everyone to go between. All in all, though, the local hires mesh well with Frankie and his crew, and everyone continues to deliver and hold up their end of things—something I'm told is a rarity for a construction endeavor. Martha O'Doyle is a regular fixture around the build site, but I think I've got her figured out now.

"You actually *asked* that woman for her feedback?!" Sage whispers to me from across the table we're stationed at in the library today. She's got a pencil twisted through her hair and a horrified smile tugging at her cheeks. "You're a sadist." I feel stupidly bashful when her foot skates up my leg under the desk.

We've been stuck in a limbo of sorts since that afternoon in the sunroom last Thursday. The next day, I had to be at Starhopper early for the plumber, and she'd been busy at the farmers market over the weekend with Indy. I'd been inundated with the restaurant and getting it all caught up where I could from Monday to Thursday this week, which means today, Friday, is the first day we've been alone together since. Friday afternoons are what we agreed would be our typical time slot for trivia studies and eventual cooking lessons, anyway. Still, that day certainly hasn't left my mind. Not her silky skin or her taste, not the way the crook of her knee began to sweat against my shoulder or how she'd circled her hips when she got close.

Shit, I'm seconds from begging her to let me dive beneath this desk to taste her again. But I know I distracted her from establishing her rules before, and I don't want to risk pushing her again in that regard. I have to jerk my thoughts into submission.

Remembering that Martha O'Doyle was the subject we'd just been discussing seems to do the trick.

"True, but guess who was too busy shopping for local artwork that she wasn't there to hover or yell at any loading trucks today?" I ask. "Besides, I feel like I picked up that method from *you*."

She innocently puts a palm to her chest and mouths, "Me?"

"Yes, you," I say, nudging her foot with mine. "You don't think I noticed how you supplied Indy and me with *usefulness*?"

She smiles coyly to herself and goes back to studying the textbook in front of her. I feel like a toddler rocking on my hands with how difficult it is to focus. I let out a dramatic sigh.

"Do you feel you know *everything* you need to know about the early Pacific Northwest and its timber industry's rise and decline?" she asks, arching a dark brow.

"Define *need*," I say, sulking. I have no idea how my brain ever got me through traditional learning.

"If you can actively study for ten more minutes," she says, "I'll show you the attic."

Intrigued and motivated, I concentrate on everything she's put before me.

Before I know it, while I'm knee-deep in the drama of timber wars, Sage reaches across the desk and runs her fingertip up my arm, hairs standing on end in its wake.

"Good boy," she tells me. And I don't think studying together will ever be a problem again. She gets up and starts sliding our books into her bag, and I follow suit. I can't wipe off the dumb look I know I have on my face, and if I had a tail, I know it'd be wagging.

She walks me over to the same alcove we visited on our first time here, this time pulling down on the attic stairs and leading me up.

"It's not a full attic or anything," she tells me. "Just an extra space I guess they didn't really account for."

It's smaller than I'd anticipated, with a circular stained glass window that makes the room feel like the inside of a kaleidoscope. It's slanted, but even at the tallest part of the ceiling it's too low to stand in. There's a big crate full of clothes, toys, and what looks like a medley of items from over the decades—a big sign painted with "Lost & Found" on the front. One corner of the room looks like it's a bit more intentional, though, with a short case stuffed with books covered in long-haired, nipple-baring men, a few jaggedly drawn pictures hung on a string, clearly done by a kid, and a stuffed animal she surreptitiously tries to kick off to the side. It's painfully intimate, like she's showing me into her personal time capsule.

"This," she says, "is where I had my first kiss." I find her smiling self-consciously at me. "Venus started letting me come up here when I was seven or eight, but no one else unless I took them up with me. I think she knew I'd need some sort of private space somewhere away from my brothers. Anyway, Shiloh Wilson was my first kiss here. I was in eighth grade, playing spin the bottle with, like, seven other kids." She lets out a trill of laughter.

"Sordid," I say. "Shiloh and Sage. Sounds like it belongs on a napkin."

"Ugh," she scoffs. "I think he lives in a yurt somewhere in Washington now."

"You crushed his heart that badly, huh?" I laugh. "Poor Shiloh."

"Bold of you to assume that I'm not the one left behind and pining for Shiloh."

Somehow I find that impossible, but . . . "You're right. I can't imagine you leaving anything more hurt or broken than when you found it."

Something sad passes across her smile, but she reaches out and holds my hand. We sit side by side in peace for a time, fingers intertwined and not saying a word, in all the colors and glittering dust suspended in the air. It's like time and worry suspend for a little while, too.

"What was it like? Finding out you got a Michelin star?" she asks. "The first one, I mean."

"Not sure I really ever let myself enjoy it," I admit. "It felt like the pressure just settled, because I knew I'd have to hold on to it. Mostly felt like fear, or panic." I search for the discomfort or the disgust in her expression. Any hint that she's disappointed that I wasn't filled with immediate gratitude or pride. There's nothing but curiosity in her eyes. "I think my adrenaline perspective is a bit skewed," I add with a laugh.

"It got worse with each one?" she says.

I nod. "The day after I found out about the third, I started a small fire. Don't even remember how. But I remember watching it burning and thinking it was proof that I was a fraud, and . . . and it sort of felt like a relief, in a way. I think by the time I actually lost the third, I'd already become so detached that it felt like another confirmation."

"You did deserve them, though. You know that, right? You worked hard and you deserved them."

I lay a quick kiss to her knuckles. "I do know, now," I say. "That's kind of one of the good things about getting fired, I guess. Like, for how much my brain has gone through everything trying to figure out what went wrong, I also remembered all the shit that went right."

The happiness on her face makes me hungry.

"What were your parents like?" I ask. All this sharing might be dangerous, but it feels like she's invited me into more than a public library attic, like each piece of her she unveils makes me feel starved for more. I want to know if she went to her prom, where she's traveled or if she wants to. I want to know what her favorite meal is and if there's a reason why she loves it the most.

I want to be the one to make her favorite meal, I think. Actually, I know I want that so badly it makes my ribs ache. And I know it's because I want to impress her. Admittedly, yeah, I'd like to seduce her, too. But I want to cook her something.

"My parents," she says, her face dividing into a dreamy grin. "My parents grew up here. They were neighbors and strongly disliked one another most of their lives—all the way up through senior year and everything. Dad went off to school out of state, and Mom stayed here." The more she smiles, the harder she squeezes my hand. "They used to do a whole dress-up thing as part of the festival, so my mom and a bunch of people wore these, like, Regency-era dresses and had to act like they were in character for a day. I'm sad they got rid of it, because I think I'd kill. But, at any rate, my dad had just come home for the summer, and I guess his jilted ex had shown up in town looking for him."

"The ex wasn't from here?"

"Nope," she laughs. "She was from the next county over. And Dad wasn't perfectly innocent or anything. Apparently, they'd met at school at the end of the semester, and he took her out a few times but knew right away they wouldn't work out. *However*, she'd mentioned her family having a houseboat over the Fourth of July at one of these big lakes in their county. And you have to understand, there's nothing big that happens here for the Fourth, and it can be a bit of a sore spot for us." She sigh-laughs again. "He wanted to see fireworks and said he wanted to see a houseboat, so he sorta used the girl. Broke up with her when they got back to land." She winces.

I shake my head and tsk.

"I know, agreed. Anyhow, by the way he always made it sound, this girl showed up to Spunes on the warpath. He was scrambling around in a panic trying to find someplace to hide. Until he saw my mom—in her giant-skirted dress." Her smile looks irrepressible. "He must have seemed truly desperate, because he managed to convince her to tuck him under it."

"Now that," I say, "is how you meet a woman. He sounds pretty slick."

"Best way to meet a woman is by letting her rescue you?" she asks, delighted. "Yeah, I guess I like that approach, too."

When I chuckle, she continues. "They didn't have us until they were much older, and I don't know. From everything I remember of them, they were just always so interested in life, always going in a bunch of directions and circling right back. They traveled a lot, and they both tried multiple career paths before they settled back in Spunes.

"I think I get my learning quirks from my dad. Like, I'll read something about a certain period in time and come across a weird word or an expression, and I'll end up going on a tangent and learning about all the slang of the era. Or I'll read that cucumbers grow better when they're planted next to sunflowers, and before I know it, I've got a whole floral operation in place."

"I like that," I say. "That you like learning new things and you'll throw yourself into them."

"You don't?"

"I like *mastering* something, I think," I admit. "I struggle when I don't feel like I'm good at it, or struggle to jump into something when I don't feel like I can see and control the outcome."

"I always felt like cooking was something more naturally acquired, I guess," she says.

"It is. It absolutely is a creative avenue and it can be some of the most abstract art out there. It's just also very measurable. If you can manage controlling the ingredients and how they're grown, how they're prepared, what quantities or what size you cut them into . . . it's all a complicated puzzle, but you can control it in the end."

She snorts an amused sound.

A minute of contented quiet later, I say, "Speaking of the Fourth, Indy asked if she could go camping with her friend Blake and her family in Gandon that weekend. I wouldn't be saying yes to, like, some weird, patriotic, Burning Man–type thing, would I?"

"Blake's good," she says. "And no, it's all very wholesome Americana. Only the good sort of weird. Very few psychedelics." She elbows me with a benevolent smirk. "And that's where pretty much everyone will be. This place will look like a ghost town."

"You don't want to go watch fireworks or anything?" I ask.

She shakes her head nonchalantly. "Nah. It's too hard to get away with the animals and everything. Anyone that could come take care of them has plans."

"Maybe . . ." *Shit*, my palm feels like it's blistering and my pulse is hammering all of a sudden. "Maybe I could cook for you or something."

She bends and kisses me. "Sure. I'd be interested in *or something*, then, too," she says. "But." She swings a leg over and settles herself into my lap, and everything in my core lurches with want. "While dear Shiloh will always be my first, I was hoping I might tempt you into being my *best* kiss up here," she says.

I have to take three steadying breaths before I reach up and thumb her lower lip, then lose my breath completely when she pitches forward and sucks it into her hot mouth. "Fuck," I whisper, my hips arching up against her.

I grip the back of her neck and bring her perfect mouth to mine. "Let me go down on you again," I beg. "I'll give you anything you want. I'll memorize that history book if you want."

A soft sound crawls up her throat and her knees dig into the sides of my hips like she's trying to squeeze them together. I feel something like desperation when I look at her face, and I'm not sure which part is my favorite—her flushed, freckled cheeks or those bright gray eyes with her long black lashes. The lips that always look a bit stained. God, even her nose is sexy to me.

Her breathing matches mine in its shakiness. "I want you," she says, swallowing like she might be nervous or shy, "to teach me how *you* like to be touched this time." Her pulse flutters in the base of her throat. This seems to be the only time Sage gets remotely shy, when it comes to her sexual side, but I gather that curiosity and desire urge her on anyway.

I can hear the blood battering my veins, all of it rushing to one place in response. "I can do that," I say. I want her to feel comfortable to touch me however she wants, whenever she does.

She makes a project of tugging down my jeans to my knees, unbuttoning them and dragging open the zipper slowly. By the time she takes me in hand, I'm panting, fists clenched in the skirt of her dress. The sight of her pretty blue nails wrapped around me makes me groan.

"*Jesus*," she says, staring at my dick, mouth open. Somewhere, my ego sheds a prideful tear.

"Make it wet," I plead.

A rough noise I've never made rips through me when she spits on it, before she gives me a long, light tug. "You can make it hurt a little, sweetheart," I say. I wrap her hand in mine and show her the pressure I like, then grunt when she keeps pumping that way on her own. The calm, studious way she watches me close makes me thrash too far, too quickly.

"I won't be long," I admit, more growl than voice behind the words.

"Tell me when," she says. Some foggy corner of my mind registers that some idiot probably didn't before. When I look away from her hand and find her face once more, her eyes meet mine. The strap of her dress slips off her shoulder in her work, a lock of hair falling across her face. Oh god, I'm already barreling for the end, and a deep and broken whimper escapes. She moans at the sound, and her dress rides up her hips, a flash of wet, pink cotton peeking through.

"I'm gonna . . ." I start to say, tilting my hips to lean to the side. She shoves me back down and takes me into her mouth, and I choke on the slew of sound that wants to explode from my chest. My vision goes blissfully white. I gather her and hold her tightly in my lap after, while my heart tries to return to its normal rate.

"That was . . . there are no words, Sage," I tell her.

She softly laughs.

"I might love the library," I say.

CHAPTER 22

SAGE

I think I've got the yips.

I remember when we were young and the boys still played sports. They'd go through a growth spurt or some random phase that'd disrupt their normal functionality. Dropped balls, tripping over nothing—silly, asinine mistakes. They called it *the yips*.

I think this is similar to whatever's happening to me. On Saturday, I dropped an entire bag of opened chicken feed in the garage, caught my belt loop on the door handle three times, stepped on a rake outside of Bud's stall and knocked myself pretty decently—some real Stooges-level shit. When Indy and I got to the farmers market on Sunday, I realized I'd forgotten the dozens of extra eggs I'd planned to bring, forgot string for the bouquets, *and* forgot to put water in the hydrangea buckets. Thankfully, Indy caught that last one early enough in the day. We sprinted over to the harbor fish-cleaning station, filled the buckets, and dunked the hydrangeas headfirst to revive them.

I delivered flowers to Savvy's this morning for her summer

cakes—nasturtiums and violas and cornflowers for pressing into frosting because they retain their color best. And I was trying to engage in something cheerful with Savannah herself when we were remarking on summer and all the bright flavors, but I think I got jumbled up in my brain while fingering some honeycomb brittle, and said something moony about "the birds and the bees." I looked at her fascinated face in horror before I turned and fled.

I think I used up any suave I had when I told Fisher I was interested in *or something*. Like, now I've built it up and put a date to it instead of just letting things happen. I'd felt too comfortable and easy, sitting there in the attic together, and now I have to get through another week of knowing he's next door, imagining the feel of his head between my legs or the sight of him in my hand. The sounds he made when I brought him his release. His taste. I've never had a relationship where I felt this safe to be curious and adventurous sexually before.

Our training "schedule" is going to have to remain pliable, we've quickly realized. He'd texted last night to ask if I'd mind him pushing us back to the afternoon so he could jump on a phone meeting this morning with Carlie, Frankie, and Walter's nephew who owns the portables company. And I'm glad, because I needed time to get my thoughts together on how to approach the rest of our summer successfully, anyway.

I think I'd like to take a page out of his playbook and try to control the ingredients in this arrangement however I can. It sounds callous in theory, but smart in the end. No hooking up when we should be practicing, and limiting those hookups to once a week.

I'm immediately questioning my wisdom, however, when Fisher shows up on the beach to meet me today, his wet suit half rolled down and bare-chested yet again. He looks so good it makes my teeth ache.

"Hi," he greets me happily. His eyes look lighter in his sun-tanned face.

"Yay." *Damn yips.* "I *mean*," I say, "hey." I need a time-out.

He breathes a laugh. "Ready?"

"Rules," I say. It's like I need smelling salts, I swear to god. "I think we should talk about having some training rules. We still didn't actually . . . establish any the other day."

He rakes a hand through his hair and squints at me. The corners of my vision pulse black when I notice one of his earrings is missing and wonder if he lost it when he was with me, the last time I tried to have this discussion in earnest.

"Yeah, sorry about that," he says. "Sorry if I got a bit ahead of myself."

"No!" I blurt. "No, don't apologize." *Don't you dare reconsider, either,* I want to say. "I did the same thing at the library." I feel my face and neck get hot, the memory of his heavy-lidded gaze slipping through. "I just think it would be smart to say that when we're training, we keep it to only that. And maybe we limit . . . other stuff . . . to once a week." I've avoided looking at his face while saying this, but jolt when I realize I've chosen to speak to his nipple instead. I look at his hand, but then it flexes, and I decide that's not safe, either, then look at his water shoes. Okay, there's the relief. In exactly no world will water shoes ever do anything for me.

"Training will stay training," he agrees. "But I don't feel like I can agree to your once-a-week proposal," he adds calmly.

I frown at his placid face. "What would you agree to?"

"I'm a grown man. I can control myself and stay on task while we're working toward something. But outside of that, I think we stay . . . illimitable."

I cough a surprised sound. "So just *no*, then?" I don't know why I expected this to be more of a discussion.

"Well," he says, leaning onto his paddle. "No *is* a complete sentence." He chews his lip in a grin. "But I agreed to your first rule, and I propose that we let part two stay fluid." He starts toward the canoe. "For you as much as for me, Byrd."

My mouth falls open in a scoff. "The *ego*, really," I say.

"It is big," he declares. Blasé and stupidly beautiful and definitely aware of the double entendre. "And by the way, your nipple slipped out of your bikini top." He steps into the water while I curse the yips again and sort myself out. "Surprisingly hot today, and yet . . ."

Ultimately, he is the one who keeps training on course, in spite of my accidental areola flash. We row for two hours with few breaks, until our arms are lead and we're drenched in sweat and too spent by the end for me to even worry about any awkwardness. We slip the canoe behind the blind and trudge back up the cliff, with little room for chatter in between trying to recover.

When we make our way to the meadow, I spot Indy and Gary lying in the grass in his pen.

"For the way she acts like he's a pest, she sure visits him a lot," I say.

"I won't pretend to understand her yet," he replies.

I shrug. "Trying has to count for something."

He raises his shoulders like he's unsure. "You, uh, want to join us for dinner tonight?" he asks. "We're bound to have extras."

Legoless marches up from somewhere and winds himself through Fisher's legs. In the distance, Sable bays a goofy *ahrooo*.

It feels like some kind of omen. I get instantly afraid that this all feels far too comfortable for us.

Fisher may not have believed in setting firm restrictions, but it feels prudent to at least put some limitations on myself in place.

"No, that's okay, thank you," I say.

He nods—in understanding, I think. And turns to head back to his place.

On Tuesday, training is all business again. He's not impolite and he's not exactly cold, but he's definitely not warm, either. He seems rushed, and it's as if he avoids meeting my eyes. I laugh when I spot a pair of sea lions with their bellies distended toward the sky, wailing out their ridiculous-sounding barks, and his only response is a tight smile that's short-lived.

On Wednesday, I send him a text asking him if he wants me to show him where to pick the marionberries. He sends me back a photo of his handsomely rumpled face, half-obscured by a mixing bowl brimming with them. The caption says: "Sniffed them out. Thanks."

When I reply and ask him what he plans to make with them, he leaves me on Read. I decide to go tackle some weeding when it cools off in the evening, and spot him at my fence, letting Legs rub his head against his scruff. I pivot to walk his way with a laugh, and his head pops up. He spots me, waves, then turns and jogs back inside. I spend the remainder of the evening in the garden, giving myself mental and emotional whiplash over the whole thing, snipping aggressively with each warring thought. I hate that I've even acquired this acute awareness of his distance. Snip. I hate that I turned down having dinner with them. Snip. I hate that I've wanted to invite them over since. Snip. I hate that I know that this is why it is probably best that I didn't. Snip, snip.

Sable wants to be let out sometime in the night, and I should be suspicious, but I'm too sleep-addled to think clearly. She comes back howling and gagging, skunked and reeking to high heaven. She needs multiple multistep hydrogen peroxide, baking soda, and dish soap baths. The ordeal does not brighten my outlook.

A few hours later on Thursday morning, I wake up feeling dejected, muscles tender and inflamed from all the previous training and the lack of decent rest. I doggedly shove myself all the way into my wet suit, and at once lose the last ounce of my motivation for the day. I text Fisher and tell him he's off the hook.

Shortly thereafter, I'm staring down at my couch and looking for some sort of inspiration to go through the trouble of uncasing myself from the suit before I crawl back to bed, when Sable lets out an excited whimper and skids across the floor.

I hear Fisher let himself in through the sunroom door and make his way through the kitchen. When he finds me in my living room, he braces himself with an arm on the frame.

"You sick?" he asks.

"No?"

He pins me with an unflinching glare, a lock of his hair flopping forward to fall across his brow. "So what do you mean I'm off the hook, then?"

"I mean," I say, "exactly that. We don't have to train today."

He blinks slowly, plants his feet, and crosses his arms. "Listen, Byrd," he says. "I'm not really a water guy."

"Of course you're not," I say grouchily. "Otherwise, you'd have gills and webbed toes like Kevin Costner in that *Waterworld* film."

"Precisely," he parries, undeterred. "And I'm not much of a boat guy, either. But I am a *winning* guy. I told you if we did this, I wouldn't want to lose. We can take it easy, but I think we should still go."

There's something so set in his expression—in his stance and the determined gleam in his eye. It makes me remember how I wanted to do this for *me*, and his warmth or his apathy toward me shouldn't get in my way.

"You're right," I say. "Let's row." I couldn't decide if I was saying *roll* or *go*, and it came out as *row*. I roll my eyes at myself. Maybe being pun-prone is inborn when you're from Spunes.

Still, I'm irritated with him for having this kind of pull over me. Even more annoyed with myself for feeling this way. Silly, too-soft Sage yet again. I let the annoyance fuel me, and I throw myself into the task at hand.

By the time we hit the one-hour mark, I am still rattled but admittedly glad he made us go. It's as if my brain is almost curtailed into focusing on the present again. Into the feel of my paddle splitting through the water and the stinging sweat I blink out of my eyes, the air that charges in and out of my lungs. There are a million aches along my spine, my hands feel raw, and the weather feels like being inside of a slightly undercooked Hot Pocket, with weird spots of cold between the warm.

"Must be a storm coming," I eventually choke out between dragging breaths when we're on our final break.

"How do you figure?" he asks, panting just as heavily from his seat behind me. "I don't see a cloud anywhere."

"Just can tell," I say.

His snort of laughter nettles me—the mix of the adrenaline, exhaustion, and insecurity blending into something acerbic.

"What?" I clip and spin around. "Think I'm being silly again?" It lilts at the end enough that it could be a joke, but his chin still jerks back in surprise.

"When did *I* ever call you *silly*?" he asks, brows darting down above his eyes.

Frustrated embarrassment clogs my throat. *I'm* the only one who is actually telling myself that. He already apologized for his earlier remarks and implications all those weeks before. He's here for me now, and he's sticking to his end of the deal. It's me working myself into these knots, and me alone.

"You didn't," I admit, voice hollow. "Sorry. I'm—" I inhale a shaky breath. "I'm having a weird day. Let's just get back, okay?" I don't face him, not wanting him to see the misery I'm sure I'm wearing.

"Okay," comes his soft reply.

By some unspoken agreement, we take it slow the rest of the way back, and I use the time to get my thoughts in order. The fact of the matter is that I don't have it in me to maintain some sort of detached, cool reserve. I never have. My mom recognized this about me before I was six. Even wrote it in her book of sage advice. "I've never seen someone instinctively go headfirst into things all the time," she wrote. "Walking, swimming, it took us forever to teach you how to use utensils because you kept trying to eat like the dogs—mouth to food directly. Watching your dad teach you to swim gave me the very specific nightmare of you diving into shallow water, though. I'm not telling you not to jump into unfamiliar waters. Just please go feetfirst."

She may have meant this one in the most literal sense, but it's one of those things I too often find I can apply.

We work in silence when we paddle into shore, dragging up the canoe and settling it behind the blind. "I'm sorry," I tell him again. "My brain and I are fighting, I think." I offer him an apologetic shrug.

"Yeah? What's that bitch trying to say?" he replies. It's playful and indulgent of him to meet me inside my metaphor, and I can't help a grateful smile. It makes it easier to talk about this way.

"She's confused, and worried, and fucking tired." I laugh. "Sable went out and got skunked around one A.M. It was a long night."

"That explains the smell," he jokes, wide-eyed and wincing. "But *what*, exactly, is the worry?"

I jump on into it, feetfirst. "You've been—different, this week. I know I said I wanted us to train, but . . . you barely even make eye contact, and I'm worried since I said no to dinner that you're trying to, like, avoid me? Outside of this, of course." I raise my hand toward the water. "You keep turning away when I laugh." I didn't mean to include that last point, and now I'm the one looking away.

I hold myself still as I feel him step into my space.

"Look at me," he says.

When I do, his expression is stern and concentrated, and I think I've officially exasperated the man. But then his hand comes up to my throat, thumb charting a line along the hollow of my jaw.

"First, I feel bad for calling even your mean brain a bitch. I take it back. I like your mind," he says. "And second, I talked a big game about staying focused." He lets out a sigh. "And it's made it so the tiniest things you do feel fucking erotic to me, and it is torture. I'm hanging on by a damn thread and trying to stick to that, but it's so much harder than I'd thought."

My face breaks into a happy beam that his shines right back at me.

"Glad you're still enjoying my pain," he adds. "But, I'm se-rious. There are the obvious things—the heavy breathing, the more vocal noises you make while exerting yourself. The sound of the zipper on this skin-fucking-tight wet suit." He flicks it with the tip of his finger. "Then there's the nonsense things, too. Like, last night I was taking out the trash and saw you in the sunroom with the light on, painting your toenails, and I swear, Sage, for no sensible reason, it felt pornographic. From, like, fifty yards away."

My head dips back to cackle harder at this, and he nods animatedly above me.

"I almost called the cops on you! Public indecency and all that. But then I remembered that one of those cops was your ex, and I worked myself into a jealous rage over *that*. Over an entirely imaginary scenario, Byrd."

Oh, I'm squeezing myself against him now, powerless, I can't help it. Big, stupid smiles on both of our faces.

"Your laugh is . . . I don't know what it is, Sage, but your laugh . . ." I feel the muscles in his back bunch beneath my hands, the ones in his stomach contracting and relaxing against mine. "I think your laugh could maybe defibrillate me."

Oh no. I can *hear* giddiness buzzing in my veins, even in the silence. The muted whoosh of jumping into the deep end and everything else going quiet and distant from above.

He kisses me with short, tasting, teasing kisses. "Please let me cook for you tomorrow, still," he says, nose skimming mine. I'm prevented from answering when he takes my lips again, urgent and just shy of rough.

"Yes," I say into his mouth. One of his hands spreads and presses firmer behind my ribs, our hips digging into each other. When he breaks away, I feel bereft.

His nostrils flare, and he looks at me like he's in pain. "Tomorrow," he says, a promise to himself, I think, as much as it is to me, before he turns and marches off.

CHAPTER 23

FISHER

I take back what I said about time gathering speed. This week has stretched every single solitary second on me. My eyes snap open while it's still dark on Friday morning, and my brain launches into the day before my body gets the memo. I go over everything I'm planning to make, prep all that I can, then pace the house in a purposeless circle.

On my fourth lap, an idea hits me. I check the clock, and when I see that it's not yet even six, the plan solidifies. Blake's family won't be by to pick up Indy for the weekend until early afternoon, and my plans with Sage aren't until after that. When I went to the store last night, I spotted a flyer advertising that today would be the first day to see the shapes in the sand.

I leave a note for Indy, scoop up a jacket and my keys, and book it for Founder's Point.

I'm the first to pull into the parking lot by the beach, aside from an elderly man clad in a bright tie-dye hoodie who appears to be setting up. There are signs all around the wooden stairs that snake their way down a smaller cliff, all indicating that onlookers are limited to observation only until the maze is complete.

"COME 'ERE!" the man hollers out to someone, but continues to walk in various directions, angled over the sand like he's inspecting it for something.

Then the guy stops and spins in my direction. "COME DOWN HERE!" he echoes.

I look around to see who he's yelling at. "Me?!" I shout back.

He nods demonstrably until he sees me start down the steps, however hesitant. I just wanted to kill some damned time, didn't want to get pulled into a *task*.

"Grab a rake," the old crab says when I make my way to him. I see he's got a group of rakes with various metal heads, their poles all covered in different kinds of decorative tape. "Rainbow one is yours," he adds.

"Oh, no," I say, waving my palms in the air. "I couldn't." I remember Sage talking about the labyrinth designs here, and I'd thought it would be nice to see. She made them sound like something, I don't know, transformative. "I don't want to fuck it up," I explain.

"Y'can't," he replies. "The entrance and exit will be next to each other, and I always begin each maze with a left turn. We'll cover as much of the sand as we can that's exposed right now. Go on. More help'll be here soon."

I screw my eyes at the guy's bright colors against the rest of the gray around us. The air feels heavy, like maybe Sage was right and a storm is imminent. "So, no other instructions? No tips? Nothing to keep in mind?" I ask sharply.

"Nope. If you like something, such as, if you like looking at that there rock—Bannet Island, the Spuners call it." He stabs a finger at a tall, jagged mound fifty yards or so into the water. "If y'like lookin' at that, then make your path work so you can face it more. If you want to look at the ground and your own god-damn feet, make your shit wrap around in a billion little angry mind-fucked circles for all I care. The point is just to *do it*."

A shock of laughter punches through my chest. "Aren't old bastards in tie-dye supposed to be friendly and, I dunno, a little more gregarious?" I ask.

He straightens and frowns at his sweatshirt. "Local girl bought it for me last year," he says sheepishly. "Think it's sup-posed to be *ironic*."

Hilarity bounces through me. "Let me guess who," I say. "Fisher?"

As if conjured by the thought, I turn around and find Sage at my back, smiling up at me like the most welcome apparition. The tip of her nose is pink in the early-morning air.

"What are you doing here?" she asks with a warm grin.

"Remembered you talking about them and wanted to come see," I say. "He yelled at me," I add, pointing at her grumpy pal. Her yelp of laughter makes me pull her into my side like a reflex.

"Amos," she tsks before lifting her chin back to me. "Go easy on him. Amos spends his summers driving up and down the West Coast, visiting with his eccentric family and then—what did you say last year?" she asks.

Amos rolls his eyes with a rattled sigh. "I've got a brother that owns an apple orchard in Southern California and a hippie sister in the Bay. I visit them and theirs and then have to unwind by trying to get into a meditative state, repeatedly."

"You gave him my rake?" Sage chides.

"He looked like a rainbow kinda guy," he says ingenuously.

She grabs the third rake and surveys the expanse before us.

"How do I do it? I don't want to mess it up," I ask her, hoping she'll be more forthcoming. I don't think I like not having set directions for where I should go, or how big I should make the circles.

"I'm never sure, either. You just do what feels right, I think."

It shouldn't be a struggle to do this intuitively, to chart a simple circular path through the sand. So I do my level best to just . . . go. But, within a few minutes, I end up closing myself in. I wave down Amos and Sage to come help me untangle myself, no way to continue without raking over one of the other sets of lines I've already drawn.

"Leave it," Amos says. "Sometimes that's just where that path needs to end." Then, with his back turned as he starts to walk away, making a new trail behind him as he goes: "It all washes away with the tide."

I look at Sage. "That doesn't seem kinda sad? To do all this just for it to wash away?" *Pointless* felt too callous to say.

"I don't think so," she replies. "Not if you can accept the impermanence of it. Sometimes people will write things that they're worried about and carry with them into the maze, and it's sort of therapeutic to leave it there—leave it behind. Other times it's about learning to enjoy the journey in a way that's more tangible than on some pithy sound bite. Even . . ." She looks across everything I've traced and meets my eyes. "Even though it takes you in circles that don't lead anywhere in particular. Even if it can't really go somewhere in the end. Once you accept the impermanence of it, you give yourself permission to enjoy it now."

Something pulls painfully tight behind my solar plexus. She's so beautiful in this moment it makes me feel close to panic, heart thumping erratically. I drop the rake, reach out for the edges of her jacket, and haul her into me again. I let my thumb skate across the bridge of her freckles before I curl down and kiss her lips. Just once. Just one to slake whatever this thirsty feeling in me is.

When we break apart, a collection of moments between us pass, her fists twisting in my shirt and her eyes searching mine. I think we've spun something together here this month, something we can maybe accept the impermanence of and still enjoy in the meantime.

We continue to work on our paths. I take a straighter approach going forward, with edges that only slightly curve. Sage makes braver ones with big dramatic swoops and multiple direction changes. I couldn't say how long it takes, but eventually, I find a way to just be. The lines all start to connect as if they had that intention all along. Until Amos comes over at some point and instructs Sage and me to find a way to merge and connect with the road he's created for the exit. I loop around, almost all the way to the water, and swerve my way to her. Amos's trail blends into the edge of the one she's made, and she and I form up the borders that finish the last leg.

The three of us step back and look at the great shapes before us. Even the turns I'd made and thought were too jarring end up curving into something better.

Voices start to flit through the breeze, and a crowd begins milling onto the sand.

"You want to stay awhile?" I ask Sage.

"Nah," she says happily. "I left behind what I needed to for now."

So did I.

CHAPTER 24

SAGE

Raking the maze this morning soothed something in me today, but it in no way made me feel calm. I guess you can be excited for every rise and dive of a roller coaster and still can't stop your physical reaction to it or the way your stomach soars.

I spend most of the afternoon getting ready, fussing over the typical, senseless things. I send Wren pictures of about eleven different outfits before I land on a matching skirt and top in dusty blue, with a flirty strip of my waist on display. I get antsy and decide to change my nail color at the last second, but miscalculate the time and end up just leaving them bare. I slip on all of my favorite rings and a simple pair of sandals before I kiss the animals goodbye and head out into the meadow.

My senses feel clear and heightened, the early evening holding its breath around me, like the sun-cooked grass itself is excited, too. The last flickers of nerves melt and heat in my veins.

I let myself inside when I get to the Andersens' front door and am greeted with a smell that makes me nearly moan. I find Fisher in the kitchen and stop to take in the view of him.

He looks entirely in command of the space around him. He's wearing a green, short-sleeved button-down that ripples with his movements. His hair still looks wet from a shower. He takes a pull from a nearby bottle of wine, and his throat works in a way that makes my chest tingle.

"Hey," he says when he spots me, his face breaking into a broad grin, one side tugging up higher. He rounds the island and meets me halfway, lands a chaste kiss to the corner of my mouth. He smells better than the meal, and for a second, I consider trying to peel him away. But for as much as we've revealed to one another, this feels like something intimate he's putting on display.

Acoustic, broken-down versions of popular songs play from a speaker somewhere, and I slip onto a stool at the breakfast bar and watch him work. He tells me he's making me a four-course meal, but will serve small portions of each thing so that it's not overwhelming. We make light small talk, laughing when he tells me how flustered Indy acted when he asked if she'd see Sam in Gandon this weekend.

"I just hope she's not too hard on the kid, I guess," he says. "I know I'm probably supposed to act overprotective and glad at her being aloof, but, I dunno. . . ." He fades off, bracing his hands on the butcher block. "My sister was very young when she had her. And people were cruel." He raises a hand to halt my condolences. "It's okay. She was okay. I think I took things more personally than Freya did. But, I also think, as a result, Indy has an intensely independent spirit. She won't entertain anything that might get in her way or hold her back. I used to be the same."

I angle my neck to study him. "You're not anymore?"

He checks a saucepan and concisely gives it a stir, the points

of his shoulder blades working beneath his shirt. "I just keep putting bits of your sage advice to good use, and it's getting easier.
The more trust I show, the more she gives," he says, then pivots
back to another task in front of me. "I just have to keep being
steady for her."

Fuck, he's perfect. No, it's worse because he's imperfect and
honest about it and he's deserving of so much love. This is won-
derfully terrible for me. "You're doing really, really well, Fisher,"
I tell him.

"Thank you," he says, his voice low and grating.

He dices with the concentrated precision of a surgeon after that, his face taking on that dangerous, passionate look I'd
thought it would. My mind tumbles into the memory of having
all that focus on me, his devotion for my pleasure. And just as
deliciously, the image of him unravels. I take it a step further
and let myself imagine being laid out before him like a feast, his
attention on me all over.

"Hungry?" he asks, gaze flicking up to mine.

"Starving."

"This," he says, sliding a shallow, wide-brimmed bowl my
way, "is a carpaccio of hibiscus-poached monkfish. I use the term
carpaccio loosely, but if it were on a menu, that is what I would put
in the title. On top, you'll find a mélange of market melons, com-
pressed with lemongrass and kaffir lime. To tie it all together, a
lobster vinaigrette."

I have no idea what he just said or described. But it sure is
pretty. Colorful and bright, exotic . . . my eyes are devouring it
before I can. I take a bite, and an artless moan escapes me almost
immediately. I put my hand to my lips and stare at him in shock.

His jaw flares. "Been dying to find out what else it'd take to
get you to make that sound again."

Heat sparks across my skin, gathers in the crooks of my elbows and the backs of my knees.

He changes out my wine for a different one when the next dish is up. The pasta course, he tells me.

"I actually hate working with dough, most of the time," he admits when he passes it my way. "But this is a wild fennel pollen gnudi, with Calabrian chili and . . ." I black out on the rest, the morsel dancing on my tongue. Whatever this is doing in my mouth is a *performance*.

When I do peel my eyes away from the meal, I find him watching me and ignoring his own—something raw, vulnerable, and searching on his face. It's almost boyish in its hopefulness, and it makes me want to grab fistfuls of the stuff and shout at him, *You're amazing, you're amazing, you're so damn incredible! You're bigger and better than anyone and braver, too, and why would you ever let anyone else make you feel like you're less?*

Instead, I take a slow drink of my wine and say, "This is unequivocally the best thing I have ever tasted, Fisher. This is—" I have to cover my mouth again and let out a hysterical sound. My nervous system is truly processing something entirely foreign here.

He makes his way around the island in a few avid strides and kisses me in a slow, bone-melting embrace. "I'm glad," he says, and again, the desire to have him stop and take me now wars with the part of me that cannot wait to experience whatever he's prepared next. Dessert might be a medical event.

The third course is a phenomenon of a beef tenderloin, and he's done something rapturous with fucking asparagus, of all things. It's almost too much for my senses. He was right in keeping portions small, because I would, without a doubt, be in some sort of coma if I were full of all of this.

Rather than being lulled, though, I feel as if all my nerve endings have been whipped into something frothy, like a featherlight touch could sweep me apart. The flavors and smells, the sight of him and the rise and shift of his forearms, sinews and veins working beneath his skin. That stubborn lock of his hair that keeps sliding forward. He ruffles it behind an ear, and I'm up, the legs of the stool scraping against the floor beneath me.

He sees me coming for him, and the dire want must be blatant in my expression because he asks, "Dessert?"

"Later."

"Thank god," he grinds out, tossing a dish towel away somewhere and meeting me the rest of the way. His hands wrap around my waist before he props me up onto the counter and steps between my legs, diving for the column of my neck like a man starved. The metal of his belt buckle is cool against the overheated skin of my thigh, my hands scraping everywhere they can touch. His teeth slide against my collarbone, and the fine grit of his stubble skims the top of my breast. I search for his mouth with mine and wriggle my hands between us to get at his buttons.

A brief moment of consciousness slips through the haze when I spot the Andersens' robot vacuum out of the corner of my eye. "Fisher," I rasp, the last syllable ending on a whimper when I feel his tongue on the hollow of my throat. "Fisher, let's go to my house," I get out quickly.

"What?" he says.

"I don't want to have sex in the Andersens' house." I laugh. I'll never be able to look Nina in the eye.

He growls into the valley of my chest, scoops me down off

the counter, and pulls me for the door by my hand in a half jog, falling back upon me with a wild look in his eyes before he opens it. Our lips press smiles together, and our tongues taste each other—small, matching laughs popping out of us like bubbles of champagne. Fresh lust laps through me when he adjusts himself before he leads us through the door.

The sky breaks open the moment we hit the porch. Great, heavy raindrops that sparkle like a shower of light in the sun. We look at one another in surprise, then break into a run.

We screech and laugh our way across the field, only stopping to taste the rain off each other's skin. He tugs the tip of a breast from my top and makes me gasp, face to the sky. I ruck up my skirt so he can grab me by the backs of my thighs and carry me the remaining way.

When we get into the sunroom, Sable barks a happy sound and promptly makes herself scarce. I roll out the mattress pad I keep in here before I close us in, my entire body trembling when I turn back to face him.

"You're shaking," he says, running his palms along my face and limbs. Probably wiping away the makeup smeared under my eyes. "Are you okay?" His face cinches in concern. I lean into his palm, holding his wrist, fingertips on his pulse, and try to steady my breathing.

"Yes." I nod. I just know I'll never be the same, and want to keep going nonetheless.

He continues touching my face as I work at the rest of his buttons, hands spreading wide and high to push it off his shoulders. I raise my arms up so he can quickly dispose of my top and bra in return, flicking it away to join his shirt in a wet heap. He struggles to swallow, and my own mouth goes dry at his look of appreciation.

I reach for his belt next, and the button of his jeans over the hard swell of him beneath. He toes off his boots in an enthusiastic way that eases my nerves and makes me laugh.

"I love your smile," he abruptly states, like the words were pulled from him. I love so many parts of him. His lopsided smile, his sort-of-big ears, his unruly hair, the ego that asserts itself now and then. I love the way he *tries*. How he tried to understand and see me from the moment we met, even when he was still trying to buy his own assumptions, how he's been trying to get better, how he always tries for honesty and to do what he says he will. How he owns it when he hasn't or can't.

"I love so many parts of you," I decide to say. It comes out like a whisper and I'm unsure if he hears me over the rain.

"Just can't think of any specifics?" he tries to joke.

I shake my head. "Too many," I admit.

He inhales sharply and nods, like he gets it, like it's the same for him, too.

I press my lips to his warm chest, my nipples tightening when they graze the skin over his ribs. He snakes his palms down the back of my skirt and kneads, then glides it gently, slowly, off. He keeps me close and corrals me to the bedroll, holding my eyes as I lie down at his feet. He shirks his jeans and briefs together, then smirks knowingly when I choke on nothing at the sight of his naked form.

When he lies by my side, he becomes singularly focused on my body. I can see him watching the blush spread across my skin. We both watch his hand circle my navel, then as it ghosts a path down to toy with the strap of my thong.

"Can I?" he asks.

"Please."

His eyes flutter closed when he touches me where I'm the

neediest, his forehead falling to my shoulder when I let out a strained, keening sound. It overwhelms my senses: the sight of his hand shifting under the scrap of cotton, the way he thrusts himself against my hip like he's helpless against it, his hair tickling my chin and his breath warm on my chest, the rain clattering and blurring against the glass above us. Everything coils impossibly tight and fast, sweeping me toward the edge. But then he brings his hand back up, fingers glistening, and paints them in lazy swirls around my nipples before he licks me off my skin. I start to break into a series of moans—his name, and please, and thank you, and yes, and yes, and yes. He brings me further and further until I'm mindlessly writhing, grinding myself into his palm and holding his head to my chest, thrashing and winded.

"That's it, Sage. Let it come, sweetheart. Don't fight it."

His words undo me. I completely fall apart, the release rushing through my limbs and unraveling in blinding light. A joyful sob bursts up from my chest. I keep falling, over and over, spinning through pleasure until I'm wrung out and spent, until I see him use that same brilliant hand on himself with a rough tug. My still-recovering heart hiccups violently in my chest.

"We don't have to do anything else," he says, like he's not throbbing painfully or like I can't feel the evident bead of moisture he's left against my leg.

"Yes, we do," I say huskily, reaching for him. "I don't think *I'll* be able to again, but I want to—I want to take care of you, too." I suddenly feel shy again for some inexplicable reason. I've been with a whopping three people, and not even in the five years I was with one of them was it ever as staggering as anything with Fisher has been.

"You can again," he deeply grates, staying my hand. "I can make you ready again."

The words alone kick up my urgency. I chase his mouth, tongue and teeth and rapid breaths. "I'm on birth control," I say.

"I haven't been with anyone in a long time. I've got nothing to report," he replies, smiling softly. I feel myself mirror the expression, grateful for this trust and comfort.

He levers up to sit, propping himself against the side of the yellow chair and gathering me back into his lap, my knees flanking his sides. His utter lack of shame—his parted, muscular thighs and the flex of him against his stomach—make me shiver. He catches it and swipes a throw blanket from a nearby basket, wraps it lovingly around my lower back before he smooths his hands down my arms. He kisses my palms before he pulls them around his neck.

He clasps my hips and slides my panties to the side with a hitched, encouraging murmur, tilts and drags me up the length of him. I bite my lip to catch a gasp, a shock of warmth flashing through me again, leaving a dull ache in its wake. I hiss a curse when he does it a second time, and his mouth tips in a crooked grin. Arrogant man. He continues to lift and squeeze in a slow, hypnotic rhythm. The way he's using me without being inside me—it's unpolished and visceral and so fucking hungry, his eyes trained on where we're slipping against each other. Another knot starts to stir and pull from somewhere deep, and I instinctively seek out more, arching at the height of another grind so that the broad head of him glides just inside and makes me gasp. Just the tip of him stretching me deliciously. A rough noise wrenches out of him, and his fingers grip me tighter, holding me still. I worry I've hurt him or done something wrong and search his face in worry.

"I'm sorry I—"

"No, I mean—yes, but no, don't. Don't apologize," he pants,

pecs rising and falling. His gaze is heavy-lidded. I mark the sheen of sweat misting across his temples and chest. "I just don't want it to end," he says. "It's too good. I just want to put off the end."

Emotion twists in my throat, because I don't want any of this to end, either. Not this summer, not this hour, not this minute. "Just be here now," I whisper, seeding kisses across all the angles of his face, along the shell of his ear, down his neck. "Let me enjoy you now," I say.

He answers me by guiding me down farther. My breath catches, and I have to stop, letting myself adjust. When I sink deeper, he buries a groan in my skin. I rise slowly before I take him completely, deep into someplace that feels essential and new.

I couldn't guess how much time passes, our movements slow and rocking and lingering together. I don't know that I've ever smiled so much during sex, if I've ever enjoyed myself this much. A disturbing sort of bliss takes over when I realize I'm going to come apart again, with him inside me and under me and around me. He talks me up to it once more, tells me he can feel me when everything pulls taut, tells me how beautiful I look and how good I feel.

"It's never been like this," I say, a truth ripped from me before I can stop it.

"I know. Never," he quickly agrees with a tortured groan, leaning forward to kiss me. "I can feel you pulling me tight. You're going to come again for me, aren't you?"

I've never been with someone who talks to me during this, who manages to stay inside my head just as much as he's in everywhere else. He reaches down and toys with me in tight circles, his eyes watching with carnal focus as I piston against him. We start to writhe more quickly, our sounds getting more broken and movements more desperate. My palm slaps and slips against the fogged-up glass when it finally takes over—this one hard and fast and incendiary. I hold on as tight as my sated limbs will allow when he folds us over and takes me beneath him.

"Sage," he grits when he tumbles over the edge, then collapses into the cradle of my hips, heavy and spent and ecstatic, his chest rumbling happily against mine.

He leaves briefly to grab a damp towel, then cleans me off with devoted care. When I return from the bathroom, he peppers me with sweet kisses across my face and a final hot, wet one against each of my breasts before he says, "I can think of only one thing that would make this moment better."

"What?" I ask, though I instantly know what he's going to say.

"Dessert."

"Let's go get it," I say, barely suppressing a squeal.

I throw another blanket at him, wrap myself in mine, and we rush back out into the rain.

CHAPTER 25

FISHER

"Hold still," I admonish.

"It's harder than you think," Sage replies.

She has no idea. I've convinced her to let me attempt painting her toenails—a difficult enough task on its own, to be honest. But I might be a sadist after all, because I also thought it would be fun for her to stay naked during this foray into arts and crafts. I've got one of her dining chairs at the foot of her bed, her feet braced on my thighs, and the rest of her less than a yard away, bare beneath a sheet. Every time she wiggles, I get peeks of her that threaten to unman me.

After dessert—a strawberry-rhubarb madeleine, with a vanilla crémeux and pops of lemon—we jogged back to her house again, crashing and colliding along the way. We made it to the bed that time, then fell into the most restful sleep I can recall. I woke to the sound of her shuffling around, bottles clicking together as she rifled through her collection. After brushing teeth and taking care of basic human needs, we wound up here.

I think subconsciously I thought that getting physical might ease this feeling in me, but I feel myself tripping precariously into that addiction. Sage is honest and curious and vibrant in everything she does. Anytime I set out to tantalize her, she naturally ends up wrecking me.

Her free heel grazes me through my briefs like she can read my mind.

"Hold. Still," I warn again. She dips her chin innocently. "I don't think I can redo these." I blow on her toes to speed up the drying process. Magenta, the color of a marionberry stain.

"What else do you want to do today?" she asks. "Indy comes home tomorrow?"

I can't think of anything else I'd rather do. "This," I admit, polishing the last layer on her pinkie toe. "Talk, eat, lie around—" I wag my brows. "Eat again. Happy Fourth of July, by the way."

"Fireworks imminent," she replies.

I find her laughing eyes, and my mouth waters. She's so damn captivating. Sleep rumpled and still disheveled from the night (and half day) before. She blinks and calms when she sees whatever change comes over my expression.

"Tell me what you're thinking," she says.

That fate is cruel and wonderful. That I am already so twisted up in this maze and don't want it to wash away. "That you're very, very beautiful, Sage." Her color heightens, and it only emphasizes the point.

From somewhere below, a phone starts to ring.

She clears her throat self-consciously. "I'd better get that," she says. "I can't imagine who would be calling me."

"No!" I say, then, more calmly, "I'll go grab it for you. Don't—don't mess up your toes."

Approximately an hour later, I find myself driving past the border of Spunes, a vibrating Sage in the passenger seat.

"Are you nervous or excited?" I say with a poorly suppressed laugh. "I can't tell."

"Both," she replies, hands clenched in her lap. "I need you to help me keep it under control, Fisher. I can't take on too much more. I *shouldn't* take on anything more."

I press my lips together to stop a smirk. "Sweetheart, it'll be all right."

"I mean it, Fisher!" she cries. "Do not let me come out of there with more than a cat. Maybe, like, a normal-sized dog, okay? I don't need any other big pets. And for the love of everything holy, do not let me near any fucking ferrets or birds."

It'd been Dr. Serena calling Sage, letting her know that a hobby farm outside of town had been abandoned when the owner passed unexpectedly. The family has no use for all the animals left behind, so Serena asked Sage to come and see if she might have room for anything. She was suspiciously vague on the variety of species. Sage has been wringing her hands ever since.

"You don't get it," she says. "Something comes over me. I swear to god if I cry, you'd better not laugh."

She stabs a vicious finger my way. I snatch it and give it a bite just to see if it'll break her anxious haze. When that doesn't seem to work, I hold her hand on her thigh.

"Hey," I say, waiting for her to look my way. "You know no one can make you do anything you don't wanna do, yeah? It's okay if you can't take on another animal. We can turn around right now and it won't make you a bad person at all."

Her head hits the seat behind her miserably. "That's the problem. I *want* to. I'll want them all. I always want them," she says in defeat.

That something that's been there since the day she cried into my chest wedges in a little further.

"Well, it's not like we have a trailer to transport anything large, anyway," I say.

She looks at me like she's already apologizing.

"Ohmygod, Fisher," Sage wails. "Feel my forehead."

"I—hang on," I say, frightened. I have a baby Nigerian Dwarf goat under each arm. I had no idea how tiny they were. Someone should have warned me. Their entire bodies each fit in my palms. I'd been defenseless. I easily finagle both into one arm and lay my knuckles against her brow. "Also, why?"

She faces me with shining eyes and nutty glee. "I think I have a fever of some kind."

She isn't warm at all, so I can only discern that she's referencing whatever spirit has overcome her in the midst of all the infant livestock. The real issue is that I can't seem to get a grip myself. I let out a shaky sigh at Bert and Ernie. At least these two are already weaned. I managed to talk her away from the emus, and the housebroken raccoon couldn't go to a home with any cats. I feel both my luck and feeble resolve wearing thin.

"This," Sage excitedly declares, "is Rosemary, and this is Ginger." She leads me and the boys into a barn and to a stall that appears empty.

"I see nothing." Shit, maybe she really is possessed.

"Look over the door, Fisher," she explains.

When I do, my first thought is that at least they will all fit in the truck.

"I mean," I say, "their names are Rosemary and Ginger. I feel like that's gotta be a cosmic sign."

"*Miniature donkeys?!*" Indy exclaims when she gets back the following day. She's been home for four minutes and is already jetting back out of the house.

"And a pair of goats," I say, laughing at her intensity. "Wait! Tell me about your weekend. You had a good time?"

"Just walk with me," she replies irritably, rushing down the porch stairs. "And yes, it was nice. We made s'mores and watched fireworks. The normal things. Nothing *untoward*." She devours the meadow with lengthy strides. "And how was your weekend?"

"Nice," I say, voice an octave too high. "Cooked. Hung out with Sage." A very different sort of fireworks display. I have no idea why she celebrated me so fervently again last night when I'd technically let her down in terms of holding her accountable. I gulp at the memory of her pushing me into the chair in the sunroom and yanking down my pants. Her on her knees and her messy, hot mouth around me. "Nothing untoward." Indy's eyes narrow at me—dubious and shrewd, the understanding plain on her face. I step past her and into the barn.

"They have to stay quarantined in here for a few days, but then Sage will introduce them to Bud," I say. We find Sage in their stall, smiling up at us with Ginger's brown-and-white-spotted head in her lap. "That's Ginger, and that's Rosemary. They're mother and daughter."

A strange look comes over Indy's face. "Rosemary's the mom?" she asks.

"Yeah. Go on in if you want."

"They're very sweet," Sage adds.

Indy unlatches the stall door and lets herself in carefully, walking over to sit beside Sage. She looks happy and young again, rubbing at the fluffy fur on Ginger's belly.

Rosemary pauses in her snacking and marches over to Indy as cautiously as Indy had approached her babe. They regard each other for a moment, before Rose lowers her head in some sort of offering. Indy presses her forehead into hers and closes her eyes.

Memories hit me with violent clarity.

When Freya was seventeen and I was sixteen, still living at home. Indy only months old, Freya balancing her on her lap, Indy gnawing on a chubby fist.

"*It's you and me, kid,*" Freya said with their foreheads pressed together. "*I guess your uncle sometimes, too.*"

When Indy got her first bike one year for Christmas, she slipped on ice and scraped up her arm.

"*You're okay. You're okay,*" Freya said, head against Indy's as she calmed her down. "*Now, you're gonna get back on that bike and pedal home, kid. You know why? Because riding a bike is one of the greatest things. You might get hurt again, but you're gonna have so much fun before that. The important thing is to have courage and try again. And what is courage, Indy?*"

A sniffle. Indy's tiny voice saying, "*Courage is a muscle.*" You strengthen it with use.

Indy turns to me now, but where I let out a wet and wistful chuckle, her face pinches closer to rage, eyes darting back and forth, overcome with what I can only guess are similar flashbacks. She blinks and looks around as if coming out of a trance before I watch it carve itself in her body language—the helpless anger when she's reminded of her mom and the injustice of the world again, the fear that she's become too attached to something that might hold her back. She gets up, fighting hard for control, and flees.

Sage gives me a baffled look. I give her one I hope conveys that I'll explain it to her later, and I head back out after Indy.

She tries to slam the front door on me at the house, but I catch it and close it quietly at my back.

"What are you doing?" she snaps. "There's obviously more going on with you and Sage."

"Indy—"

"Just because you're lost or going through some shit, do not tell me you're gonna abandon your whole life and give it all up to slum it on some farm!" she spits. "What a cop-out."

"That's *enough*," I seethe. "Say what you feel, but don't you dare disrespect that woman when she has been nothing but kind to you."

She scoffs and paces angrily, slapping at a tear. "I can't do it, Fisher. I lasted three years in that place without Mom. Without anyone. The town cautionary tale my whole fucking life. Don't make me be the *new* sob story in another small, shitty place. Don't make me trade one for another." And then, more vehemently, "You already signed me up for school! I'm doing everything I'm supposed to do! I don't want to get *stuck*."

More memories. *Whore* spray-painted on our driveway in big red letters. Freya, after driving me three hours to the nearest airport, waving goodbye to me with a toddler Indy in her arms. The feeling that I could finally breathe when the plane lifted off.

"I thought you were having a good summer here, Ind. You seem like . . . like you've made some friends?"

She looks at me in frightened outrage. "I'm making the best of being here! Why wouldn't I do that?! I'm just doing what I thought I was supposed to do," she sobs.

I pull her into a tight hug, even as I feel like I'm breaking, too. "You won't get stuck, Indy," I assure her. Because I know she's right. I can't abandon my life. I've done that before. I *have* to stay steady for her now, after deserting her twice. She deserves that—feeling like someone wants her to get what she wants. Like someone still sees her and puts her first. And I still want to make that comeback again. Especially from a better place, mentally. "We're going back to New York at the end of summer. I promise." And just like that, some of the sand gets carried away, taking a piece of me with it.

CHAPTER 26

FISHER

Sage and I struggle to get our training in for the following two weeks. She focuses on getting everyone adjusted to their new routines, coordinating immunizations and food, plus her regular garden work. The gopher is back and wreaking considerable havoc.

Everything seems to be delayed or on back order in the construction industry, too, so our plan has officially been shifted to getting Starhopper to a place where the bathrooms and the open areas can be of use, without being an eyesore for festivalgoers. Basically, my job has been reduced to placating and ass-kissing Martha O'Doyle every other day, assuring her that the building will not collapse and that both the lawn and patio areas will be cleared of all debris, in addition to writing up a menu that is both *"approachable* and delicious," with help from Sage.

The times Sage and I get to sneak away together, it feels unfeasible to focus on anything else but her, but we manage. For the most part, at least. Neither of us seems too stressed over the cooking aspect of things, despite the fact that her knife skills make my eye twitch. But my creativity is finally loosening up, so I find ways to drop off things most days, and save myself from recalling the bungled way I found her chopping red onions last week—hunched over her cutting board with goggles over her eyes, elbows splayed out in a way that would have sent my mentor into a violent rage. It's not entirely selfless, believe me, because the way she applauds me is addicting in its earnestness. Five days ago, she'd spotted me walking across the meadow with a plate in hand (lobster corn dogs with preserved lemon remoulade, and brown butter honey mustard for dipping) and had almost leaped from her riding mower without turning it off. She'd jogged up to me with her hands outstretched, sporting a tiny pink shirt with two hummingbirds on the front and tiny lettering that said, I LOVE HUMMERS. After I fed her, she taught me how to use the mower and let me finish the job.

I am determined to enjoy this thing we've got for now, but I can't deny that I'm also markedly aware of the time clock over our heads. It leaves me in a controlled state of panic-stricken, one that only briefly ebbs when I'm with her. Inside her. Beside her. Talking with her. Listening to her.

The biggest blow that comes for everyone, though, is even more out of our control. A fire is raging on the California border, so bad and so widespread that our air quality becomes highly unsafe. There are days when the smoke is so thick, I can't see Sage's house across the meadow.

On one of these smokier days, when it's too terrible outside for any of the crew to safely work in the orange haze, I screech into Sage's driveway after dropping Indy at summer school and stomp through her front door. I feel trapped in by all this cloudy ash, restless and frenetic and short of breath. Irritated that anything is cutting into our time, I think. I tousle Sable's ears before I trample past, on the hunt for Sage.

I find her in her living room on her green sofa, curled over the journal I often find her with these days. She looks up at me with rounded eyes, sees my hands opening and closing at my sides, and springs for me. I moan savagely when she climbs into my arms and her legs wrap around my hips.

"Can I be rough?" I ask, voice a husk of itself, unnerved and carrying her upstairs.

"I think asking sort of subjugates being *too* rough," she replies with a smile and a hot kiss. Another throttled sound leaves me when she nips my neck. "But *god* yes."

I shove out of my jeans when we get to her room, and she rapidly peels out of her shorts next.

She climbs the bed on her back and elbows, but I grab her ankles and drag her back down, fall to my knees, and lose myself between her thighs, until she's shoving at my head and her legs are shaking against my ears.

"One more. Give me one more," I beg, coming at her from a new angle, until I think she's as dismantled as I feel, saying my name in a way that makes me think it ought to be the only one she ever says, cursing and whimpering and writhing against my face. Her legs drop to the floor with a small thud when I let them go. I pick them up and scoot her back onto the bed, kiss and taste along her flushed and freckled chest, and flip her onto her stomach.

"Lift up for me, sweetheart," I say, gently kneeing apart her legs to spread her wide. When she does, I tuck a pillow beneath her hips. And as I watch myself disappear into her, I feel as if she's holding on to me, keeping me anchored even though I'm supposed to be the one in control. My fingers spread on top of hers and weave, hands both clutching the sheet. I conceal my face in her neck so I can breathe her in, keep my body flush with hers as much as possible so I can feel her everywhere.

And instead of hard or hasty, I end up wanting to draw it out, to stave off the inevitable and savor it as much as I can again.

CHAPTER 27

SAGE

While Fisher and I continue to wait for clearer days, we focus on studying for the trivia contest and begin on some basic cooking lessons. I can tell he finds my knife skills dismal, but he remains patient and . . . uplifting.

I've also discovered I can make him blush when I say *Yes, Chef,* just right, and I'm delighting in abusing this power.

"I have something I've been meaning to tell you," I say to him one Friday night, when Indy is staying the night at Blake's. She's only been over once to see Gary since the day she met the donkeys, though she's still helped me out every weekend at the market. And despite the lingering awkwardness I feel from her, I see Fisher most afternoons, and I've been over quite a few times for dinners with them both.

Tonight, we've dragged a folding camp chair down to the estuary and angled it to watch the wooly sunset, since the smoke is finally thin enough that we might be able to see it. We share a bottle of wine and a blanket between us. His lap is appallingly comfortable.

"Tell me," he says into my ear, running his nose down the side of my neck.

"I know this year's secret ingredient for the cooking competition." I pass him the bottle and a sly smile. He moves a piece of hair behind my ear.

"What kind of espionage are you partaking in?" he asks in mock amazement. "And what is it?" he says more flatly.

I wag my brows. "I have a farmer friend in the other corner of town. You know how we like to stick together," I say.

"Of course. Legen-dairy how tight those circles run," he replies.

"Oh no, he's been pun-etrated!" I muse.

"No, really. I get it. Easy to bond with others who are also outstanding in the field."

"Oh my god, that was another one, wasn't it?"

"I prefer my farm and garden puns subtle," he states. "Make you seed between the lines." His mouth clamps down on a laugh as a snort tears through me.

"That was atrocious, Fisher."

"Herb your enthusiasm and tell me the secret ingredient, Sage." He captures my mouth in a distracting kiss. His favorite thing to do, I think, those sudden kisses that throw me off course.

I smile against his mouth. "Imagining you looking these up is my new favorite thing," I say. "And you'll love this. It's marionberries." We've coincidentally made all sorts of different things with them the last few weeks, for every course.

A slow grin spreads across his face, hot caramel dripping over a dessert. "We've got this in the bag," he states. An intoxicating thrill goes through me because I think he might be right.

But this thrill doesn't last. I'm not sure if it's from too much exposure to the smoke or what exactly triggers it, but I notice my vision start to go blurry when we trek our way back to my place. Dread grips me tight when I realize a migraine is impending, the first one I've had in eighteen months. In the short walk from the top of the trail to the sunroom entrance, I go from thinking I might be able to take something in time, to fully nauseated and in pain.

Fisher tries to convince me to go to the ER, but I go into full isolation mode. I don't want sound or light, and most definitely do not want to ride in the car anywhere. I only want to shut my eyes and wake up when it's over. I had these more often when I was younger, but it seems as I've gotten older, they've spread out and make up for it with their intensity.

I try to get Fisher to go home. I even tell him through slitted eyes and gritted teeth that I'll feel *better* if he goes home, that I won't be self-conscious on top of being in pain. But even though I sequester myself in my dark bedroom, I know he stays, because I don't hear a peep from Sable or Legs all night. And when he hears me throwing up in the upstairs bathroom, he comes in to hold back my hair. He tucks me back in bed when I'm done, then frequently replaces a cool towel over my forehead throughout the night while I sleep in scattered, fitful increments.

Early the following morning, I open my eyes to find that the pain is still there, but it's settled into a dull roar. I can tolerate some light and sound, and the nausea has dissipated. I start to get up and try to get ready. I'm supposed to meet Indy directly at the market and still need to load up all my goods.

When Fisher sees me in my kitchen, he jolts up from the seat he's been in and the screech of the chair on the floor makes me flinch, my hands going up to my head.

"Shit, Sage," he says angrily, but blessedly quiet. "Please go back to bed."

"I'm okay. Market today. Need coffee and food." My eyes squint more with each choppy sentence.

"I already told Indy I'd meet her," he says.

I blink, confused. "No, I'm working at it today," I explain.

He holds my face in both palms. "I know, and I saw all the stuff already in your garage fridge. I'll get everything loaded up and will meet her," he says rapidly, barely more than a whisper. "You need to go back to bed."

Fuck, I'm going to cry again, which is only bound to make my head throb harder. "Animals," I remember.

"Already all fed and let out."

This forces my eyes open again. "What do you mean?"

"Everything's watered, too. It's covered. Please, will you go rest?"

"How'd you know where everything was? How much to give everybody? Bud was fine?"

He breathes a laugh through his nose but frowns sympathetically. "I've been paying attention," he says, shrugging like it's the easiest thing in the world to him and like he hasn't just given me a glimpse of what it would be like to truly have a partner in life. I feel like I'm a fizzy drink of emotion about to uncork. "I'll make you something to eat if you'll go back to bed," he urges.

I shake my head like a toddler. "Want to watch you make it." The pain has me loose-lipped and stripped of self-preservation, I think.

He huffs a sigh, resigned. "Go sit over there. I'll be right back."

He steers me to the chair in the sunroom before he takes off into the still-fuggy meadow. I spot him jogging back, his strong arms loaded down with bags. He comes back to me first, pulling a pair of headphones from one of the bags before he delicately places them over my ears.

"Noise-canceling," he explains, then pushes a button that mutes everything else around me.

I watch him assemble an omelet with so much dedicated care I feel like I'm watching something else. Maybe it's the lack of sound that heightens every motion, but it feels as if it's some other ritualistic thing entirely. I already knew he could do the one-handed egg-cracking thing, a skill that inspires major jealousy in me. But then he runs the eggs through a mesh sieve, scraping and whisking constantly as he strains them, and I know the metal on metal must be noisy outside of my silent cocoon. The bend of his elbow where his forearm and biceps meet becomes the most mesmerizing body part to me.

He proceeds to whisk the strained eggs even more in the bowl, swirling and checking until the consistency looks like water from over here. He's pulled out a frying pan of his own and forks a chunk of butter into it. And when he finally pours the eggs into the pan (where he also seasons them), he simply watches, never looking away to do anything else. He takes a rubber spatula he's also brought over and carefully rolls it in on itself, before he smoothly glides it onto a plate and glosses butter across it some more, a lock of his hair falling forward as he dips. He rapidly dices up some micro-chives that he sprinkles on top to finish.

When he brings it to me, I feel almost embarrassed to eat it, this thing that he put so much attention into. But once I've got it and a fork in hand, he immediately goes back to the kitchen and starts to clean. I take a shaky bite, and of course it's the most delicious omelet I've ever had, no matter that it's only eggs and butter.

He brings me a glass of juice next, and doesn't leave me any room for arguing or pushing before he tells me he's headed out to load up the stuff from the garden and go to the market.

When he's gone and my belly is full, I drag ass back to my room on weak legs, admitting to myself that he was right in telling me I needed more rest. The migraine's talons have let up a bit more, but I still feel like crying when I lay myself down. I've spent so much of my life observing others, trying to learn the things I was missing, trying to make myself significant to *them*, but this man who has known me a month has made himself feel crucial to me.

The last thought I have before I drift off to sleep is: I am fucked.

CHAPTER 28

SAGE

Three days after the migraine, the winds finally begin to shift. It looks as if it will be clear enough next week to resume training, but it also means the fire continues to spread in another direction and that Silas and Ellis are among the hundreds of crews being called out to assist. The night before they have to leave, during the second-to-last week of July, I make dinner at my house for the two of them and Fisher. Indy chooses to stay home, and Sam stays at Wren's. And while the night passes in relative cheer, with only a few complaints from Silas about Fisher not being the chef again, when it's time for them to leave, a surge of foreboding grips me.

"Be careful," I say, beseeching Silas. "Please."

His brow comes together when he hears the catch in my voice, and he crushes me into a hug. "You okay?" he asks me quietly. "He's being good to you, right?" He shields me conspicuously from Ellis and Fisher on the porch.

"Yeah, Si," I say, trying to swallow the sudden lump in my

throat. "He's really great to me." I'm in so far over my head. Even when everything seems to be going wrong—a migraine and my flowers struggling in the polluted air, the restaurant taking way longer than anyone hoped, all our training delays . . . I am deliriously enamored. He is silly in private in the sublimest ways—with the funny voices he does with the animals and in how he plays with me. This morning, he joined me in the shower and began tracing shapes over all the places I have freckles.

"*God, Sage*," he said, sounding spellbound. "*I want to count every single one.*"

I'd snorted, disbelieving and self-effacing. Turned the water off and swiftly covered up with a towel. "*That*," I said, "*would waste a whole day.*"

"*That's it*," he replied. "*On your knees.*"

My mouth fell open with a shocked laugh, even as a thrill zipped through me. He'd kept me under his steady, penetrative gaze, wet and powerful and so handsome it hurt.

"*Why?*" I asked. "*Because I admitted I'm worried about my oral game? Trying to see if I'm cursed with false modesty?*" I've divulged all kinds of things to him I never thought I would—namely, how stunted my sexual relationship with Ian had been. How I always felt like something was wrong with me when I couldn't get there quickly enough, how I'd be self-conscious about communicating what I wanted and would get shy anytime I tried. How everything else other than sex always felt like an afterthought. Fisher, I've learned, treats everything like its own special course.

"*No*," he replied, gripping my chin. "*I already* know *your modesty is—misplaced*," he said. "*I just have a lot more nice things I'd like to say to you right now, and I think I'd like your mouth full while I say them.*" He smiled full-out at the look in my eyes. "*Then you'll have to listen without brushing me off.*"

I jump when I realize where my thoughts have traveled, with my brother at my front, a quizzical look on his face.

"Just don't do anything stupid," I tell him before we send them on their way.

When he sticks half his body out of the car window to wave from the end of the driveway, I realize he, once again, never agreed.

Late during the night, I spot the first visible star I've seen in weeks. I text Fisher to see if he's awake and jokingly tell him to bring me a midnight snack. He sneaks over at 12:01.

When he walks through my sunroom door, he finds me on the bedroll waiting. I sigh audibly at the sight of him drawn in moonlight, and his face crumples, sliding the sandwich onto an end table before his hand goes to his chest like he's been struck.

"What is it?" I ask.

He leans against the door, too far away. "I think," he says, then coughs to clear his throat. "I'm wondering if we should start to pull back."

Now I'm the one who feels like they've been pelted. My heart does something that cannot be healthy inside my chest. "I'm confused," I say. "Why?"

He looks at me with unfiltered agony. "I think you know why."

Oh. Of course he knows. Of course he sees that I'm too far gone and wants to spare me whatever he can. My throat gives a nasty pull, like soft hands on tough rope. I toss my head back and implore gravity to make the tears slow to rise.

He comes to kneel before me. "I'm in too deep, Sage," he rasps, voice thick. My head snaps back down. "I—I don't know what I'm supposed to do. I'm trying to do all the right things. I *promised* Indy, and she has no one. I've let her down before, and I think she needs someone to prioritize her, and . . . I'm sorry. She still thinks that a bigger life means a better one, and I have to let her learn and support her, anyway. And I do want my star back. I don't want to let Carlie down again, either, but mostly I want to see if I could do it again, you know? And I'm so sorry, Sage, I know you didn't ask for this. I know we were supposed to accept the impermanence of this thing with you and me, and enjoy it in the meantime, but I just keep digging in, and now I'm drowning in you, Sage." His eyes are swimming with tears.

"Fisher," I say, the first tear escaping, more following each of my unsteady strokes along his face. "It's too late for me. I've *been* too far dug," I confess. His trembling hand comes around to cradle the back of my neck. "Just love me until then, anyway," I say. "Please."

He dives for me, desperately tender and so perfect it stings. And I'm sunk a little more for it.

CHAPTER 29

FISHER

I'm not sure how I got this far without realizing I was getting in too deep. I think I knew I'd wanted her badly, that much has been obvious. And over our time together, I'd found myself deciding that I'd find a way to keep her as my friend, at least, that I'd maintain that in some capacity after I leave. But then I met her in the sunroom that first midnight. She'd sat up, starlight shining through the glass, draped in a sheet with a smile my way like I'd brought her the cure for something terrible, rather than some basic sandwich on a paper fucking plate. And right then and there, that wedge in my chest pierced home. I realized that infatuation was the shortness of breath, the adrenaline, the idea that we could ever just be friends and it wouldn't kill me each and every day.

Love is this. Love is breathing. A sweet, deep, aching relief. And it's somehow even more disorienting.

We throw ourselves into training with every available minute we have, even Sage becoming especially militant about it. We complain that all the muscles in our shoulders feel like they've been ripped and rebuilt a hundred times over, but our determination seems to harden right alongside.

I don't give a voice to it and neither does she, but I think that we're both hoping that whatever magic keeps the festival winners in Spunes might work on us, too.

I do, however, talk to my therapist about all of it. I'm hoping that she'll tell me what I want to hear—that making a big life change on the heels of another monumental change is okay, maybe even recommended. Maybe she'll tell me to leap off the culinary industry ladder I climbed, forget ever getting back the star, and drag Indy with me whether she wants to or not.

Dr. Deb does not. She doesn't tell me it's *not* okay, either, which is one of the most annoying things about therapy, if you ask me. But, even as I talk it through, I'm all too aware of how I sound. I know I'm in that spot early in love where everyone is in the beginning. You think that no one has ever felt as much or as strongly as you have before. You convince yourself it would be different with you, you could make the distance or the obstacles work.

Because it's her, everything in me says. It's Sage.

It's become routine for me to go over sometime around midnight and stay with her until 3:00 or 4:00 A.M. before I head back to the rental. I've never been more exhausted, but it's a few more hours together to savor. Ironic that it turned out to be me sneaking out this summer.

The night before our first trial run on the real racecourse, one week before race day, I wake to find Sage's place in bed beside me empty. I pad down the stairs and shuffle to the sunroom, where she is curled in her chair and reading.

"Found you," I softly say.

Still she startles, then exhales into a smile. "Scared me," she replies.

I sit on the ottoman and prop her feet on my lap. "What're you reading?" I ask.

She slides it away. "Nothing, just . . . just a journal. Notes and stuff."

"Can't sleep?" I ask.

She shakes her head. "Almost time for you to head back."

I think she means back to the rental, but it steals away my breath nonetheless. "Okay," I say. The rest of the unspoken hangs in the ether. Neither of us have outright said the words yet, but I try to say it in every other way. I make as much love to her as she'll allow. I try to infuse it in every touch. "I'll see you in a bit," I say before I kiss her goodbye.

I meet her by her truck with coffee and a bagel a few hours later. We silently work to strap down the canoe and drive over to the other end of town, holding hands on the seat between us. The course winds down through the river at the easternmost border of Spunes, under the main bridge, out to the bay where it wraps around, finishing at Founder's Point. It means we'll have a stronger current pushing us along, but we will also face rougher waters and some potential waves.

When we get to the launching point, we discover that we're not alone.

"Hey, Sage," Officer Carver says, his fiancée bouncing around at his side. "Fisher," he says, nodding to me in greeting.

"Ethan," I reply with a nod of my own.

"*Ian*," he corrects. I pretend I didn't hear. I reserve maturity for people I actually like. I've never been more jealous of this guy or liked him less. He had Sage longer and before I did, and he'll still be in her orbit when I'm gone.

"We should race!" Cassidy cries. "It would be great practice, right, babe?"

"I'm game," he says.

I look at Sage, dark circles under her eyes and a mulish set to her jaw. "Let's do it," she states. *That's my girl*, I think. Flexing her courage muscle.

Cassidy quickly recruits an unsuspecting passerby to count us down, and we all make our way into our starting places. Sage and I share a look, unwavering and hell-bent on beating these two.

"Ready," the power walker with a quaking poodle in her arms calls. "Set. Go!"

Sage and I launch with utter finesse, the canoe hardly rocking as we push off from shore. We paddle through the water rapidly to start, then steady our strokes when we've edged a boat's length ahead. We focus on our breathing, our sequenced timing, and maintaining our pace. We execute everything we've worked so hard to learn, and not once do either of us look back. Not when I can no longer hear them behind us, not when we cross under the bridge at the halfway mark, not even when we round the final bend and see Bannet Island reaching up from the waves.

We make it the fifteen and a half miles to Founder's Point in sub two hours, barely longer than last year's winning time.

Sage holds her paddle in the air and screams in celebration, somehow invigorated enough to have the energy to run in circles.

She knocks the (very little remaining) wind out of me when she crashes into me with a hug.

"We fucking did it," she says, salt water and sweat plastering her hair against her temples.

"We fucking did it," I agree. I give up on the rest of my breath, spend it on kissing her instead.

And it might be petty or dickish, but we don't wait for Ian and Cassidy before we scoop up our canoe and leave with our heads held high. I admire Sage's lifted chin and smug grin in the passenger's seat, windows down and hair blowing wild. I've never, ever been prouder of anything.

The crowd of people stockpiling in the park around Starhopper the week of the festival is startling at first. There are already a few campers parked at Martha's place, portable grills smoking from their tailgates, and folding chairs creeping onto the sidewalks. I see her issue a verbal dressing-down to a disheveled couple when they roll out of their converted van before she directs them over to the long-term parking. I spot Amos from a distance, too, and he flops his hand at me in an apathetic wave. A lady walks by me and asks for directions to the library, and it takes me a minute to realize that she thinks I'm a local. For some idiotic reason, it feels mildly like a compliment.

After I direct her and suggest a few more stops, I continue loading the crew's supplies inside Starhopper before I lock it up for the week. It's enough busywork to occupy my hands while I sift through the remaining tasks ahead in my mind. Tying up loose ends, even though it's more reminiscent of suturing something.

After we got back and changed this morning, when Sage left to start her day, I finally ripped off the Band-Aid and called Carlie. We talked about Marrow and how things have been running under Archer since I've been gone. And it's so strange to me—I can't pinpoint when it happened or how, but it's like that whole world feels more foreign than everything here, despite the fact that I've only been here nine weeks.

"*So,*" she said. "*What do you need from me?*"

"*What do you mean?*" I'd asked, confused.

"*I mean, do you want to change up the menu at Marrow?*" she went on. "*I'll help however I can. We'll get the star back and get the blogger scene amping up again, too.*"

I don't want any of it, I thought, then immediately had to suffocate a pang of guilt and reach for the gratitude I have for her giving me my job again. It doesn't feel like it used to, anyway. It won't. It won't feel like the kind of work I want to blur my way through. I know I can have fun with it again. Maybe because I also know it's not the sum of my worth, either. It's not life or death—just some of the great shit in between.

I told her I wanted to be able to change or tweak menu items weekly in the future, based on product availability and anything particularly exciting that I find. She let me know she'll be on board. It feels like a step in the right direction, whatever that looks like.

Walter ambles over from the diner to help me string up the lights I promised O'Doyle for the festival, then invites me into his diner for lunch—on him. He serves me a surprisingly good cheeseburger and some fries. I am also happy to report that I do not spot Pegasus the chinchilla anywhere on his person or in his restaurant. I don't find anything out of place, actually.

I think of my parents' tiny, tidy deli with its similar vinyl-cushioned booths. How younger me would have killed for any sort of validation on their behalf.

"Hey, Walter," I say, glancing around. "Nice place."

His chest puffs out with pride. And then the diner phone rings.

When I see his smile fall and hear him say "Yeah, he's here" into the receiver, my stomach plummets through the floor. "Where's your phone?" he asks me next.

"What is it?" I say, already headed for the door. My phone must be back at Starhopper. "Indy?" The corners of my vision pulse and spot in fear.

"Indy's all right. Wren has her," he says. "Go get Sage."

CHAPTER 30

SAGE

I knew it. I've known something was coming. Almost every night for the last week, I've woken up and needed to curl my fists in my sheets to keep from clawing at Fisher like I was falling. Most nights, I've had to get up and read or write in my journal instead. But this afternoon, I woke up from a nap gasping, like some connected thread was trying to pull my lungs from my body.

Silas got separated from his crew on a ridge and fell down a mountainside. He's alive but sustained major burns to 20 percent of his body, in addition to inhalation injury. He's been put in a medically induced coma to keep him on a ventilator and to allow them to manage his pain.

Fisher says nothing when he peels into my driveway, only holds my hand when I silently climb into the truck. I'm not sure how many traffic laws he breaks on the four-hour drive, but I know it should have taken us over five to get to the hospital where Silas is placed.

Voices all sound like they come from far away as I make my

way down the hospital hall. I keep my lips clamped together and my jaw clenched tight. Until I see Ellis.

Ellis with his head in his hands. The Ellis that works so hard to protect everyone and everything that he's left no room for himself in between. The Ellis that had to become a man too young, who has carried the weight of the world since he was thirteen. The one who told me when Mom was gone when my own dad couldn't get out the words. He looks up at me, and I see his face dip into something like shame, then rearrange with a viselike grip, like he doesn't want to burden me by breaking.

Silas—somehow I know Silas will be okay. He'll find a way to turn any scars into stories. But god, *Ellis*.

He pulls me into a hug and raps his fist gently against my spine.

"When we pulled him out of there," he says, "his first words before he passed out were, 'At least nothing got my face.'"

I sob-laugh hysterically.

CHAPTER 31

SAGE

The next forty-eight hours pass by in a daze. When Silas shows no signs of infection and his vitals all continue to look good, his doctors tell us they'll be taking him off the ventilator and out of the coma.

Day three is when I finally see Ellis cry. He never leaves the bench outside Silas's room. I'm not sure if he sleeps. It's only when Wren shows up to the hospital with Sam and Indy and pulls him away that he lets himself fall into her arms.

You'd think Silas had a funny mishap by the way he himself behaves, rather than having nearly one whole leg and a chunk of his side covered in third-degree burns. I understand that he's high as a kite, but it's like he is actively trying to agitate the rest of us to avoid our pity. He's a ruthless (albeit sloppy) flirt with all of his doctors and nurses, happily showing off his bandages and letting himself be poked and prodded with a dozy grin.

Fisher gently herds me to one of the hotel rooms he's rented nearby on day four, where I proceed to shower and collapse into my own sort of coma, tucked securely into his side. I know if I had the energy, I would be panicking about spending some of our last days together this way.

When I wake alone in the room on day five, I find that he's brought me a bag of things from home, including my journal and a few books I'd had on my nightstand. A swarm of emotions collide behind my sternum. I set out to find him, and like his chemistry has altered to magnetize with mine, my feet carry me to where he's asleep in a lounger by the pool. I rouse him with kisses until he softly wakes.

"Where's Indy?" I ask.

"Wren took both kids back," he says. "She thought the festival would be a welcome distraction."

My chest caves a bit when realization dawns on me. By now, we've missed both of the buy-in competitions. Tomorrow is the race, but it all feels so trivial in light of everything else. My chin still wobbles nonetheless.

I remind myself that it's absurd, that life is not a meritocracy. Just because you do everything right, even if you know you deserve it, doesn't mean that it will all be perfect in the end. Just because you accomplish a dream doesn't mean it'll make you happy forever. Sometimes wonderful people get sick, and sometimes people who were terrible to you have everything go according to plan. It really is what you do with it, what you take with you when you go to bed at night that counts. I try to remind myself that *I* know I can do it, that I proved this just the other day. I got my win.

So why does it still feel like I'm losing so much?

"*Hey,*" Fisher coos, pulling my head into his chest and rubbing circles on my shoulders. A labyrinth pattern he traces onto my skin. "Shh. You need more rest. Let me get you back to bed."

"No," I say. "I don't want to sleep. But yes, take me to bed."
Love me, love me, love me, I silently beg. *Before we're out of time.*

It's the least scenic place we've made love yet, but we make that hotel room feel like hallowed ground. We bring each other to the edge time and time again, until I can't tell if we're making demands or desperate invocations.

His hands tangle in my hair when I taste my way down his warm skin, his fist tightening against my scalp when I tease my lips across the tops of his thighs, a litany of my favorite raspy pleas in the air.

He toys with me endlessly with his hands in turn, coaxing up heat into a slow rolling burn. He follows every subtle response, whispers curses and words of praise, and knowingly tells me, *Not yet, not yet*, in a way that makes my body surge toward it more. Before I can recover from the first, he rolls me onto my side, lifts my knee, and enters me from behind, my head lolling against the cradle of his arm. He stretches and fills me, his hand sliding across my hip to touch me where we're joined, until I'm impossibly on the verge again, until his deep, broken whimper in my ear sends me over the peak once more.

It's like every release makes me need him more desperately. The closer he is, the closer I want him. When I don't think I can take any more, he shifts me under him again, cupping a hand to my hip. He waits for me to meet his eyes before he says, "I love you," as he enters me.

"I love you, too," I whisper back, voice tight and airy.

A tear streaks down my temple when it ends.

CHAPTER 32

SAGE

"What the *fuck* are you doing here?" is how I am greeted by Micah in the hallway outside of Silas's room the following morning—no matter that I have not seen him in nearly five months.

"Micah," I say, scooping him into a teary hug.

He mutters a "Higreattomeetya" over my shoulder to Fisher before he grips me by my shoulders and gives me a small shake. "Why are you here?" he says.

"Um," I reply with blatant annoyance, breaking his hold. "Our brother lit himself on fire?"

"I fell off a mountain!" comes Silas's hoarse shout. "Don't tarnish my reputation!"

"You should not be shouting!" I yell his way.

"*You* are supposed to be at the race," Micah says. "You don't need to be here. You gotta go."

"Micah, no."

"*YES!*" Micah, Silas, and a newly approaching Ellis all say.

"We already missed the buy-ins," I say, then risk a quick look at the clock. My hopeful-rising lungs rapidly deflate. "There's no chance we'd make it in time now. There's—there's no point."

"Sage," Fisher says, his warm hand circling my arm. "Let's go. You deserve to do that race. We fucking earned it."

My eyes fill and start to spill over. "We can't win. There's no way for us to win," I say. There's no use denying it.

"We do it anyway," he says firmly. "It's all worth it anyway." And I know he's talking about us, too.

CHAPTER 33

FISHER

I'm not a praying man, but I'm doing my damnedest to call upon some sort of entity the whole way back to Spunes. For all that she's given me this summer, I have to try to come through for her, somehow.

The start time comes and passes while the map time says we're still two hours away.

"Maybe it didn't start on time," Sage says. "You never know. Maybe there were, like, delays of some kind."

"Happens all the time," I say optimistically.

But the remaining drive doesn't get any less tense.

We don't have wet suits, but we've got all our minimally required gear, at least. I fishtail onto the launch point road, an hour and fifteen minutes past the first round of start times, and park directly in front of the entry gate.

"You'll get towed!" Sage cries.

"By who?! Everyone's here."

"Valid point."

We fly out of the cab, throw on our vests as we go, and work to untie the boat.

Sage drops it from her end when the crowd parts.

Still on the beach are Ian and Cassidy, one of Walter's nephews and his husband, and three other teams I recognize as people from around Spunes. Patty Munty and Wren are standing up to their knees in the water. Indy comes walking up to us from somewhere off to the side.

"The competitors from out of town already all started," she says. "We couldn't get them to stop. But we got everyone else to wait."

"To be fair," Patty says, "it wasn't that hard. They all wanted to wait."

"Once Indy told them everything that was going on," Sam adds.

Sage lets out a weepy laugh and throws her arms around a bright red Indy. I swallow stiffly and nod my thanks to everyone. We get our canoe slotted into a spot at the starting line and make the rounds shaking hands and giving out more grateful hugs.

Sage doesn't hesitate to thank Ian or Cassidy, either, because of course she doesn't. She's too full of grace, my lovely girl. I decide to treat her actions like her advice and offer him my hand, too.

"Appreciate it, *Ian*," I say.

He meets my eyes and shakes my hand with a nod. "Yup. Needed another chance to beat you, anyway," he replies.

I laugh and clap him on the shoulder before I swing back to the boat.

We get our paddles set how we need them and look at each other once more. Disheveled and in regular clothes and shoes, with the same shared determination between us. I lunge forward and give her a firm, quick kiss.

"Let's fucking row, Byrd," I say.

Patty makes her way to the small dock, megaphone and bright orange starting gun in hand.

"Ready," her saccharine voice shakes through the speaker. "Set. GO!"

We slam off the shore, but it is an instantly wobbly start. I slip and nearly topple us to the side, and Sage gets her paddle tangled up with one of the checkout boys' from the grocery market. We chaotically work our way through the initial scramble and manage to secure ourselves a position in third.

The fatigue is already so much heavier, though, only thirty minutes in. I am painfully aware of the leaden feeling in my muscles, the fugue in my brain. Days of shitty meals and sleeping on foldout hospital chairs and in an unfamiliar hotel bed are making themselves known. I can hear it in Sage ahead of me, too—frustrated noises slipping through her breathing.

Still, we push on. I dig my paddle into the salt water, flex and pull like my life depends on it. Until we accidentally bump into the back of the second-place team, and a burst of energy has us clumsily overtaking them.

We're approaching the corner that leads us down the home stretch, with Ian and Cassidy at least two canoe lengths ahead. I can see them going all out, too, their whole bodies rising and falling in heavy strokes. But this is when I remember one of my late-night conversations with Sage, lying in the sunroom under the stars, and talking philosophically about how futile it is to live your life constantly comparing journeys.

"*You just gotta row your own damn boat,*" Sage had said.

So, we do. And we do *our* best. We keep in time with each other and stick to our practiced technique.

We row our own fucking boat and ignore the rest.

And when we gain the inside corner on them, they get flustered, faltering and flailing. But Sage and I keep steadily surging on, bright buoys marking the finish line a meadow's distance ahead.

There are the actual prize-money winners already being celebrated on the beach, but this is still our race.

Ian and Cassidy are a steady presence in my peripheral vision, but I keep my eyes trained forward on Sage and the sea.

When we win by a few measly feet, Founder's Point erupts. Everyone that I know from town is waiting for us on the sand, having driven over from the starting line if they weren't already here. It looks like Sage's high school students showed, too, loads of teens with various signs that say things like MISS BYRD IS HOT, and FUCK 'EM UP, MISS BYRD. Walter rips off his shirt and spins it above his head like a helicopter. Wren and Patty are hugging and sobbing in celebration. Venus and Athena Cirillo run into the water and start splashing around in glee. Hairstylist Bea holds a tablet in the sky with Silas on FaceTime. When we bring the canoe to shore and footslog hand in hand out of it, Martha O'Doyle crashes forward and wraps her arms around us both. Even the construction crew from Starhopper is here, applauding and whistling.

Indy and Sam make their way through the crowd, too. Indy's hug is especially tight.

I can clearly pick out the audience members who are not from town by the looks of dumbfounded concern on their faces.

It is the most ridiculous, ludicrous, small-town, corny scene.

And it's one of the great honors of my life to be a part of it.

CHAPTER 34

SAGE

I try to stop and soak up the scene on the beach, to close my eyes and hear the cheerful sounds, to look around at this whole place that's shown up for me. To savor it down to my bones. I think even if we hadn't "won," this alone would've made me realize what a victor I am.

When the rest of the Spunes racers cross the finish line, too, we keep the celebration going. Ian and Cassidy make their way directly to us, and Fisher pulls me into his side.

"Congratulations," Cassidy says, though it's obvious she's struggling not to break into a sob. I give her a tight squeeze.

Ian grasps my hand after he shakes Fisher's, too. "Good work, Byrd," he says to me. "You earned it."

"No shit, Ian," I say with gumption, patting his hand. "And thanks."

I spend the rest of the day in my dirty, smelly, salty-wet clothes, enjoying garbage carnival foods like corn dogs and funnel cakes with my Michelin-starred love. I indulge myself with

him and all the little favorite things I've loved to partake in over
the years, and some I've never been able to before. I do my first
photo booth session with a man that I love. I dance barefoot on
the blacktop with him that night, under the lights strung up
around the new restaurant patio.

When we get home later, we don't rush into bed together, instead taking turns to greet and love on all the animals we missed
so much over the past week. When I leave the barn and find Fisher
in the goat house, he's fallen asleep with Bert and Ernie in his lap.
And maybe it's the exhaustion of the day finally catching all the
way up, but I have to cover my mouth and swallow back a cry at
the sight. It's like the cruelest tease of the life we might've had, if
our paths had found a way to converge. Instead, I know this loop
is coming to an end, and I have to find a way to appreciate it for
the beautiful maze it's been.

We allow ourselves six more days of blissed-out and *now* after the
festival ends. No worries or talk of the future, even though they
are supposed to leave on day eight. Just Fisher bringing me a snack
in the garden, now. Indy lying in the grass with Gary keeping
vigil, now. Fisher running after one of the goats when he escapes
from his pen, hauling him back under his arm like a chastised
child. Legoless rubbing against Fisher's chin at the breakfast table.
Fisher opening the sunroom door at 12:01, sometimes to make me
see stars, other times to lie together and look at the moon.

It's day seven that things start to slip.

"What if," he starts to say. "What if we tried long distance
for a while?"

His question only leads me to more. "With what in mind?
When would it become . . . not long distance?"

He scratches the back of his neck. "I'm not sure." A million more loops take shape in my mind—like, what if Indy decides to leave after she finishes high school, would he want to come here then, to live? Could I make it three years, and would he still want the same things?

I blow out a torn sigh, remembering Silas still in his hospital bed and how fleeting life can be. I imagine living for phone calls and FaceTimes and scattered trips. Never living for the present. Always waiting, always anxious for the next time. I can't expect promises from him, either. How could he give up or severely downgrade his career, limiting himself by staying? I can't ask that of him, either, not when he's as brilliant as he is. He deserves to get that back for himself, to conquer his own win again.

I think of one of those articles I'd read when I broke down and googled him all those weeks ago, how he'd talked about wanting to hit Pause on the inevitable. I think that might be what this is, too. Once he's actually away, it will all unravel eventually.

I'll think that giving him space will make it easier to keep him. I'll act fine when phone calls go missed or get rescheduled, because I won't want to waste any of our time fighting or on any negativity. He'll think I'm apathetic instead. Or maybe it will all be the other way around. I don't know.

I think trying to stave off the inevitable would only make it worse in this case. I can't imagine not having him *and* feeling like I'm continually losing him, over and over. I'd rather savor this wonderful thing we have, for what we have left.

"I can't," I say, voice so empty it sounds like a breath. I look around at my parents' house and all my displaced animals, and for a moment, I regret hemming myself in.

He shuts his eyes, but nods in understanding.

Another loop: What if he asked me to come with him? People

who work in New York live in other states, right? Maybe I could bring the farm somewhere out there? Even as I spin up in the thought, something breaks in me at it. I *love* my home.

I think if he asked, though, I wouldn't be able to refuse him. Part of me wonders if he knows this, too, and that's why he won't.

That night, he doesn't come to the sunroom.

CHAPTER 35

FISHER

I try to reach for that blurring ability again, and I find that it's fucking gone. I'm not spared any of the sharpness when I load up our suitcases and pack up my knives; I only grow more desolate by the minute.

And I'm trying so hard to think of this time as a beautiful thing and to be grateful for it for what it was. Indy and I have come so far, both individually and together. I have finally broken through the numbness of my burnout with my career. I'm actually not dreading it.

I tell myself to put on a brave face for everyone. Remind myself that courage is a muscle and that maybe if I use it this will get easier.

I start my goodbyes with the animals. Legs keeps his back turned to me, his tail twitching in disgust. Sable stays happily unaware, wagging around by my side. I've managed to win over Bud with treats and nose rubs, so I give him both, and he snorts his thanks, flaps his lips against my palm. I indulge myself with giving the donkeys the same. I shed my first tear over the damned goats.

I expect to have to draw her out, but I find Sage in the meadow, waiting for me halfway. She's shrouded in one of her bright robes, a strained smile on her face and something clutched in her hands.

She's always surrounded by so much life. Her garden and her creatures and just . . . her. Like some sort of mythical thing.

Except she's also real, which makes it so much worse. My fantasy and the reality I'll likely always dream of wrapped up in one. I feel like the life she breathed into me is leaving already.

"I wanted to give you something," she says, and all I can think is, *More?* "Do me a favor though and don't . . ." Her throat hitches on a swallow. "Don't open it too soon, okay?"

"Okay," I say, my voice pathetically choked.

She hands me the little brown book I always see her with, and I know I won't have a problem doing what she's asked. The idea of cracking into something that's touched her so much would be like repeatedly ripping open a wound.

I asked Indy about saying her goodbyes, but she refused all my offers to take her to Sam or Blake, and she shuts herself in the truck now.

"Thank you, Fisher," Sage says. "For the best summer. Thank you for loving me, as is."

I think of everything I wanted to say and regret not writing it down.

"Thank you, too," I brokenly tell Sage. And god, fear almost bowls me over right then because will I ever not find her in everything? Will I ever be able to not make everything about summer and Sage again? I'll see some spotted cows and I'll imagine her robe the night we met. I'll taste berries and think of her lips. I'll hear any pun and break into a sob. "It's been a privilege to fall in love with you, Sage," I tell her helplessly. Her expression shatters, and I kiss the tears from her cheeks before I have to wrench myself away.

CHAPTER 36

SAGE

TWO WEEKS LATER

My watch has gone off twice today with a redundant message that states something to the effect of, *"Hey, your heart rate looks like you're dying, but you also haven't moved. Like, at all. Don't you have to pee?"*

I learned by day three that you don't have to pee as much if you don't hydrate as much, and maybe I've cried enough, anyway, that the water doesn't have to find an alternate route. I'm not sure how that all actually works, but who knows, maybe like the heart my fucking watch won't shut up about, that part of me is just broken, too.

I get out of bed every day, at least. It's been two weeks, and I still manage that. This is the good thing about having creatures that rely on you. It force-starts me into some semblance of a routine. I make sure everyone is fed and their needs are met before I let myself fall apart some more.

The only thing I can't bring myself to handle is the garden.

Anytime I pass it, I feel like it's mocking me, my naivety on full display.

I thought being with Fisher would be like cut flowers in a vase. Something lovely I let in, even knowing it couldn't last forever. The problem is, I messed up and planted him here in all my places. I gave him my dirt, my heart, my home, and now he's been uprooted again and I'm left with the upturned mess of it all.

The day before I am supposed to head back to school to set up my classroom for the year, I wake to find Wren on the pillow beside me. I'm not sure why my nervous system doesn't muster up any shock or startle at all.

"How can you stand it?" I ask her. "How can you stand seeing Ellis everywhere you look?" I had a summer with Fisher, and no corner is the same. She and Ellis had each other since kindergarten.

"Time," she says. "Time's the only thing that increases your pain tolerance. Eventually, you see the good that came from it more than the pain."

I think it's those words he used that shred at me the most, when he said it had been a privilege. Because it was, wasn't it? Even feeling how I do now, I would do it all again for the privilege of loving him, of being loved by him. He didn't fix me, and I didn't heal him, but we loved each other wholly.

"Now," she says, "you get up. And you brush your goddamn teeth because your breath *stinks*. And you keep going."

CHAPTER 37

FISHER

I try to see New York through Indy's eyes, like I'm experiencing it for the first time again. I try so hard to make all the small shit matter. And in certain ways, it genuinely does. I take her to Broadway shows, seeing them for the first time myself. I take the time to absorb all the great tall buildings and the incredible food around every corner. Work has been different. I've enjoyed it most of the time, but it's still been work. Somewhere along the way, getting the star back stopped mattering, or maybe it never did and I only thought it had to.

I try to remain steadfast and to remember all that I learned over the summer with Sage. Try to compartmentalize things into that ring of a journey and accept that that's just where it had to end.

It never quite sits right, of course. Too many things slip through.

It's the obvious things, at first. Like every time I work with a recipe that has those little green herbs bearing her name—which happens more often than you'd think. It's cinnamon freckles on top of a dessert, and noticing the flowers that get brought to the restaurant every couple of days. Carlie frowns when I make the request for the first time, but obliges me by allocating some for my back office with each delivery, too.

It's when Indy comes with me to work one day after class in early September, and Carlie happens to mention something to do with adding goose on the menu for fall. Indy shoots off the counter she'd been seated on, visibly stiffening. I have to discreetly shake Carlie off the subject. It's awkward to explain.

A week after that, Indy and I are walking around the park and eating our newest favorite ice creams. My latest is an Earl Grey, hers is a marionberry cheesecake. We come around a corner and find the Hans Christian Andersen Monument, a secondary statue of a goose at his feet. We both throw away our treats in the nearby garbage, not even halfway done.

Marrow's most recent reviews start rolling in, praising the new menu and the fresh approach. Praising me. It feels nice, I suppose. Nice, but not nearly as nice or as good as when I nail my mom's stroopwafel recipe for Indy one weekend, or when she tries to make me dinner one evening, catches a kitchen towel on fire, and we laugh about it the rest of the night over Chinese takeout.

That same night, Indy opens up to me a tiny bit about Sam and summer. She tells me she had feelings for him but that she knew they were incompatible in the long run. Indy wants to see the world, Sam wants to end up in Spunes. She worries about falling for someone at her age, because back in Nebraska, that's all she saw, time and time again. Young people falling young, getting stuck, and cutting their lives' adventures short. I stumble with the right thing to say, but I end up telling her that I'm proud of her for having her priorities and for having her head on straight. It feels like a lie. I desperately wish I could talk to Sage about it.

The worst times are when I just want to hear what Sage would have to say about something. Or when I'm suddenly distraught when I think of something I don't know about her. Like, why didn't I ever ask her what her favorite color was or her favorite song? Has she ever been to a concert? What's her go-to ice cream?

Is she doing okay? *Jesus*, is she doing okay?

Frankie is still there working on Starhopper, so I've gleaned what I can from him. I know that Silas's recovery is going well and he was released to go back home last week. I know that Sage returned to work last week, too.

When I think I'm wearing on Frankie's nerves, I've taken to calling the diner and ferreting out what I can from Walter.

"She came in with Ellis and Silas today for lunch!" he calls to share one day in late September. I clutch my phone so hard I think my fingertips bruise. "She looked like she was doin' okay," he says.

What does that mean, Walter?! I almost say. *What did they talk about? What was she wearing? Does she wake up in the middle of the night like I do?*

I thank him instead and try to go back to pretending.

Every time I think about calling her directly, it feels cruel. The more time that passes, it feels crueler. I break down when I look up her social media. All her Instagram has is pictures from around the farm, bouquets she's arranged. I have to do some serious covert stalking on Micah's page to find a photo of her face. I hold my phone and stare at the screen like a madman.

It's October when everything changes.

Most nights when I get home, Indy is responsibly sleeping. Sometimes I'll find her dozing off on the couch.

Tonight I walk in and find her pacing, with Sage's book propped open in her hands.

"Have you read this?!" she says.

A little piece of me snaps. I've given Indy so much trust since we came back. We've been doing so well until this moment. "No, and that wasn't yours to read, either," I say angrily. "Give it to me, Indy. Right now."

I reach for it when I notice she's been crying. That she's continuing to *sob*, actually. Big, shuddering, full-body cries.

"HAVE YOU EVER COOKED A GOOSE?!" she bawls. I flinch, jolting back with the book in my hands.

"What?!"

"HAVE. YOU. EVER. COOKED. A. GOOSE?!" she howls.

I don't know what to do with my hands again. "Indy . . . I did my externship in France. Of course I have."

She shrieks before it blends into a fresh wave of weeping.

"D-did you know g-geese bond for life?! D-d-did you know th-they can get—can get *depression*?!"

"I did not," I clip. I try to pat her arm soothingly, but she jerks away with a scream.

"And I just LEFT," she says.

"Indy, honey, sit down."

"*No*," she sniffs, then sucks in a deep breath, trying to pull herself together. "All these buildings everywhere make me feel trapped in all the time, and today was one of those days. And I guess . . . I guess I wondered where I could go see some birds other than all the freak pigeons waddling around. So I went to the park."

"Indy, you are not supposed to go anywhere but directly home after school." She's been doing so well. She's been great at checking in, and I've given her freedom and trust in return.

"Christ, man! I know!" she yells, cutting me a glare. "You're missing the point!!"

"Which is . . . ?!" I'm yelling back now.

"I thought I would go to the park, and I thought I would journal," she explains. "It's something we've talked about in therapy before. I w-wanted to go find some grass and some dumbass bird and give it a try. How come no one ever talks about how bad this place smells?!" she abruptly pivots.

"Wh—"

"It *stinks*! No one ever talks about how bad it stinks around all these humid streets! I never hear them talk about it smelling like hot garbage in the movies!" She's belligerent now.

"So you . . . went to the park?" I ask warily, trying to get things back on track.

She drags her wrist across her nose wetly. "Yes," she says. "I went to the park. I wanted to journal. Sage was always doing that and, well, you know. You get it. She just seemed to get it, I guess. She seemed to get *life*."

I'm afraid if I open my mouth I'll start crying, too. I grind my teeth together so hard my jaw creaks.

"I knew she'd given you that, and I just thought—I needed a prompt or, like, an example of what to write. So I took it. I'm sorry, but, Fisher, you need to look at it. And I'm so sorry—" She breaks off into another high-pitched wail and coughing sobs. "I'm sorry I pushed you to leave. If-if you wanted to stay—"

I pull her into a hug. "Shh, hey. It's okay. You didn't do anything wrong. I had reasons to come back, too, okay? I did have a whole career and life I'd built here, and I thought I needed to hold on to that, too," I say. "We would have had to agree on something together," I add. "And anyone would agree that a cross-country move wasn't something to do on a whim, all right?"

Her chin trembles, but she nods into my shoulder, then pushes back a few feet. "You just need to go through that," she says again, pointing to the book. "But I think you were right. I think finding your people is what makes the difference," she says with another heartbreaking cry.

"Or finding your bird?" I offer. Her shoulders fall, and she wails again. "Okay, okay, that was too soon, I know." I try and fail to suppress a small laugh. "Let's go get you a snack before bed."

After I get her settled down, I sit beside her on the couch. "You know before, when you talked to me about Sam and about getting stuck? You know what I really wanted to say but worried it might be the wrong advice at the time?" I ask. She looks up at me from swollen, red eyes. "I wanted to say, 'So what?'"

She frowns, her chin rearing back.

"What I mean is that, yes, some people feel called to do huge things, and yes, many of them are important and great and they have a great deal of money or great titles and see great things. And if you want that, I will support you getting all of it, however I can. But you know what the bravest thing of all is? The most extraordinary thing?" I let out a relieving breath I feel to my very soul, because I also know the truth in what I'm saying. "To live by your own standards and no one else's. To be happy by your own measure. You want your own flock of geese and a garden in Spunes? You want to make the same people you've known your entire life a little happier just by being in it? By doing the small things? Maybe it's that you see your flowers in their stores and on their tables and in their hands, like Sage. Maybe you love passing knowledge on to your community through books, like Venus and

Athena do. Maybe you sign up for all the things around town, like your mom always did." Tears stream silently down my face, but I laugh. "Remember when she petitioned to save that town rock? How proud she was?"

She tearfully nods.

"So. So what if you happen to meet the love of your life in some tiny town, and so what if you get stuck there? If it's a life that's filled with joy, by your standards? I can't imagine a bigger, more fulfilling feeling."

When Indy ventures off to bed, I pick up Sage's notebook with shaky hands and make my way onto the couch once more.

I open up the cover and read the first page:

Sage Advice

Bits and pieces of advice I might leave you, for when I'm not there to tell you myself.

XOXO, Mom

I bring a fist to my mouth. She gave me what has to be her most treasured thing. Of course she did, this incredible woman who had to teach herself how to not overwater everything, who can't stop herself from giving. The most generous person I'll ever know. My heart pulverizes even more, and the knot in my throat hardens.

There are pages and pages of notes and advice. Words to remember when life doesn't make sense, mixed in with more practical thoughts.

Things like:

> Baked goods are always welcome, to literally any-
> thing. New neighbor? Need to say you're sorry? Just
> want to brighten someone's day? Bring them some-
> thing from Savvy's.

Or,

> Life's short. Go to the library. Live a million dif-
> ferent stories and see a million different places in one.
> You might not have control over some things, but you
> can always foster your imagination.

There are some places marked with fresh tabs, and I know
she's marked them for me.

> Busy hands and idle minds have knitted many a
> brow. Find a hobby to occupy your hands with, pref-
> erably outside. Sometimes thoughts just need space to
> roam before you can sort them through.

Sometimes courage is just quietly trying again, she's written
beside it. I know it's her by the different handwriting alone, and
my fingers press against the words like I might reach through and
touch her skin again.

Another tab,

> Time will always give the best advice. Take care of
> your moments and the years will follow suit.

I notice other small notes written in different-colored ink in the margins. A different handwriting from the original again, this one slightly varying over the years. It makes me imagine a younger Sage with her tongue between her teeth, a concentrated furrow in her brow as she curled over this notebook. Then a gangly teenage Sage, scribbling in it moodily. My sweet, beautiful, impossibly kind, and lonely girl trying to make sense of her world using notes from the past.

My chest feels heavy, every breath weighted and scraping me raw from the inside out. I miss her so much I think it could swallow me whole.

So, I keep reading.

CHAPTER 38

SAGE

I finally made my way back to my garden a few days ago. I knew if I let it go much further, I'd kill off any chance at fall flowers, so I figured it was time.

Also, I have decided to pursue my grower's license along with my business license so I might start selling the blooms professionally. Who knew having my heart crushed would lead me to finally take a risky leap? Women with newfangled bangs and Taylor Swift in all her eras are sighing collectively at me.

I was all but too late to save the garden, though. I think there must be a whole gopher megalopolis that has taken up residence. And, because I am not in a sound emotional state, I had to call all around Oregon to locate a humane relocation service. They can't come until next week.

For now, I have decided to make the gophers my friends. I am currently sitting on the border of my destroyed dahlia patch, tossing pieces of a tortilla to one that keeps popping up to snatch them. Maybe if I keep them fed, they'll go easy on the rest of my plants.

I also have Gary in my lap, a steady supply of treats being doled out to him to keep his depression at bay, with Sable at my feet.

If an artist were to paint this whole scene, I think they'd name it *Me and My Demons*.

The gopher suddenly scurries back down in his hole with a renewed surge of panic just as I hear Rosemary and Ginger start to bray in the distance. Sable jumps up with a booming bark.

"What the . . ." I trail off, then recall Nina Andersen telling me they'd be heading back this month. Last year, they kept putting off their return until after the holidays, so I was honestly surprised they were returning for fall this year.

I should probably have warned her that I've added some additions to the farm, but they're not typically this noisy. I take a deep, steadying breath of cool, briny air. Test out a smile to make sure my cheeks can still do it naturally, then push up from my seat with Gary in my arms, ready to welcome them home.

Gary jerks violently when we round the corner and propels himself from my grasp with a chorus of noise. He's too fat to fly, but he does his best to do something between that and a running waddle when he sees Indy across the meadow. The bird and his girl collide in the distance, Indy falling to her knees with an unrepentant cry.

I turn just in time to see Sable nearly knock Fisher to his ass when she jumps up on his chest.

I pull my flannel robe tighter and self-consciously pat at my hair while something claps inside my chest. I try to hold still, I really do. I'm not certain he's not a mirage. Maybe this is some sort of fertilizer-induced hallucination. But my feet keep carrying me his way nonetheless, and he keeps getting closer and more here. And then he's there before me. A little too thin, hair a little too long, ears just sort of too big. Still walking around with far too much of my heart.

God, I'll kill him if he's here on some whim. If I've been clawing my way through missing him only to have to start over again.

"What are you doing here?" I croak. I want it to sound flat or wary, but it's so obviously full of hope. His eyes fill with tears, bright green with all the gray mist floating around at his back.

"I seemed to have lost an earring," he says. "Have you seen it?"

My hand automatically goes to it in my ear. I'd found it three days after he left, in the corner of the sunroom.

"And," he adds, stepping dangerously close, "you knew I wouldn't be able to keep this if I'd opened it here." He holds up my journal. My first tear escapes and my chin starts to tremble.

"It was a gift," I say. "I want you to have it." And then, "I'm keeping the earring either way."

He huffs a laugh and loses a tear of his own. My hands are quivering with the need to grab for him, but . . .

"What are you doing here, Fisher?"

He blows out a shaky breath, his hands moving restlessly like he's trying to stop himself from reaching for me, too.

"We're moving," he replies.

I slap my palms over my eyes. "You can't," I sob. "You can't move your life just for me."

He pries my hands away and looks down at me, one side of his mouth tugging up apologetically. "First of all, you can't tell me what to do," he says. I let out a watery laugh. "Second of all, I'm so sorry I left." His voice cracks on the last word, and oh, god, I feel my face doing that scrunching thing, my lips locking together and trying to hold back a gut-wrenching sob.

He presses on. "I fell in love with you, and with this place, and it should've been enough to make me stay. I should've been able to show Indy that, too, but I was scared to fuck it up again. We're better than how you found us, but we're still working on ourselves." He makes a frustrated sound. "Can I hold you? Please?" I step into his chest in answer and we both shudder in relief. "We both know that life changes," he continues. "But for once I'd like to be the one to change it, for something great. Something Sage.

"So yes, I can move my life here. Indy and I both made that choice. I currently have a month-to-month lease agreement for that house back there." He jabs a thumb over his shoulder to the Andersen place. "I also have connections with the Main Street Business Coalition. More commonly known as the mob." He pulls me even closer. "I can move to be with you, because I'm doing it for me, too. Me, and Indy, and this menagerie of pets, and Walter, and your brothers, and most importantly, for Martha O'Doyle."

I let out a blubbering, happy sound. "But what about work?"

He grimaces. "I am, technically, unemployed once more." He chuckles. "But I've got some things in mind," he states. "Plus a few other ideas in the works. All I know is that I can cook anywhere, Sage, and I didn't want to wait for the logistics and the minutiae to work out before I could start a life with you. I want every minute of it, every second."

"Starhopper?" I ask, like I still need him to convince me before I'll let myself feel the gravity of his words. The place is still under construction, and I'd wager it will take a few more months to be fully ready.

He shakes his head. "That job's already promised to someone," he says. "But I'm not opposed to taking a lesser role there for a while, and I do happen to know the boss. She's not pleased with me, but she is happy for me right now." He shrugs. "Nothing's for certain, except that I certainly fucking love you." I push up and kiss him because I think I'll die if I don't. He hums and I almost weep anew when I hear it. "I did promise a Taco Tuesday and I should try to see that through, at least."

I can't stop myself from touching him now. I reach up and trace his face, and he nuzzles into my palm. Real and warm and mine.

"You once told me you thought you were a lot of nots," he says. "I want you to know that to me, you're everything. I love that you're full of terrible puns that you're not afraid to follow with profound wisdom." He thumbs my temple like he's caressing my mind. "You're all the shapes made perfectly to hold me, and you're all my favorite colors." His lips press against my chin. "You're definitely my favorite flavor," he says lowly into my ear, and I feel my laugh rumble through our embrace softly.

"I love you so much," I have to say.

"I love you, too. Please bring me home."

EPILOGUE

THE FOLLOWING JUNE

"How much longer, Ind?" I finally call up the stairs. I've been quietly pacing in the sunroom for the last forty minutes and couldn't last any longer. "I wanna get there early in case she needs help!"

When she doesn't dignify me with a response, I stomp back away from the stairs and through Sage's kitchen—*our* kitchen, officially, as indicated by my knives on the counter and the sous vide still out from the night before. The Andersens ended up wanting to come back for Christmas, so we'd only stayed for a month in their place before we moved in with Sage.

Back in the sunroom, I find the new pictures along the display shelf. Indy's report card from her sophomore year, framed—all As. A family portrait of all of us on Founder's Point, my parents included, from when they visited over Christmas last year. We attempted to build a sand-snowman on the beach. We made it as far as his base and had frozen wet hands that we all proceeded to thaw at Walter's diner. Beside that picture is another recent one of Indy and me in the truck, wearing twin expressions of apprehension, our mouths pinched in serious lines. It was the first time I took her out to teach her to drive, since she has recently earned her learner's permit. There's a picture from last year's festival, too. It's Sage and me pulling onto the beach, with a bunch of the faces of people we love celebrating around us, our eyes stuck on each other.

I pick up the photo from New Year's, which also happened to be the soft opening for Starhopper. It was a town-only event outside of Carlie herself, where one of Walter's many nephews (this one a great-nephew, I think?) came to deejay. Desserts were made by Savvy's and Wren, and floral design was provided by Sage. It was her first big gig, and I am proud to say that I've never heard so many compliments on floral arrangements at an event centered around food. The official grand opening took place a week later, with hordes of patrons from out of town, many brought in by the allure of watching a meteor shower that was happening that night from the observatory or from the lawn outside.

Starhopper has been a huge draw for Spunes and tourism these last six months. And working there under Archer has been somewhat refreshing, actually. I've been enjoying the low pressure and low stakes. I do still have some other ideas in the works, though, and my determination is gaining. Once Walter quits playing chicken and makes his retirement official, I'm going to do all I can to purchase the diner. I won't have a backer this time; it will be mine through and through.

I hear Indy hustle down the steps, and I return the photo to the shelf, just as she slides into the sunroom to brush past me. "Let's go!" she says, like I'm the one holding us up. I yell a quick goodbye to Sable and Legs before I follow her out to the truck and head into town.

The soft opening was Sage's first real gig, but tonight's thing is a much bigger deal. Starhopper and the whole of Main Street itself have been shut down for exclusivity.

Indy splits off when we make it inside the restaurant, spotting Sam and some of her friends by the drinks. It feels like something hot pokes inside my chest when I see her getting along so well with them.

I'm not the least bit surprised when I turn and find Sage at the very top of a ladder, in bare feet and a pretty green dress I've already peeled off her once today. She reaches for something and I spot the tattoo on the inside of her elbow, a canoe spilling over with flowers. I got my own version the same day on my forearm: a whisk and a spatula in place of paddles. Her high-heeled shoes are waiting at the bottom as she adjusts the garland hanging from a rafter.

I make my way over to her from the side, and she does a double take and wobbles just slightly. "Dammit," I grumble as I dive for the ladder and steady it. "You're gonna give me a heart attack."

She smiles over her shoulder before she makes her way back down, and the irritation melts away the second she's on the ground in front of me, replaced by a different sort of heart race. She's got her hair in messy waves, partially pulled back in some sort of fancy ponytail. Big, dangly earrings that are dull compared to that glimmer in her eye. Lips that look berry-stained. Only a few rings on this evening, one bare finger in particular I intend to adorn very soon.

We'd taken a weekend trip over to Gandon back in March for Sage's birthday, and I'd been hit with an idea based on some of their summer advertisement signs. It took a whole lot of hunting and coordinating, but I found (and purchased) a glass-bottomed canoe, complete with lights around the rim for night rides. I've had it hidden over at Silas's for almost two months, but at the first hint of a warm summer night, he's going to bring it to our beach and have it waiting for me behind the blind. I'm going to take her out on her favorite stretch of water and ask her under a vast, starry sky to be my wife.

"Well," she says with a meaningful look. "What do you think?"

"So beautiful it hurts," I tell her.

She pulls me down for a kiss that's probably too passionate for public display, but that's my Sage. All heart, full force, and making every moment matter.

"I meant," she says, punctuating it with a quick nibble on my lip, "what do you think of the wedding?"

Oh. I take the time now to look around the room, and I'm stunned that one person managed this. Well, one person and her brother, I guess. Micah got released from his contract and has been moping around Spunes since spring. Sage, in trying to keep him constantly busy and distracted, also recruited him to help with all the floral installations for today's nuptials.

Speaking of which, Ian and Cassidy stroll through the Starhopper doors now. We all nod to one another in polite greeting from across the room. Contrary to the couple from today, those two ended up eloping to Mexico this past February.

I help Sage with the last of the setup, then move the ladder and tuck it away. She walks by me at some point when I'm busy fixing some sort of sprig in a napkin, swats my ass, and whispers, "I've changed my mind; this is my favorite suit on you," in my ear. The only other one she's seen me in is a wet suit. I'm half a step from dragging her off to a supply closet when the emcee announces that it's time to head to the observatory.

Chairs are stationed around the circular room, and everyone files in and takes their seats. There are probably only twenty of us or so, just enough to make for a very intimate ceremony. The rest of the town will be at the reception, no doubt. By the telescope in the middle of the room, next to Athena Cirillo acting as

officiant, stands a visibly emotional and suit-clad Walter, waiting
for his bride. Sage has strung up a garland, with dangling strands
of crystals and lights throughout the dimmed room, with moss
and various star-shaped flowers along the aisles at our feet.

"You're amazing," I tell her. "This is amazing."

"So are you," she says to me. I shake my head at her. I'll never
know why I got this lucky. Of all the places in all the world I
might've ended up, the idea that fate might've landed Indy and
me anywhere else grips me with terror some days. I think because of how hard I want to hold on to this life, how badly I wish
I could slow it down.

The elevator dings at the back of the room, and we all turn
in unison just as Silas and Ellis begin to walk Martha O'Doyle
down the aisle.

Turns out, Martha and Walter had been living their own star-
crossed story throughout the years, pining from a distance until
something inspired them to finally take the plunge. They decided
to quit wasting their days and to be with the one they love.

That night, I dance in a conga line, I eat delicious food and cake
that I didn't have to make, and I witness the horrifying sight of
Walter peeling a garter from Martha's leg by his teeth.

I dance as much as I can with Sage, even if it makes me hungry to get her home. And whenever we're separated throughout
the evening, I find that I still watch the woman I love. She's the
one I intend to make my wife, who helps me parent Indy, and
who I'd be honored to raise more children and even more animals with one day. She's the woman who has taught me to let go
of so much so that I can wish and dream for more.

I plan to savor every bit of it.

ACKNOWLEDGMENTS

Well, well, well. Look at us! We made it here again, somehow. This book was a self-imposed labor of love (aka, I made it harder than it needed to be because I put pressure on every single sentence). Every book feels like it might be the last, and I'm so happy that's not the case. This is hugely in part due to the many people I'd like to acknowledge.

First and foremost, I need to thank my husband, whose hours are even more lengthy and unpredictable than mine, and yet he always manages to put in extra time on the home front to free me up to write. Thank you, honey, for distracting the kids and taking care of our very real lives so often, so I can tend to these pretend ones. Thank you for letting me talk it out with you when I need to, even if it freaks you out a bit, and for giving me the space to be quiet when I can't talk about them another minute.

Thank you to my powerhouse agent, Jessica Watterson, who didn't know she'd be moonlighting as a therapist when she signed me. You've been a champion for my work from our very first conversation when you said, "You should be on shelves," and you've helped make so many of my dreams come true. Your faith in me so often restores my own. Thank you for seeing this book, with its simple concept on the surface, and knowing it was much more underneath. Thank you also to Andrea Cavallaro, my foreign and film/subrights agent, and to the entire Sandra Dijkstra team for taking my work to so many exciting new places already.

To my editor, Cassidy Graham, thank you for making this the best book it could possibly be and for your patience with me transitioning from this being a solo endeavor to having a team behind me and flanking me on all sides. Thank you for pushing me to strengthen the weak spots and for cheering on the triumphs. Thank you for holding my hand through our shared vision for this book and for Spunes as a whole, even when I was clutching a little too tight. I am so happy to have you on my side and can't wait for everything we'll do together.

To Kejana and Alyssa, more teammates I'll likely never get over having. Thank you for all the marketing and publicity work you do, for setting me and my work up for unparalleled success. I feel indescribably lucky to be part of the SMP team, and god, I hope I never embarrass any of you with my chaos.

To Liza Rusalskya and Kerri Resnick, thank you for creating a cover more beautiful than anything I ever imagined. I welled up when I saw the sketches for the first time because they were *them*.

To the readers who became friends (and sometimes counselors), you know who you are, THANK YOU. Your tireless campaigning for my books gives me the boost I need when I'm low. I wrote this one for that me who thought this was an impossible dream because I didn't have a degree or experience, and at every step I was reminded of just how much my characters and words have stuck with you. Through your posts and proclamations I was reminded again that I could and *should* keep going.

To the authors who took the time out of their extremely busy lives to read this, as well as my previous work: Rachel Lynn Solomon, Amy Lea, Julie Soto, Ava Wilder, Lana Ferguson, Rosie Danan, Liz Tomforde, Erin Hahn, Elsie Silver, Livvy Hart, Jessica Joyce, Austin Siegemund-Broka, Emily Wibberly, Jen Devon, Melissa Grace, Elena Armas, and Lyla Sage. It's terrifying to have someone whose work you adore read your own, but it's deeply affirming when these extremely talented people enjoy it. I know how hard it is to read when you're a writer, so I'm truly grateful.

To the friends and family who support me, I'll never be able to convey what you mean to me. You're an integral part of me pursuing this dream, because I know I have safety in all of you either way. I love you.

ABOUT THE AUTHOR

Jessica Prangley

Tarah DeWitt is an author, wife, and mama. When she felt like she had devoured every rom-com available in 2020, she indulged herself in writing bits and pieces of her own. Eventually, those ramblings from the Notes app turned into her debut novel. Tarah loves stories centered around perfectly imperfect characters, especially those with just enough trauma to keep them funny, without ever being forcefully cavalier. She believes laughter is an essential part of romance, friendship, parenting, and life. She is the author of *Rootbound, The Co-op,* and *Funny Feelings.*